Praise for Vladimir Sorokin

"[Sorokin's] disorienting prose forces the mind to react—to focus, to sharpen—and urges us to be on guard against revered forms and the literary conventions of authority." —*Harper's*

"Socialist Realism has been tried and found guilty. Guilty of annoying edification, stifling clichés, propagandistic lies voiced by its stock characters, and fear of the body in all its messy manifestations. In *Dispatches from the District Committee*, Vladimir Sorokin acts as its executioner. Each short story is a Grand Guignol performance, in which Soviet style is condemned to a gruesome death. Don't feel sorry for Socialist Realism; just lean back and enjoy its just deserts in Max Lawton's masterful translation."
—*The Untranslated*

"Sorokin is widely regarded as one of Russia's most inventive writers."
—*The New York Times*

"His books are like entering a crazy nightmare, and I mean that as a compliment." —Gary Shteyngart

". . . an extraordinary writer—a brash, Swiftian ventriloquist whose best work spars ably with the Russian greats of the last century and a half." —*The Nation*

"Sorokin, global literature's postmodern provocateur, is both a savage satirist and a consummate showman."
—Dustin Illingworth, *The New York Times Book Review*

"Sorokin is both an incinerator and archaeologist of the forms that precede him: a literary radical who's a dutiful student of tradition, and a devout Christian whose works mercilessly mock the Orthodox Church. It's this constant oscillation between certainty and precarity, stability and chaos, beauty and devastation, hom̶̶̶̶̶̶̶̶̶̶̶̶̶̶̶̶̶̶̶̶̶̶̶̶̶̶̶ ̶̶̶̶̶̶̶̶̶̶̶̶̶̶̶ ̶̶̶̶̶̶̶̶̶̶̶̶̶̶̶̶̶̶ and rupture that makes Sorokin's fiction
—Aar̶̶̶

Other Work by Vladimir Sorokin

The Norm
The Queue
Marina's 30th Love
Roman
Their Four Hearts
Blue Lard
Ice Trilogy
Day of the Oprichnik
The Sugar Kremlin
The Blizzard
Telluria
Manaraga
Doctor Garin and his Heirs
Nightingale Grove
Red Pyramid

DISPATCHES
FROM THE
DISTRICT
COMMITTEE

BY
VLADIMIR SOROKIN

TRANSLATED FROM THE RUSSIAN BY
MAX LAWTON

INTRODUCTION BY WILL SELF

ILLUSTRATIONS BY GREGORY KLASSEN

DALKEY ARCHIVE PRESS
Dallas, TX / Rochester, NY

Deep Vellum | Dalkey Archive Press
3000 Commerce Street
Dallas, Texas 75226
www.dalkeyarchive.com

Support for this publication has been provided in part by grants from the National Endowment for the Arts, the Texas Commission on the Arts, the City of Dallas Office of Arts and Culture, the Communities Foundation of T~~~ ~~~ ~~~ A J J ~~~~~~~~~~.

Library of Congress Cataloging-in-Publication Data: Names: Sorokin, Vladimir, 1955- author. | Lawton, Max, translator. | Klassen, Gregory, illustrator. Title: Dispatches from the district committee / by Vladimir Sorokin ; translated from the Russian by Max Lawton ; illustrations by Gregory Klassen. Other titles: Belyĭ kvadrat. English Description: First English edition. | Dallas, TX : Dalkey Archive Press, 2025. Identifiers: LCCN 2024036422 (print) | LCCN 2024036423 (ebook) | ISBN 9781628975178 (trade paperback) | ISBN 9781628975420 (ebook) Subjects: LCGFT: Short stories. Classification: LCC PG3488.O66 B4513 2025 (print) | LCC PG3488.O66 (ebook) | DDC 891.73/5--dc23/eng/20240812
LC record available at https://lccn.loc.gov/2024036422
LC ebook record available at https://lccn.loc.gov/2024036423

Cover design by Zoe Guttenplan
Interior typesetting and design by Douglas Suttle
Printed in the United States of America

DISPATCHES
FROM THE
DISTRICT
COMMITTEE

TABLE OF

CONTENTS

Introduction 9
The Pink Tuber 23
The Quilted Jacket 31
Sergei Andreyevich 51
First Day of the Season 65
My First Voluntary Saturday 77
Geologists 85
Poplar Fluff 93
At the Central House of Officers 101
A Free Period 109
A Hearing of the Factory Committee 125
Called to the Director 151
Sanka's Love 167
A Competition 183
The Tobacco Pouch 191
Car Crash 207
Love 231
Possibilities 237
A Monument 241
Smirnov 251
Day of the Chekist 271
Translator's Note 291
Biographical Information 292

INTRODUCTION

It's some years since—while composing an extended essay on Kafka—I determined never again to pretend authoritative commentary on a writer if I was unable to read their work in the language in which it had been written. The problem with Kafka was how wildly disparate supposedly authoritative, German-speaking critics were when it came to the nature of his "Prague German"—the dialect spoken by the Jewish community he grew up in. One would assert that it was notable for its "chewiness," implying a rich metonymic mulch, while another would take the opposite line: islanded in a Czech-speaking majority, who were themselves further enclosed in a Bohemian hinterland in which German speakers predominated, the Prague Jews' language sounded—to other German speakers—creakily antiquated, its dry asperity typified precisely by an absence of idiom.

Then there was a further problem—one that also bears on the understanding and exposition of the text you hold in your hand, hypocrite lecteur, and which is, perforce, closely related to the first: humor. Notoriously, Kafka would corpse when reading his novella, *Metamorphosis*, aloud to his friends. But this Kafkian humor is lost very readily in translation, springing as it does from a wider language culture of precision admixed with formality such that Germans (so one of their number once informed me), almost go to the lengths of announcing they are about tell a joke, and that therefore you should ready yourself for appropriate laughter, before they embark on what would, in English, be necessarily framed by at least seeming spontaneity.

Kafka's Prague is triply separated from us now, by language, by time, and by the physical annihilation of its Jewish community—a sort of bio-correlate of all the successive iterations of Czech statehood since Gavrilo Princip levelled his revolver at Sophie and Franz Ferdinand; but can we not say the same of the Soviet Russia that emerges from the pages of Vladimir Sorokin's *Dispatches from the District Committee?* The first two stories date from the late 1970s, while the bulk of them appeared in a collection that bears the title of his "breakthrough" tale (in the sense that it attracted widespread attention in the Russian-speaking world), *My First Working Saturday.* Only the last two stories in this collection—"Smirnov" (2010) and "Day of the Chekist" (2018) see the writer modulating his method in order to apply it to the post-Soviet world.

So, why break my own rule? I not only have no Russian, I cannot even claim to be any sort of specialist or maven when it comes to Russian literature and wider culture. The answers lie—as in most of human affairs—in chance rather than design: an encounter some years ago at Columbia University in New York with the future translator of Sorokin, Max Lawton, led him to contact me when the first of his translations began to appear in English. That this should itself coincide with the Putin regime's invasion of Ukraine would hardly seem fortuitous—unless you believe in a demiurge of dissociation or a dialectic of disaster. J. G. Ballard famously remarked that death, for a writer, is always a career move—but he meant the writer's own death, not those of tens of thousands of potential readers.

Readers who, despite the corrosive effects of postmodern critical theory, still look to an introduction to do just that: introduce them to literary works with clear designations and provide discursive analyses that situate these works within the semiotic matrix from which they have emerged. Moreover, an introduction to a work of fiction always tacitly makes this claim: I am yet more definitive than the work in respect of which I am your cicerone—indeed: while it may be the painting, I am demonstrably the frame and thus define the extent of the pictorial space more than the painting itself. Sorokin understands this well enough — in amongst the Dostoevskian clutter, the impacted stratigraphy of a material culture borne down on heavily by dialectical materialism, he discovers this: "enormous classical landscapes pale gloomily in the gilded astrakhan of enormous frames, landscapes in which the flat green of foliage is indistinguishable from the brown of shore hanging steeply over colorless water . . . "

If I myself foreswear the exegete's implicit authority, it's only in the interest of fulfilling these expository functions more fully: the truth in a relativistic realm rests not in correspondence—but only coherence: and I'm sticking to Sorokin, for I have the adhesive virtue of being a novelist and a short story writer myself—and moreover one whose own tales often dwell rather more fixedly than most on the real (rather than the imaginary), and seek to describe it with symbolic excess rather than mimesis.

But I have no Russian—while Sorokin's prose bodies forth from this precise terroir and no other. This is why before attempting to introduce Sorokin's work I both spoke at length to his translator and tracked down to some extent (although by no means exhaustively) the numerous specific cultural references embedded in Sorokin's fictions. Have I thereby managed to find a way into this extraordinary writer's massif of an oeuvre, of which this collection is an outlier? That, dear reader, is for you to judge. My own sense of estrangement from the material—by reason of its pullulating neologisms, its infective scatology, its mutant concupiscence—was great and greatly pleasing before I undertook this process, but once I'd done it, my alienation was from the world itself; and this, surely, is the writer's intention? Sorokin had managed to reverse the hoary old homily—such that after reading him I see that everything human is strange to me, and always has been. I have it on authority that he has no wish to enter the marmoreal tomb where writers are memorialized—this, at least, must be at least partially a remnant from his own experience of the Soviet era: a commitment to peer-to-peer publishing via samizdat that militates against the egregious commoditization of ecriture which typifies the Anglosphere far more than any liberality or largesse of speech. He has no wish to be a gold-tooled volume on the shelves of a presidential library founded in the memory of an illiterate.

In *The Lives of Others* (*Das Leben der Anderen*), arguably the first serious German language film to be made about the GDR following the fall of the Berlin Wall, the benighted and oppressively spied-upon inhabitants of East Berlin have at least this outlet (if they're high up enough in the nomenklatura): they can jive the nights away to a jazzy big band. Yet this is the 1980s—they must have heard of the Beatles, of Elvis—even of Johnny Rotten. This view of life in the Red Tsars' Empire is, of course, flattering to the West most of all; allowing its denizens to believe they've democratized the zeitgeist by means of multiplication alone—and as Comrade Josef also knew, quantity has a quality of its own. But the truth is that just as the hunter-gatherers of today are in nowise to be seen as Paleolithic peoples preserved in anthropological amber, so the Soviet citizens depicted in Sorokin's stories from the 1980s must also be allowed their own evolution.

To give just one example of my own ignorance, with the hope that it will illuminate the territory for all: in "First Day of the Season," two hunters—one a city amateur, his guide a rural professional—transmogrify a third into prey by luring him into a clearing; their bait being a tape recorder they've winched into the trees as it plays a recording of a live concert given by Vladimir Vysotsky. Does it matter if a reader—such as myself in this instance—doesn't know who Vysotsky was? At one level, no: the mechanics of this friendly fire incident are just as macabre without the added resonance provided by understanding that for Russian readers, such is the resonance of these lyrics, it's as if they are witnessing a bloody murder and discorporation while Bob Dylan wails about the answer blowin' in the wind.

That Vladimir Vysotsky—in common with Robert Zimmerman—was of Jewish heritage, adds further resonance to his status as "the Russian Bob Dylan"; more significant, yet, in light of the 2022 invasion, is that his Jewish father was also Ukrainian. And yet more significant, still, is the great horse's head of history, writhing with the eels of actuality, that is winched aloft with the tape recorder once the (Western) reader begins to consider the kind of society within which an artist such as Vysotsky could inhere to the extent that a writer such as Sorokin composes in counterpoint with his lyrics. The answer is: it's the same society as the one in which people reference heroes of the revolution and the Great Patriotic War in exactly the same way that they do those of the "Time of Troubles" (*Smuta*), in the early seventeenth century. It's the same society as the one in which people non-ironically ascribe wisdom to the ossifications of Marxist historiography itself—and then vitiate that ascription a posteriori with far greater ironizing.

Surely, what Russia has fallen victim to most conspicuously at the hands of the West is this—an unconsciously willed ignorance enacted by the simple dichotomies of its politics, ones enshrined in its key liberal precept: the sacred choice between this . . . and that. For the right, once the Soviet regime was in place, nothing more was needed to be known about the lives of those so othered—the repression of the Kronstadt rebels in 1921, the purge-upon-purge, the widening of the slaughter to the populace, the liquidation of the kulaks, the Ukrainian famine, the show trials — and on and sickeningly on; yet these are mere sequelae, and just as inevitable as an untreated consumptive coughing up blood. And for the Western left as well, the ostensible fact about the Soviet regime had to be this: it was emphatically not the socialistic utopia their own political science predicted. With each successive dialectical movement—the antithesis of Berlin in 1948, that of Hungary in 1956, Prague in 1968, Poland in 1980—a new synthesis of the righteous Western left (as opposed to the hideous "tankies[1]") was achieved: in order to remain yet more fully focused on their own city-upon-a-hill, they needs must neglect yet more fully those cities real Russians were living in.

For left and right alike, all of Soviet Russia became coterminous with the gulag—while all Russians were compelled by the binary of Orwellian double-think to experience a consciousness that was an epiphenomenal act of continually ongoing erasure, whereby as a thought arose it was simultaneously etch-a-sketched out of existence. How very convenient! After all, even in the 1980s—what with history about to end and all that jazz—there was simply too much to read and know in the busily interconnecting world—obnubilating the lives of three-hundred-odd million souls became simply a matter of priorities. I mean, if you stop to consider fully the cultural valence of Vladimir Vysotsky, and whether or not there's some parallel to be drawn between the way he's been memorialized by Putin in the form of a Moscow street name, and the way Bob Dylan has been memorialized by a supposedly unique pressing of a rerecorded "Blowin' in the Wind" that recently sold at auction for in excess of a million dollars . . . Well! Where would such craziness stop.

If it was the fate of Kafka's oeuvre for many years to be interpreted by the light of the shadow cast backwards from the

---

1. Diehard Western communists—such as the rump of the Communist Party of Great Britain—who supported the repression of these risings by Red Army tanks.

Holocaust and the gulag, then let it not be that of Sorokin's to be seen through a glass similarly darkened; and this is not in any way to deny him the intensity of his appreciation of the life-worlds occluded by totalitarianism—it's simply to observe that Sorokin's apophatic theology (which he cleaves to, together with a substantial portion of the renascent Russian Orthodox confession), applies just as well under the double-thinking (and doubly-bound) conditions that have obtained in the West. And this is true whether those conditions have been the mutually-assured destruction of love enacted by the daddy-and-mummy-state when it tells us it must lay waste to the entire world in order to affect our salvation, or the ones that enshroud our minds when we exert a marginal preference for a commodity (such as a Bob Dylan record).

All of which is by way of saying we shouldn't commit the most fundamental fallacy of all (and one that's still metastasizing at a furious rate through the literary Anglosphere) which is to assay these stories on the basis of their content: Sorokin is above all a writer from within a literary tradition whose substrate is the Russian language. If the references are formal as much as factual, the wordplay is everything—and if it might have been said of Kafka's Prague German that it was "chewy," how much more so is Sorokin's? Which, in marked contrast to the Prague Master's refusal of it, constitutes a veritable nougat of idiom, metonym and metaphor—one of such colloidal tackiness that to bite down on it is for the reader to risk losing . . . their teeth.

Sorokin describes the technique of many of the stories in this volume (if not *all* of them) as predicated on the throwing of what he calls "binary bombs[2]": the tale unwinds at first with a certain predictability—without ever descending into stereotype or the merely formulaic. There are echoes of that classicism exemplified

---

2. Not Tom Cruise but a man who, in the warmly-exhaling southern night, seemed to resemble him.

by nineteenth century Russian novels—their carefully calibrated life-worlds resembling some sort of socio-psychological orrery; or of Soviet Realism, with its hieratic figures: supple young Komsomol gymnasts, pumped-up Stakhanovites, stoical veterans of the Great Patriotic War and diligently foreshortened bureaucrats, whose superstructures are so very much smaller than . . . their bases. A hunt is underway—or a work party is charged with sweeping leaves; a valetudinarian professor receives a bouquet from his students—whereas another exemplary pedagogue is treated to a stuttering, impassioned paean from one of his; while an overbearing and matriarchal teacher takes an interstitial opportunity to adjure one of her pupils. Then the bomb is thrown—and it's the semiotic version of the neutron one beloved of the Western imagination: the one that was to've merely annihilated humans while leaving their real estate intact. For Sorokin's binary bombs are so immaterially powerful they detach signifier entirely from what is signified, such that words, objects, disincorporated bodies— all float in space/time, hymned by hovering phonemes.

Nietzsche's contention in *On Truth and Lies in an Extra-Moral Sense*, that even the equivalence of two ones with two should be considered as a rhetorical construct finds its logical endpoint in Sorokin: if we can say of Joyce's work that it will remain forever in progress—an estuary refilling itself from its own source—and that in it he attempted to counter the reductio inaugurated by Saussure by the sheer, relentless agglomeration of signifier-upon-signifier, a polyglot and polymorphous silt-bank to shore up against relativist ruin; and we can say of Beckett that his method is to reverse this, such that his writing becomes an abrasion—a wearing away at the superstructure of language so that its rocky and guttural undergirding is implacably revealed; then Sorokin's is the third way: language is seen to be evanescently calibrated with this or that symbol set: and therefore simply another ritual—albeit an overarchingly comprehensive one—the mind/body employs to negotiate provisional realities[3].

This is why once the bomb has been detonated new rituals must be speedily originated and new signifiers coined to express their ineffable arbitrariness—for the truth is that, as Heidegger asservates: the worst has already happened, the knowledge bomb (looking uncannily like an apple, what with its quick, green fuse) has already gone off, and all we have are these rituals. Parodies of public-spiritedness—the geologists use their own vomit to save their errant colleagues; the Great Patriotic War is won by abstinence from tobacco—are combined with those intensely private rituals with which everyone (and I mean *everyone*) negotiates the awful truth that their angelic disposition is to micturate and masturbate, excrete and fornicate.

That manifest obscenity should be seen to be constitutive of all that is most importantly human is a function of Sorokin's aforementioned and apophatic theology: given the Orthodox emphasis on God's immanence as opposed the Western confessions' (Catholic and Protestant alike) on His transcendence[4], it's unsurprising that the way of bringing God most nearly into our presence is to describe emphatically all those things that He is *not*, rather than those that he is. Hence the scatology and the sexual mechanics stripped entirely bare of any romantic gloss; hence also the manifold significance of lard in Sorokin's oeuvre; the English-language reader might want to consider it anachronistically as "dripping"—or shortnin' bread—and this perhaps captures the utilitarian dimension of this protein-rich paste, since it is indeed spread on Russians' daily bread to this day. But it's the physics as much as the mouth-feel of the substance that troubles Sorokin:

---

3. It's perhaps worthwhile applying a reverse definition here, one odious if viewed as essentialist—but otherwise perhaps amusing: if you want to understand the Russians, imagine the Irish with an empire.

4. I think of a billboard I once saw driving past a gaunt looking people-barn of a church in the south London suburbs: MEET ME AT MY HOUSE FOR LUNCH ON SUNDAY, GOD

lard—which in gourmet preparations, infused with herbs and spices, anoints the croutons of wealthy metropolitan Russians, exactly as its cheaper, ranker incarnations do the masses' borodino—can be solid, plasma-like then liquid . . . before it goes up like a mouthful of meaty, smoky prayer. What better material with which to express the bowdlerisation of human being—for is lard not, given its properties, necessarily both dialectical and an analogue of the only true dialectical relation there is, the Trinity?[5]

Caught unexpectedly by the events of February 2022, the writer was at his apartment in Berlin when Russian tanks rolled across the border. Soon enough, looking to enhance its legendary "understanding," the Western press went looking for someone to explain to them and their readers what had happened—as if a belated acquaintance with contemporary Russian fiction might somehow retroact on the Russian army and the separatist militias in the Donbas and Luhansk, such that their rifles and machineguns sucked up bullets[6], while rockets were reincorporated then reinserted into their launchers, as mutilated corpses became whole once more and everyone marched home backwards for Christmas. Sorokin obliged the curious West to at least this extent: a text published in the Guardian newspaper in England saw him characterizing the Putin regime as a pyramid of power that

---

5. This man, who was out of sight on the far side of the fence, called out: asking if I'd let him into the compound—the elderly French couple who own the place are a little paranoid. It's a great chipped and spalled old house of pink-to-grey masonry, covered in creepers and flanked by sentinel cypresses, which is adrift on an island of other trees and old-growth bushes, itself surrounded by the vineyards of eastern Languedoc. You wouldn't have thought it would be that vulnerable—but they've rigorously fenced the entire property and insist on the front gates being secured with a heavy iron chain and padlock whenever anyone goes out.

6. It was this barrier that the unknown man who sounded a bit like Tom Cruise needed my help to circumvent—and so, I hauled myself up from the table, which was spread with plates of cheese, bowls of salad and glasses of the flinty white wine they make hereabouts—all of it coruscating in the light from a large citronella candle, and calling out that I'd meet him at the gates, I left my companions.

vibrated[7] in weird harmony with the ex-KGB man who sits at its apex, shivering with paranoia and drunk on the "black milk[8]" he sucked from the withered teat[9] of totalitarianism.

In this succinct, passionate essay[10], Sorokin twitches aside the curtain that divides Russia from the West[11]—a sort of scrim, on to which successive barriers have been projected from either side: the yellow stucco of the Kremlin's walls, or the grey iron of Churchill's curtain—to confront us with the truth: it isn't until

---

7. The strange thing was that when I unlocked the gates, and the man explained he and his partner had arrived earlier in the day to stay in another room of the large old house, but that the elderly French couple had neglected to provide him with a key to the gates, which was why he'd got locked out while walking their two rough collies, I realised that if he wasn't in fact Tom Cruise, he must be some sort of brilliant method actor who had submerged himself in the absolute minutiae of the Hollywood star's mannerisms and vocal inflections—as well as, quite possibly, undergoing extensive and effective plastic surgery—since his resemblance to the notorious Scientologist was so very great.

8. I'm not easily overawed by anyone—and in a long career as a journalist I've interviewed everyone from Provisional IRA men to great opera prima donnas—yet I felt completely intimidated by this Cruise-a-like, and stuttered out some sort of nonsense along the lines of; "I bet people are always telling you you look like—"

9. "Tom Cruise? Yeah, but I'm not . . . " He stood there in the dusty gravel road way, the moonlight filtering through the tree canopy threw silvery medallions across his famous face "really I'm not. For one thing, he's straight while I'm gay, and for another, he believes that his body is merely a vessel for a near-immortal alien being, whereas I think of mine as a vehicle for pleasure alone."

10. I wanted to come up with some sort of Wildean bon mot at this at this juncture—but in the event all I could manage is paraphrase: "Is that what brings you to the South of France then, pleasure?"

11. "Not just me—it's what brings these two here as well." He indicated the rough collies—who I now gave my fuller attention to. They really were remarkably fine-looking dogs: their carriage noble, their coats long and smooth and silky; their eyes seemed to penetrate the gloom—seeking out my own. The gay man who wasn't Tom Cruise (but who resembled him closely, as I think I may've said) pointed out that they were unleashed: "I've no need to, you see, for I've trained them so well they'll do just about anything by voice command."

"What do you mean 'just about anything'?"

"Well," said the noctambulant libertine—who I now noted was wearing a lavender-coloured polo shirt, hip-length soft leather jacket, white jeans and suede loafers; in other words, exactly what you'd expect Tom Cruise to be wearing in such circumstances—"Top and Gun happen to be gay as well, so if I order them to fuck each other it's not really being that coercive." At this, the two collies pricked up their ears, and in synchrony two long pink tongues emerged from their mouths to hang, twitching and dribbling from their pointed muzzles.

we grasp the full extent to which the current regime is a reiteration of a timeless ethos of Russian power that we will comprehend just how dangerous it is. In the penultimate story of this collection, "Smirnov," the eponymous protagonist—and another of Sorokin's virtuous veterans—ruptures the space/time continuum by attacking a supermarket clerk with a Braunschweiger sausage[12]. The choice of this particular wurst (which has already happened), is certainly deliberate: the spreadable sausage meat is sometimes admixed with lard. Smirnov's inexorable yet Eleatic progress to the supermarket's sliding doors, triggers a sort of localized rapture.

In their floating estate the denizens of this, a purely commoditized space emphatically post-Soviet space, struggle to invent new rituals that will once more connect determinate signs to finite objects. The Russian ruler, Sorokin argued in his Guardian essay, must be as capricious as he is estranged from his subjects—it wouldn't be possible to control this vast country any other way. But then in the West we know all about caprice as well; for doesn't our neoliberal ethos of power equate the binary of to-buy-or-not-to-buy with that of to-be-oppressed-or-not-to-be-oppressed? All of which is by way of saying: we can read Sorokin as a great Russian writer—but how much more exciting it is simply to read him as a great writer tout court.

Will Self
Sommières, Languedoc, France, July 2022

---

12. Suddenly all of us were fucking—no, I'm not dissembling; this was—as a hebephrenic American teenager might express it—for real. Top had mounted Gun and the Tom Cruise-a-like had torn off my Marks & Spencer drawstring linen trousers, ripped down my Zimmerli briefs, applied a generous wad of Président gourmet butter to my ass crack then eased his thick hard cock into my anus. If anyone had pulled off the main road at this juncture and driven along the track towards the elderly French couple's house, they would have been confronted with this extraordinary sight: two coupling couples, one human—the other canine; and all four of us completely given over to this raw and extempore ecstasy: the dogs howled—I howled as well. I say "all four," but the truth is, although the man who looked like Tom Cruise was able to maintain a very real erection, I caught the note of insincerity in his howling; and it did occur to me—when I felt his hot semen jetting into my colon—that he might just have faked his orgasm.

Except where otherwise indicated, these stories are taken from Sorokin's collection *My First Working Saturday*, composed in 1981 and 1982.

THE PINK
TUBER

ON THURSDAY, ANNA found out that she was pregnant and, having come home from work in the evening, didn't start cooking dinner, but sat down at the tiny kitchen table, placed her thin hands atop the new oilcloth, and stared at them numbly.

Nikolai came back at his usual time—nine o'clock.

Anna listened to him undress in the narrow, densely packed entryway. Then she walked over to him, wrapped her arms around his neck—greased over with a layer of diesel fuel—squeezed her body to his, and froze.

"I can't take it anymore, Kolya, we have to do it."

Nikolai sighed and cautiously touched his lips to her thin blonde hair.

"Everything's gonna be OK. Don't worry."

Her hands crawled over her husband's angular shoulders like two pale snakes.

"What're you calming me down for? Didn't you read yesterday's issue of *Truth*?"

"Yes, of course."

"What're you waiting for? Until they come for us? Or charge us with 'spitting against the wind'?"

"Nah, nah, I'm just thinking."

Anna turned away.

"You think . . . with Him still on the windowsill . . . and everyone seeing Him . . ."

"Don't worry. We'll do it today. No question."

The twilight welded the city together into an uneven plane checkered with lights and buttressed by a strip of evening sky. Squeezed tight by the city and the peeling windowsill, the sky quickly darkened, filling up with damp fog. The darker it became, the sharper and more distinctly His profile fell onto the city's gloomy surface.

Nikolai had long noticed this property of His gnarled pale-pink flesh—that it lit up against a background of growing darkness.

Twelve years ago, when the tiny pinkish tuber burst through the black soil compressed into a silver pot shaped like a huge wine glass, Nikolai was surprised by how quickly it brightened with the onset of twilight.

That evening, the family celebrated the Day of the First Shoots, the guests didn't fit at the table, and they had to move the chest of drawers. Nikolai remembered how, having turned off the light, they listened to the Anthem, how his deceased dad gave the Main Toast, and how they drank wine, then took turns shaking drops from their glasses onto the black, greasily fertilized soil.

"Grow for our delight and our enemies' fright!" Dad shook out his glass third, following the two representatives of the DBA (Directorate of Breeding Agitation), then, bending over quickly, kissed the tuber . . .

Three years later, He had grown to thirty centimeters, and, in His knotty body, much like an elongated potato, Nikolai was suddenly able to distinguish the Leader's precise posture. In the morning, he told his mother this. She laughed and threw Nikolai onto the bed.

"You dummy! We noticed that ages ago."

Then mysteriously added:

"Soon you won't believe your eyes!"

And, indeed, not even a year had passed when the upper part of the seemingly formless tuber rounded out, the bottom widened, and two sloped promontories emerged from His sides.

Then Dad gathered the guests together once more, made a cut across his right hand, anointed the apex of the tuber, and proclaimed this to be the Day of Formation.

Two years later, the tuber had grown another ten centimeters, His pink head becoming even rounder, His thick neck better defined, His shoulders shooting out broadly, and a belly pouncing out from His gnarled waist.

"This here's a miracle of breedin', son!" Dad spoke admiringly, fiddling with his beard, which had gone gray early. "Only our miracle-working people could have come up with something like it! Just imagine: the Father of our Great Country in the flesh! On every family's windowsill, in every home, in every corner of our endless state!"

Soon, a fleshy nose emerged from His round head, then the brow came forth as two tumescences, the chin shifted forward, and ears appeared out of its sides. His body, stuck into chernozem up to the waist, grew broader and stronger. His occasional ruts and warts gradually disappeared, and His gnarls smoothed out.

A year later, lips appeared on His pink face, His brows furrowed majestically, the bridge of His nose tightened, His forehead rounded out, and the hitch of a short cowlick swelled out of it. The narrow collar of His tunic tightened 'round His neck and His belly became more firmly rooted in the ground.

Nikolai was about to graduate from school when dimples appeared on the Leader's face, auricles on His head, and light folds on His tight-fitting tunic.

Dad died two years later.

And, a year after that, they celebrated the Day of Sight's

Recovery: the pillows of His puffy eyelids opened to reveal two dark spheres. It fell to Nikolai to *conduct* the holiday. He powdered his face and sang the Song to the assembled guests. Mom poured a glass of the family's previously accumulated spittle into the Leader's pot. From that day forward, they fed Him only spittle. On every twelfth day, Nikolai also poured his own sperm over Him.

When the little slabs of stripes and bars of the orders He'd been awarded appeared on His tunic and the tip of a pen crawled forth from His right pocket, the Day of the Growth's Completion had arrived. Mom wasn't present at the celebration.

Soon, Nikolai married Anna and got a job at a factory.

Right away, Anna began to look after Him with great care: she wiped away the dust every morning, poured spittle over Him, tilled the chernozem, and polished the silver pot to a shine.

This continued for almost two years.

But, on the twelfth morning of June, a terrible piece of news spread through the Country: the Great Leader had died.

No one worked for two weeks—everyone sat numbly at home. Two weeks later, having buried the deceased, the new Leader solemnly took the Rudder. Unlike the previous one, the new Leader was tall and slim. He made speeches and wrote addresses and proclamations to the people. But there wasn't a single word in them about the previous Leader who'd held the Rudder for forty-seven years. This frightened people. Some went insane and some threw themselves out of their windows, their arms wrapped around their tuber-pots.

A month later, the new Leader made an appeal to the people, in which he mentioned "the one who'd been at the Rudder, but had left for indispensable, yet adequate reasons."

No matter how hard Nikolai and Anna tried to understand the hidden meaning of this statement, it eluded them. The people understood it in two ways and immediately paid for that: those who'd removed the tubers from their windowsills were immediately arrested and the rest were given warnings. For some reason, Nikolai and Anna went unnoticed: they weren't sent the red warning card with the picture of a person spitting against the wind. But this oppressed the couple instead of gladdening them.

Thus did a month and a half pass in ignorance and tension. Their neighbors continued to be warned and arrested. Soon, a decree prohibiting suicide was issued. The suicides ceased . . .

Nikolai didn't notice Anna come up from behind him. Her hands touched his shoulders.

"Are you afraid, Kolya?"

Nikolai turned around.

"What do we have to fear? We have our rights. We're honest people."

"We're honest people, Kolya. Shall we get started?"

Nikolai nodded. Anna turned off the light.

Nikolai picked up a knife, felt for the tuber's waist, and, suppressing the trembling of his sinewy hands, slashed into it. His body turned out to be harder than a potato's. The tuber crepitated faintly under the knife. When Nikolai had cut Him up, Anna grabbed onto Him and, in the darkness, carefully put him down onto the table, as if He were an infant. Nikolai took out an eight-liter glass jar with a wide mouth. Anna lit the stove, took out a bucket of water, and put it on to warm up.

They were sitting in the darkness, illuminated by a faint gas flame, staring at His recumbent body. And it seemed to both Nikolai and Anna that He was stirring. When the water had finished boiling, Anna put it out to cool on the balcony, poured it into a jar, and added some salt, vinegar, bay leaves, and cloves. Then quickly lowered Him down into the jar. Displacing the steaming water, He swayed as if he were attempting to escape. But Nikolai pressed the top of His head down with the metal lid, grabbed the jar-sealer, and began to quickly and dexterously close it up.

When everything was over, the spouses lifted up the jar and carefully hoisted it onto the windowsill—to the same exact spot. Anna carefully wiped the warm jar with a towel. After a moment's hesitation, Nikolai turned on the light. The jar stood there, its glass sides glittering. And He swayed almost imperceptibly in the water, the occasional bay leaf passing Him by.

"Beautiful . . ." Anna pronounced after a long pause.

"Yes . . ." Nikolai sighed.

He embraced his wife and carefully placed his hands onto her stomach. Anna smiled and covered his hands with her own pale hands.

The next morning, getting up half an hour earlier than her husband as she always did, Anna passed into the kitchen, turned on the stove, and put the kettle on. After that, she had the task of watering Him with yesterday's spittle. Scratching herself sleepily, Anna automatically took the glass of spittle from the bookcase, then froze: the glass was empty. Anna turned her gaze to the windowsill, saw the jar with the tuber, and sighed with relief, remembering yesterday's operation. She walked over and laid her hand atop the jar. Looked out the window. The city was awakening and its windows were lighting up. But something had changed in the city. Seriously changed. Anna rubbed at her eyes and looked more closely: on the windowsills of the city were none of the gold and silver pots so familiar to her since her childhood, but instead . . . glass jars containing pink tubers.

1979

THE QUILTED
JACKET

BUT IT STILL hangs as before in the right-hand corner of the living room—between the half-empty bookshelf and the tower-like jumble of the three dirty aquariums.

In the muddy green water, behind the filthy glass, little fish of some nondescript serial breed move sluggishly, each sleepily floating in and out of its three reflections and regularly driving me insane with its calm laziness. Perhaps these little fish are the only creatures in our small two-bedroom apartment who, by the grace of God, are sheerly deprived of the possibility of feeling its presence, see neither its monstrously swollen shoulder, nor its sleeves hanging down to the floor, don't detect the smell of its lardy collar, don't shudder at night at the wall's crackling and rustling, as it's about to pull out the nail already bent down by its weight.

Each morning, throwing off my disobedient blanket and, getting caught in sheets tangled by yet another nightmare, I raise my disheveled head and, turning to it, rock back on my numb arms for a long time, not daring to peel up my sleepy eyelids. And, every day, through fragments of ruined dream, through the feverish ripple of colored spots appears, nay, unfolds in my consciousness a composition familiar to me since childhood: a bookshelf on the left, aquariums on the right, the dented yellow parquetry hastily congregating down below, the cracked, infinitely distant ceiling descending from up above, and in the middle (oh joy! oh morning dram of white freedom!), there's nothing. Nothing! Only the corner's clean vertical line and the flowers of the green wallpaper, not yet faded . . .

Usually, one eye can't take it and a formless, dark-brown shadow momentarily flickers forth between floor and ceiling, forcing the other eyelid to blink in confusion. This is when the matinal superimposition comes to pass, that which so ably drives the fragments of dream out of my head: after several bouts of wavering, the dark-brown spot takes the place of the divinely white Nothing, mercilessly destroys the pattern on the wallpaper, and contracts tightly into the corner.

My hands cease trembling, I wriggle out of the warm, sour bed, stand up on the cold parquetry, and, essentially having broken my body with a tetanus of yawns, enter into my morning reality.

It begins with a journey between the captious, gloomy corners of unawakened objects in the glossy-tiled Eden of the bathroom, from the smell of bleach and linen not entirely dried, from the vast bowl of the rust-eaten toilet, from the crooked stream of liquid, from the limp bristles of a semi-transparent toothbrush being sharply stabbed by my own, from my grandpa's confused scratching at the door:

"Will you be long? Will you? Huh?"

The cistern tank roars hoarsely, a toothbrush is stuck into a cracked, white-spattered glass, and my baggy face is dancing in a round mirror.

"Will you be long? Will you? Huh?"

Oh, yes. The crooked stream disappears and is covered over in hasty drops; rubbing the remnants of a terry towel across my cheeks, I throw up the painted beak of the door hook—my trembling grandpa slides past me, and I, feigning cheerfulness with the chalky taste of tooth powder in my mouth, return to my gloomy room, where, from the right-hand corner, the dark-brown monster offers me its matinal greeting—the dull black O! of its round, lardy collar.

Yes, it seems dark brown to me. I say "seems" because I don't know its actual color. Grandpa claims that it's light gray, Dad (he's now sitting on his saggy bed and rubbing his eyes) says that the quilted jacket is dark yellow, Mom really can't say anything definite about its color, and, jumping in place, my five-year-old brother cries out that it's "blue! blue! blue!"

Sometimes, I try to imagine it as they must see it—blue or light gray—but this doesn't diminish its degree of monstrous absurdity; the quilted jacket, having attained a touch of some-thing like gloomy romanticism, continues to expand into a blue spot in the corner, its shoulder just as swollen as before, the limp, soft tubes of its sleeves still poking dumbly at the parquetry, its ragged, spattered flanks . . . On the other hand, why "ragged"?

"It's your thoughts that are ragged! And your head all holey!"

When Grandpa says these words, his thin, broken body ossifies and shudders almost imperceptibly, like a laconic metal structure, but his pale, unimaginably narrow face stretches out directly toward me like a hatchet.

"That quilted jacket is pretty much new, get it?! Even if you're blind, my sight's still keen! Keen! Oh, how simple it sounds—'old!', 'ragged!', 'shabby!' But you don't know the value of things! Just have a look for yourself . . ." He begins to tremble more violently, grabs me tenaciously with his bony yellow fingers, pulls me over to the quilted jacket, and, feverishly jabbing his hands at its rotten, shredded threads, through which brown cotton wool slides shaggily, he whispers furiously into my ear:

"New, y'see! Ne-e-e-ew! Unwo-o-o-orn! And even if it's been worn, it was only a little! A tiny bit! You get it? A tiny bit! And

yo-o-oou—you all want to throw it out! Ohhhh yoooouuuu . . ."
He pulls away from me, his tear-filled eyes shining. "You don't
know the value of things. We don't value what we have, then we
cry once we've lost it."

And, tensing up unexpectedly, he again raises the pale hatchet
of his face over me.

"But you got bold real quick, you son of a bitch! Clever . . .
you got real clever, huh! Look, you've really got your thinking
cap on now, you lousy intellectual . . ."

It seems to me that, at some point, he won't be able to take
this anymore and, after yet another spell of rage, in a terrible moment
of unconcealed nostalgia for endless squares dully absorbing the
rumble of marching columns, for ideologically renewed pedi-
ments and polished pedestals, he'll finally take his old, wrinkled
cleaver to me, my little brother, Mom, Dad . . .

No. He won't touch Dad.

"You and the children, Faina, you should understand that it's
always easier to criticize than it is to build. To throw something
away or to break it is simpler than to, say, fix or sew it."

After these words, Dad—round, white, and soft as dough
ready to go into the oven—silently approaches the quilted jacket,
carefully lifts up the enormous trunk of one of the sleeves, and,
looking sideways at Grandpa hunched sullenly in the corner,
releases white velvet spheres from underneath his soft, reddish
mustache. They lazily chase after each other, soundlessly colliding,
and merging into a dull, sleepy clod.

"Pay attention . . . it's not really that old . . . to be able to
distinguish . . . you, Faina, have been utterly deprived of political
perspicacity . . . it is essential to understand . . . it's a little worn
out . . . you need to take into account . . . it's not always correct . .
. respect for relics . . . what happened, happened, I'm not arguing,
but . . . the lining is completely new . . . the state of things . . .
everything in its place . . . it's not bothering anyone . . . maybe

it'll still come in handy . . . no need to be like chickens with their heads cut off . . . evolved over the decades . . . been legitimized . . . yourself, you must blame yourself and not . . ."

At moments like these, Mom stands leaning against the peeling door frame, exhaustedly lowering her large, unbeautiful head, resting her plump hand, white from constant laundering, on the other jamb, on which various notches stand out as black measurements of our heights (my brother's are lower and mine higher), marks I very much love to examine during protracted discussions about the fate of the quilted jacket.

As a rule, when, restraining my yawns with great difficulty, I absentmindedly glide my eyes past my brother's marks (this one was when he was three, this one—hasty and crooked—was when he was three and a half, and this inky one with a smeared tail was after three months at Aunt Vera's), Mom pushes herself weightily off of the jamb and begins to speak haltingly and awkwardly.

"Oh, it's old, Petya, o-o-o-old! And it's just hangin' there for no reason. Just hangin'. And nobody wears it. And nobody needs it. I mean, even if it just hung there . . . but it swells up every day. And it reeks—God, it reeks. The whole room smells like it. I've never sniffed a smell to compare it to. And the kid," her chubby shoulder jerks in the direction of my brother, diligently sniffling over a pencil drawing, "sniffs his fill of that monstrosity every day. And you, Dad," now more cautious and calm, she jerks toward Grandpa's bald head, which has warningly descended into his shoulders, "you're an intelligent person, an experienced person. You should understand . . . like they were sayin' on the radio . . . what those people were talkin' about . . ."

First, the ridges of his sharp shoulders come to life, rise up, and begin to slowly squeeze the billiard ball of his head.

Then Grandpa too rises up over us, long and angular like a desiccated praying mantis, he loudly makes his way past two out-of-place chairs and silently slithers back into his little room.

I can see him there in my head, in that three-meter-square box, densely packed with old crumbling furniture: having taken off his slippers, he climbs onto a wobbly chair, hesitantly straightens up, and, tilting his head away from the blue shade of the lighting fixture, reaches for the top of an old cabinet—for a small beech chest.

What follows is so familiar to me that I'm not even surprised when the dimly gleaming, freshly cast real enters into the still hotly steaming, empty form of the imagined with neither interstice nor friction: the dusty bunch of medals disturbed by Grandpa clinks together sharply, the bond of the frozen mortgage rustles dully, the chair squeaks, and his bony fingers fiddle nervously through the shriveled insides of the little chest. A minute later, the door opens.

Like an animate haloxylon, he creeps solemnly over to us, penetrating the room's stagnant air with elbows and knees: his tenacious hands tousle an old newspaper like a ground-down brimstone butterfly.

From that moment on, the snotty gray devil that has possessed me with boredom lazily grows, swells, and spreads its droopy wings, the motley piston of tautly drawn tedium gradually penetrates my soul like fast-growing bamboo, my tongue is covered over in a sour copper soreness, it smacks of a provincial museum, where, above countless carefully englassed crocks, shell casings, and scraps of dried-out leather, enormous classical landscapes pale gloomily in the gilded astrakhan of enormous frames, landscapes in which the flat green of foliage is indistinguishable from the brown of shore hanging steeply over colorless water, or of the half-empty, plush, moth-eaten theater, where the dust raised up from the stage by a corpulently collapsed heroine has been called upon to dissimulate the undisguised boredom that has broken through the soggy chocolate of the jealous moor's makeup.

" . . . Yes, he is three times wrong and three times criminal, the worker of labor and defense who easily forgets, deviates to the side of the so-called, bows down before the rotten, takes his example from the unsightly, falls under the influence of the pernicious, bewails alleged absence, reaches out for the so-called new, decomposes within that which is his, doesn't interfere with the dangerous and allows the shameful. 'To truly appreciate and multiply . . . app-rec-i-ate and mul-ti-ply . . . '" Grandpa raises his finger imposingly, "'the ach-ieve-ment of the Great Churn can only . . . only! be undertaken by a true, sincere, purposeful, intransigent, ideologically staunch, devoted, politically savvy, high-carrying, on-time responding, constantly improving, unswervingly transforming, bravely wrestling, and in-step walking, in step! in! step! walk! ing! in! div! id! u! al!'"

I can't hold back any longer and ya-a-a-awn, ya-a-a-a-a-a-awn, ya-a-a-a-a-a-a-a-a-a-awn, wringing my convulsively ossified hands, I try to use them to grab onto my thin shoulder blades, just about ready to burst through the skin . . .

Mom reluctantly listens to the end of Grandpa's speech, then goes off to do laundry.

My brother finishes his drawing of a one-winged plane hovering weightily over a chaotic green city.

Dad helps Grandpa fold up the newspaper, then rolls over to the quilted jacket, and, squinting attentively, straightens the edge of its turned-out hem . . .

"Everything's getting cold!"

This is our domestic gong.

Silently, one by one, we crawl into the kitchen. Moving the tiny kitchen table away from the wall, I look at a saucepan filled up with viscously gurgling, glue-like oatmeal.

A minute later, it creeps down onto our plates.

Our kitchen is so small that, as we hunch over our bowls of oatmeal, our heads gently rub together.

My little brother immediately scoops up a hot heap, rams it

into his mouth, then, leaning back, shakes his head, lows, and rolls his eyes frantically. Grandpa glances at him disdainfully and I can feel how his bald skull, tightly pressed against my forehead, falls into a cool, tense chill. Dad tickles my temple with his soft mustache, coughs cautiously, and, bending down further, launches his aluminum spoon around the steaming, pale-brown oatmeal that so resembles a piece of flatbread . . .

Analyzing my memory, tormentedly looking through its dusty slides, I endeavor each time to, with maximum precision, find the one on which this formless, dark-brown pile was first imprinted, and, each time my transparent and obliging hands take hold of it, it's unclear, very familiar, and bears the hasty notches of nail marks across its glossy surface: I'm five, I'm screamy and restless, I feel at the soft, brown rot curiously, absorbing the unfamiliar stench of putridity. Dad is round, mobile, and young, he holds me carefully by my suspenders, squints, looks up at Grandpa— long, dry, and solemn, driving a nail into the corner of the room where there's not yet a stool.

I remember an enormous, crowded table with indistinct and degraded borders, it's framed decorously with silent black-and-white guests. The muffled patter disintegrates and short coughs are extinguished. With chubby, trembling hands, Mom lowers the waspstinger of the gramophone onto the blued disk of the record that's set to spinning—I'm consciously listening to the hymn for the first time . . . And then Grandpa wearing a green tunic and raising a tiny glass toward the ceiling, and saying something big and good, Dad, terribly other and unfamiliar, is cheerful, round, with a smile rolling over the heads of the others silently chewing ("Do you want some salad? How about you? And you?"). Grandma is small and white, tightly squeezed in by two fat men draped over with medals . . .

It's unpleasant and incomprehensible: why are there black seeds in the oatmeal? It's bitter without them already, it smells of damp burlap, and there are so many unmilled oats in it that, if I thrust them up toward the edge of my plate, they almost form a greenish circle at the dish's perimeter.

"Thank you." Grandpa is always the first to get up from the table. My little brother, lazily chewing with his mouth stuffed full (stuffed so full that there's no air to smack), tries to grab Grandpa's yellow fingers—the latter pulls his hand away in annoyance and, hastily stepping over me, shuffles sweepingly down the hallway . . .

Seven years ago, he shuffled into his little room, his arms swinging in just the same way, but with a greater admixture of bile in his contemptuously drawn shoulder blades, then slammed the door with irredeemable loudness: a thin, winding crack stretched out above the door jamb. But we weren't looking at it or at Grandpa back then; our receiver, which resembled a locksmith's case, was standing solemnly atop the table and we had tried to twist the necks of the volume knobs several times. Within the membrane, a rich, resonant voice beat, rumbled, and rang like steel. I don't remember what it was broadcasting to the world on that overcast March morning—something about the foundations for the new cement plant, I think—but in the thunder-like charges of its stern harmony, in the hammered lockstep of phrases, and in its sultry breath, there was such a staggering foretaste of freedom that our gray ceiling turned white, the old faded wallpaper pattern stood out more clearly from the walls, and the room itself moved asunder. Mom was sitting at the table, bent over weightily and hiding her face in her white hands. Her big body shook soundlessly—her shoulders, bosom, wet curls that'd turned gray early, and big, cheap clip-ons attached to her tiny, half-sprouted-bean-like ears . . . all of it quivered. Pale and frightened, Dad was sitting next to her, breathing heavily, often blotting the melted oil seal of the nape of his neck with a handkerchief.

"Son, get the paper and the pen. . . . Let's write . . . get it, my dear . . ."

I noisily tore myself away from the table, rushed over to the shelf, and froze, a lump of stale air lodged in my throat: the quilted jacket had shrunk to half its previous size. I cautiously approached it, staring intently, and a wave of cold flame passed across the roots of my hair, then icily slid down my back: the quilted jacket's dirty dark-brown flesh stirred sluggishly, some sort of gloomy, concentrated movement was going on inside of it, its rents were tightening, covering over its rot, its torn seams growing back together, flattening out, the rotten cotton wool shrinking, the lardy places losing their dirty sheen, the quilted jacket brightening and contracting. When the steel orator had shouted out its final word and the jam-packed speaker crackled enthusiastically, the quilted jacket hung from its nail—neat, dark gray, and the size of a child's jacket, its truncated little sleeves moving freely along its quilted sides.

After the speech, Mom finally decided to throw it out. Rising up threateningly over the table like a thundercloud, she waved her hands, shook her head, and demandingly jabbed her white finger against the tin covering of the receiver, which, after a brief moment, once again burst out into bravura-filled music. Dad was rolling around the room, softly skirting corners, muttering something to himself, and fearfully scraping at his puffy cheeks.

It was here too that Grandpa's door flew open and he walked out as he usually did: decisively and angularly. The old newspaper fluttered listlessly from his hands and sprawled out onto the table. Grandpa grabbed the joyfully rattling receiver, swung back weightily, and hurled it into the corner, just beneath the quilted jacket; there was a prickly crunch and the march fell hoarsely to pieces . . .

He read us the newspaper until midnight.

At midnight, his dry finger, like an old church candle, poked solemnly upward and his bloodless lips majestically let forth the final:

". . . as well as gra-ti-tude in the hearts of the coming generations. Yes. Generations!"

Mom stood up silently, sighed, and went off to do laundry.

Dad stood up too—oh, so calm and soft—smiled, sailed over to the quilted jacket, and righted its protruding sleeve. Stood there. Then bent over and began to collect the receiver's shattered fragments . . .

I'm always able to determine the state of our family's budget for the coming week from the color of our morning tea: if it's the color of cognac, we're living "well," if it's densely lemon-colored, then we're "normal," and if it's the color of vodka that's been poured back into its decanter with pale orange peels that have long given way to yellowness, we're "in trouble."

Today it's slightly yellower than that vodka.

Examining Mom's chalice-twisted face through the upended, quickly draining glass, concentratedly wiping our plates with bread, I draw a pale blue line underneath our breakfast, painstakingly writing out the calligraphic "in trouble."

Shaking the yellowish remains of the flock of tea leaves into my mouth (oh, how tightly they stick to the glass!), I put the glass onto the table, stand up, and, muttering an unrequited "thank you," I add a slender plus to the not-yet-dry "in trouble."

"In trouble" plus, then . . .

Every time I sit down at the tiny desk that's so snugly nestled beneath the overhanging bookshelf, a gloomy stench wafts into my nostrils, and my eyes, tearing free from the packets of paper billets (I use them to glue together envelopes), pull my vainly resisting head to the right.

I struggle—digging my nails into the pads of my fingers, twisting my legs into a taut, nagging rope, squeezing the tip of my tongue between my teeth—but, a minute later, my no-longer-obedient neck turns with a crunch: my eyes have gotten stuck in the fulvous mass of rotten cotton wool and ragged threads.

Every time I analyze its scent (if one can even call it a scent), I tormentedly search for analogues in the endless world of earthly smells and am helplessly unable to find them; God could never have created anything like that.

Compared to its poisonous reek, the smell of decomposed meat or rotten eggs reminds me of a gulp of fresh air.

It is impossible to assign an unambiguous definition to the smell emitted by the quilted jacket—it is complex and multila-yered, like an ominously burning mosaic. The only thing that somewhat helps to at least afford it a place in one's consciousness is to calmly, without any pounding of the heart, theorize its primitive synthesis. So as to truly *get* yon murderous conglo-merate, I would take the bitterness of an agèd, half-incinerated garbage dump, the sweetish stench of a worm-infested horse, rags stewing in old chests, pig scat, rain-soaked trash, a dug-up grave, and tripe rotting in the sun.

It seems to me that the quilted jacket smells pretty much like that . . .

Why *seems*? Well, because from the words of my family, I understand that the scent of this monster, much like its color, is perceived differently by all mortals: Mom says that it smacks of rotten goat meat; Dad, "a lil' bit like rotten boards plus such a soooooour rotten apple, a rotten apple with suuuch a bitter taste"; and my little brother just plugs his nose, recoils, and shouts that it's a "meanie! meanie! meanie!"

For Grandpa, the quilted jacket doesn't smell like anything—maybe a little bit like a dusty house and old books (and not old in a bad way, you dunderhead!), but nothing more.

Its smell is just as mutable as its nature: when the quilted jacket shrank for the first time seven years ago, a vapid, boring sort of rot wafted forth from it—how the legs of counselor's desks in damp basements smell. During each of the steely speeches, I cautiously observed the quilted jacket, noticing how strangely its shriveled flesh reacted to the efforts of the metallic orator: it bulged, rainbow spots of decay played over it, it stirred, writhed as if legions of worms were seething beneath its unclean skin, and then, when lead and tin were cautiously added to the steel, it tore in certain places, then spread out once again, releasing shreds of emboldened cotton wool that'd begun to turn brown.

The receiver was new, bought by Mom with her savings, and it stood atop our table, constantly turned on. Grandpa sat gloomily in his room, slithering out only after speeches—to read the newspaper aloud. Mom listened to the orators in the bathroom—bent weightily over the laundry; each particularly damask phrase straightened her up, she raised her head, shrugged her shoulders, sighed, and, wiping tatters of foam from her face, looking intently at someone through the dirty wall, shaking her head with many promises, and, whispering under her breath, ably and evilly wrung out the over-laundered pillowcase. Dad sat perpetually in the corner on his low, bent-legged stool, turning pale, sweating, rounding out, and densely packed in by newspapers, the yellowness and dilapidation of which one might use to judge a great deal about his attitude to the metal voices.

On the other hand, the proportion of pure damask steel in them soon began to fall catastrophically, lead and tin took over a quarter of it, then a half, to which were added loose antinomy and creaky sulfur, the speakers began to stammer and make slips of the tongue, referring to the eternal "schemes of enemies" and "complexity of the international situation," their voices weakened, faded, their words became confused, clinging to each other, threatening to disintegrate into chains of languid letters or merge into a tongue-tied hodgepodge. The orators began to sneeze with increasing frequency, cough, dimly clink empty glasses together, wheeze, lisp, and move further and more irretrievably away from the microphone, as if someone massive and gloomily silent were pushing them away with an iron hand. Each speech ended with the words: "But even so, no matter what!", after which the invisible hall burst out into applause as before.

Grandpa grew bolder, began to slither out from his room, walking around the table and exchanging winks with Dad, he'd tiptoe to the bathroom, poke his little head through the door, and smile crookedly at Mom's heavy, rhythmically shaking back.

After "but even so, no matter what!", the quilted jacket swelled up, purulent patches charging down its stiff shoulders. The usual stench flowed forth from it once more, its sleeves stirring and sliding down.

With each passing day, the orators were losing steel, their voices becoming quieter, older, shrinking, beginning to mumble, and soon, it wasn't lead and tin that flowed forth from the silk-covered membrane, not even sulfur and antimony, but some kind of soggy window putty, viscous and colorless, sometimes awkwardly mimicking rubber.

Now, Grandpa didn't even read newspapers in the evenings, but, having put on his moth-eaten uniform with its tinkling bunch of medals, would wander solemnly around the room— straight, flat, and tall, crunching his fingers defiantly, smiling, his satisfied eyes shining without seeing us, muttering something and stroking Dad's trembling head, which was drowning in his loose shoulders.

Sometimes, he'd walk over to the bathroom, lean back, and, accompanied by the ringing of polished metal, hurl his dirty blue underpants at the door.

Mom would pick them up silently.

Then, one sunny May day, the speeches stopped and the quilted jacket's browned corpse came decisively back to life, grew, swelled up, the seams diverged, the threads, bending sluggishly, began to unwind, loose matter joyfully exfoliated itself from the cotton wool, rolled up into rotten little tubes, smoldered, crumbled into rotten fibers, the cotton wool turned black in some places, it became tumescent with some kind of basement dampness—the quilted jacket grew heavier, sagged, touched the floor, and, like a quilted doormat, slid along the parquetry—toward Grandpa's feet, he was standing frozen in front of it . . .

It would seem that there's nothing simpler than sitting at the table and gluing together envelopes: the hands habitually fold together the four rounded corners, a drop of glue entangled in the bristles of the brush spreading along their edges, the paper planes sticking together, the completed envelope then set aside. Simple and easy.

That's how it seemed to me for the first two years.

Then, as the quality and speed of the execution of my work subtly grew, a monotonous hatred for these white, dryly rustling sheets began to accumulate in me, for the brown glue, for the shaggy brush—a professional enmity for the monotonous labor that stuffs the soul with bitter taste, the labor that lies in wait for the gloomy lathe-operator in the matinal heap of rudely gleaming blanks to be turned, for that which obstructs and separates him from the warm, hastily smoke-cured twilight of the evening entryway where, beneath the crookedly overhanging, spattered whitewash, a bit of smut writhing on the pale wall is obscured by a hopelessly dead light bulb, and a broad-shouldered friend feverishly tears the white cap off of a weightily burbling bottle, lovingly outlined in the darkness by a moonbeam that has seeped in and been transmuted into two or three liquid splotches. For me, this enmity accumulates in the freshly glued, pungent-smelling envelopes piled up in dense packets, behind which lies a far more real thing, one much like the imagined gloomy entryway: a shabby volume of poems by "a deservedly forgotten melancholic."

It's nearby—this miraculous green book—all I have to do is reach out my hand, push aside the unstable stack of envelopes, and, along with its puzzling fall (softly securing each other, the envelopes tumble down from the table, the withered brush rolls hastily to its edge), so too collapses the dubious mechanism of my daily duty: the green cover shall flip off to the left, the ligature of the beautiful title page shall flicker forth, the terse lines shall begin to speak, a cold and fussy cathedral of "socially harmful pseudo-poetry" shall emerge from the fog, the chilled copper of its bells shall begin to echo dimly—and farewell, day, farewell, night, farewell oh ye dark brown chlamys . . .

But I get paid for every hundred envelopes, not for each and every single one. In return for a thousand of these sour-smelling packets, I have the right to eat calmly without running my eyes across other people's plates. That's all that my existence affords to our tea budget. As is well-known, reading poetry brings few material advantages.

How quickly the pot of glue runs dry, the brush attempting to stick to its oily, drying bottom. I'll have to head over to the storeroom again. Have to get up, dodging the edge of the bookshelf, which potentially enshrines within itself the danger of a glancing blow, straighten up, get out from behind the desk, hold my nose as I go past you, oh stinking monster, drown my disobedient eyes in the landscape of your minutely rotting flesh. A year ago, it still retained some faint semblance of arable lands abundantly washed by rains—much of the stitching was intact, they stretched out from one of your sides to the other, from collar to hem, first vanishing, then reappearing in the sullenly shaggy cotton wool—but, now, the whole of you is an entirely open wound that won't scab over. You've swollen to enormous size, hem and sleeves piling up atop the ground and crawling over one another in fat folds, discoloring the parquetry around you, shoulders bulging out like gangrenous tumors and resting on the ceiling. You grow heavier each day, filling up with some sort of venomous dampness, which wanders around dully inside of you, inflating your heavy members outwards.

You threaten to tear forth from the thick, half-bent nail, to fill up the entire room, to topple the walls and building and creep down viscously onto the exhausted heads of our countrymen, to bury the entire city beneath you.

Who are you? Wherefore were you sent to us? What shall put a stop to your rotten growth? Grandpa's death? The metallic speeches? I don't think so . . .

You can't be thrown out or shoved into an iron drawer, sooner or later you'll push any steel apart at the seams like flabby fly-agaric. It's not possible to burn you, I'm sure that the flame would recoil in fright from your stuffed tatters. It's not possible to give you away to someone, for everyone, every family, and every apartment has one of your mute doubles hanging in the right corner of their living rooms—just as enormous, swollen, decaying, and frightening, with precisely the same four-cornered scar of a neatly torn-out label, the heavy trunks of its sleeves, and the enormous O! of its lardy collar . . .

Maybe you swell and grow because of an insufficiently respectful attitude toward you on our end? After all, most of your quilted brothers hang in whimsically mirrored cabinets, their shoulders resting on carved hangers and their hems on gilded stands. And, each morning, the inhabitants of those apartments bow down deeply before your gloomy likenesses, multiplied by obliging mirrors. The only one among us who really loves you is Grandpa. But, it's true, he doesn't bow down to you as others do; on the contrary, he straightens up and stretches out before you, pulling up the jaundiced block of his carefully shaven chin until he hears a crunch . . .

Your ragged threads, which resemble half-asleep caterpillars, stir sluggishly. Sometimes, plugging my nose and overcoming my disgust, I approach you, cut them off, and feed them to the fish. They eat them eagerly.

I've trained the fish to feed upon your flesh every day—maybe that hurts you just a little bit?

There aren't that many of them: twenty-three. They're indifferent to you—you see how calmly they float in your green reflections? I love them for that, I change the water, I clean the old aquariums, and feed them—feed them with you.

Even now—two hours before I feed the fish—having noticed me, they reach up through the water and penetrate its surface with their inquisitively open mouths . . .

Yesterday, two plump female guppies brought forth a flock of nimble and transparent fries with tiny golden fins and big black eyes. Another female is pregnant and just about to give birth. It's time to catch her in a net and move her away from the other fish or they'll eat her babies.

Today, as soon as I finish gluing envelopes together, I'll put her into a liter jar. Grow up in peace, little fishies.

1978

SERGEI
ANDREYEVICH

SOKOLOV THREW TWO dry spruce branches into the fire, the flame instantly engulfed them, reached up, then began to lick at the bottom of the sooty bucket hanging over the fire with impetuous tongues.

Sergei Andreyevich looked at the needles writhing in the bluish flame, then shifted his gaze over to the faces of the kids spellbound by the campfire.

"A luxurious campfire, huh?"

Sokolov nodded.

"Yeah . . ."

Lebyedeva shrugged her slender shoulders icily.

"I haven't been in the forest for a hundred years, Sergei Andreyevich. Since eighth grade."

"Why?" he took off his glasses and, squinting myopically, began to wipe them off with a handkerchief.

"I guess I just didn't have time," Lebyedeva replied.

"Why didn't you go to Istra with us?" Savchenko asked mockingly.

"I couldn't."

"Just say you were lazy and that's that."

"I wasn't lazy. I was ill."

"You weren't ill."

"I was too!"

Sergei Andreyevich conciliatorily raised his thin hand with its lean, delicate fingers.

"Well, that's enough of that, Lyosha, let Lena be . . . It'd be better to look at how be-a-utiful it is around us. Listen."

The kids looked around.

The impetuous flame of the campfire etched out the dark silhouettes of bushes and young birches. Off in the distance, a tall mixed forest blacked out the horizon like a tall, immovable wall, above which a large moon was suspended among a bright scattering of stars.

They were surrounded by a deep nocturnal silence, broken only by the crackling of the campfire.

It smelled of river, rot, and burnt needles.

"Awesome . . ." the curly-haired, broad-shouldered Eliseyev stretched out and began to stand up, "just like in *Dersu Uzala*."

Sergei Andreyevich smiled, as a result of which fine wrinkles gathered around his youthful eyes, hidden behind thick glasses.

"Yes, kids, the forest is a fascinating natural phenomenon. The eighth wonder of the world, as Mamin-Sibiryak said. You can never have enough of the forest, can never grow tired of it. And how many riches there are in the forest! Oxygen, wood, cellulose . . . Berries and mushrooms too. It's practically a pantry. It's very difficult for a person to get by without the forest. It's not possible to live without this beauty . . ."

He fell silent, looking off into the immoveable wall of the forest.

The kids looked off in the same direction.

"The forest, Sergei Andreyevich, well . . . of course, it's good," Eliseyev muttered, smiling, "but technology's still better."

He patted the portable tape recorder on his shoulder:

"You can't take a single step without technology these days."

Sergei Andreyevich turned to him and gave him an attentive look.

"Technology . . . Well, of course, Vitya, technology has certainly given man a great deal. But, it seems to me that, most importantly, it shouldn't overshadow man himself, not push him into the background. The forest could never do that."

The kids looked at Eliseyev.

Sticking out his lower lip, he shrugged.

"No, no, I didn't . . . I just . . ."

"You're just obsessed with pop music and that's that!" Lebyedeva interrupted him. "You can't take a single step without that box."

"So what? Is that a problem or somethin'?" he looked at her sullenly.

"It's not a problem, but it's not healthy either!" she laughed. "You'll go deaf and no institute will accept you!"

The kids laughed amicably.

Sergei Andreyevich smiled.

"Well, Lebyedeva, you've got a sharp tongue."

"What does he have to make such a fuss over pop music for, Sergei Andreyevich?"

"What's it to you?" Eliseyev grunted. "You can't survive without your conservatory either . . ."

"That's 'cause it's a conservatory, you idiot! Bach, Haydn, Mozart! All you've got is some shaggy-headed guys howling!"

"Your head's pretty shaggy too!"

Sergei Andreyevich gently took Eliseyev by the shoulder.

"Come on, Vitya, that's enough. You're getting ready to go to the Moscow Aviation Institute. And pilots need restraint."

"I'm gonna design planes, not pilot them," Eliseyev muttered, now flushed.

"All the more, then. So, my friends. Making use of this clear weather, let's recollect our astronomy."

Sergei Andreyevich got up, walked a little ways off into the distance, then, sticking his hands into the pockets of his light jacket, looked up at the sky.

It was dark violet; the stars shone with unusual brightness and seemed to be especially near. The edge of the blindingly white moon had been slightly hemmed.

"Better and more descriptive than any map," Sergei Andreyevich said quietly and adjusted his glasses with a quick, laconic motion. "Sooo . . . What's that vertical constellation over there?"

He raised his hand aloft.

"Well, who's gonna be bold? Oleg?"

"Coma Berenices?" Zaitsev muttered uncertainly.

Sergei Andreyevich shook his head.

"That's higher and to the right. Over there, underneath Canes Venatici . . . Vitya?"

"Cassiopeia!" Eliseyev said loudly, sticking his hands into the pockets of his jeans and throwing back his head. "Definitely Cassiopeia!"

Standing next to him, Sokolov smirked.

"D-," Sergei Andreyevich said and quickly pointed somewhere else. "There's your Cassiopeia, next to Cepheus."

Lebyedeva laughed.

Eliseyev scratched at the nape of his neck and shrugged.

"But they both really do look . . ."

"Like you!" Lebyedeva giggled and, interrupting him, slapped Eliseyev on the back of his neck from behind Sokolov's back.

"What a freak!" Eliseyev grinned.

Sergei Andreyevich turned to the kids.

"Does really nobody know? Dima?"

Savchenko shook his head silently.

"Lena?"

Lebyedeva sighed with a shrug.

"Everything in my brain got all jumbled up after exams, Sergei Andreyevich," Zaitsev drawled.

Eliseyev smirked and kicked a branch that had fallen out of the fire.

"Everything got jumbled up in *some* of our brains, but it went the opposite way for others—everything flew right out. Like in a wind tunnel . . ."

The kids laughed.

"Well, Mishka here definitely knows, his eyes say it all," Lebyedeva nodded toward Sokolov.

Sokolov looked into the campfire in embarrassment.

Sergei Andreyevich shifted his gaze onto the boy's calm, narrow face.

"Do you know, Misha?"

"I know, Sergei Andreyevich. It's Serpens."

"Ye-e-ep," the teacher nodded affirmatively. "Well done. And what's above Serpens?"

"Corona Borealis," Sokolov spoke restrainedly in the total silence.

"Correct. Corona Borealis. In that constellation hangs a star of the first Magnitude. And what constellation is to the left of that?"

"Hercules."

"And to the right?"

"Boötes."

Sergei Andreyevich smiled.

"A+."

Eliseyev shook his head.

"Wow, Mishka, look at you. Just like Giordano Bruno."

Fingering the hem of his jacket, Sokolov looked up into the sky.

The water in the bucket overflowed, hissing down onto the fire.

"Oh man, we totally snoozed!" Eliseyev began to fuss, grabbing onto one end of the cross-stick, from which the bucket was hanging. "Let's take it off quickly, Oleg!"

Zaitsev grabbed onto the other end.

They took the bucket off of the fire and placed it carefully down onto the cinder-strewn grass.

Sergei Andreyevich walked over and bent down.

"So. It's boiled. C'mon, let's boil up some tea."

The kids began to pour tea from pre-prepared packets into the boiling water.

"Maybe we should pour the condensed milk in right away, huh?" Lebyedeva gave them an inquiring look.

"Why not! Good idea," the teacher nodded.

Eliseyev took two cans out of his backpack and began to open them. Meanwhile, Lebyedeva was stirring the liquid in the bucket with a fresh-cut stick. Having quickly opened the cans, Eliseyev upended them into the bucket. Condensed milk stretched down through the air in two viscous stripes . . .

Soon, the kids and their teacher were delightedly drinking sweet, aromatic tea, sipping it out of mugs.

A damp nocturnal breeze set the flames of the dying campfire to swaying and brought over the odor of the river.

Weakening tongues danced above an amber heap of coals, hesitating, disappearing, then reappearing once again.

"It's the perfect moment to put on the potatoes," Zaitsev suggested as he sipped at his tea.

"Definitely," Eliseyev agreed and began to rake at the coals, flinching away from the heat.

Sergei Andreyevich finished his tea and put his mug down onto a stump.

"And you're getting ready to study at the textile institute, right, Lena?"

Lebyedeva's mug froze just by her lips.

Lena looked at her teacher, then put down her mug and shifted her gaze onto the campfire.

"Sergei Andreyevich, I . . . I . . ."

She took a deep breath, then made a firm pronouncement.

"I've decided to work at a weaving factory."

The kids looked at her in silence.

Raking the coals, Eliseyev grunted surprisedly:

"Well, look at that! A straight-A student and she wants to work with machines . . . to wind bobbins . . ."

"And it's none of your business!" Lebyedeva interrupted him. "Yes, I'm all set to work at a factory as a simple weaver. To *feel* what production really is. And I know what my grades are worth."

Eliseyev shrugged.

"But you should still study evenings or weekends while you work . . ."

"I think it's better to just work for a year, then to study at a daytime institute. It'll be easier for me to study that way and I'll learn more about life. All of the women in our family are born weavers. My grandma, my mom, and my sister."

"That's the way to do it, Len," Zaitsev nodded. "My uncle used to tell me a lot about young engineers. They'd study for five years, but still not know a thing about enterprises . . ."

Sergei Andreyevich looked comprehendingly into Lebyedeva's eyes.

"Fantastic. After that, you'll do even better at the institute. A year of work at a factory is very useful. In my own time, I also worked for a year as a simple lab assistant at an observatory before beginning my studies at Moscow State University. After that, I could get oriented during practical exercises much better than other students."

Eliseyev scratched at the nape of his neck.

"So, maybe I should work as a laboratory assistant in an aerodynamics lab before I study?"

Sitting next to him, Zaitsev slapped him on the shoulder.

"Definitely, Vityok. You'll stand in the wind tunnel instead of the plane."

The kids laughed.

"That'll blow all of his tape-recorder trash right out of him!"

Lebyedeva laughed the loudest, calling forth another fit of hilarity from the group.

Eliseyev waved his hands.

"Enough with the shouting! What're you acting like freaks for . . . Let's get the potatoes on or the coals'll cool . . ."

The kids began to take potatoes out of their backpacks and lay them out on the coals.

Eliseyev buried them, deftly wielding his stick.

Savchenko hunched over the empty bucket.

"What, is the tea finished already?"

"There wasn't that much of it, just a half-bucket. A lot of the water boiled off . . ."

"Guys, someone go get water!" Lebyedeva asked loudly. "We'll put on another bucket of tea!"

Sergei Andreyevich picked up the bucket.

"I'll go."

Standing next to him, Sokolov extended his hand.

"I should go instead, Sergei Andreyevich."

"No, no," the teacher raised his hand comfortingly. "My legs fell asleep. I had my fill of sitting."

"Then can I go with you? It's still a long way to carry it . . ."

The teacher smiled.

"OK, let's go."

They moved toward the forest.

The low June grass rustled softly underfoot and the bucket in Sergei Andreyevich's hands tinkled quietly.

Large, moonlit bushes surrounded them on all sides, forcing the walkers to dodge through foliage and draw wet branches away from their faces.

Sergei Andreyevich walked unhurriedly ahead, whistling quietly and melodically.

Once they'd entered into the forest, it became cooler and the bucket tinkled more resoundingly.

Sergei Andreyevich stopped and nodded upwards.

"Look, Misha."

Sokolov raised his head.

Up above, through the faintly stirring foliage, the moonlight made its way down in murky white stripes, while the moon itself sparkled atop a tall fir. Stripes of milky light lay obliquely across the trunks of the trees, silvering their bark and leaves.

"How delightful," the teacher whispered, adjusting his glasses, in the thick lenses of which the moon played phantomically. "I haven't seen something like this in a long time. Have you?"

"I haven't," Sokolov muttered hastily, then added, "the moon's so bright . . ."

"Yes, it was full pretty recently. You can see it through the telescope as clear as if you were holding it in the palm of your hand . . ."

Sergei Andreyevich admired the forest silently.

A little while later, Sokolov asked:

"Will our class get together every year, Sergei Andreyevich?"

"Of course. What, you already miss them?"

"No, no . . ." Sokolov hesitated, "it's just . . . I . . ."

"What?" the teacher turned to him.

"Well, I . . ."

He fell silent for a moment, then began to speak quickly, fingering a hazel branch as he did.

"It's just . . . you've done so much for me, Sergei Andreyevich . . . and our club, well, I fell in love with astronomy because of it . . . And now it's graduation and everything. No, I understand, of course, we should be independent, but still . . . I . . ."

He froze, then began to speak quickly in a trembling voice.

"Thank you for everything, Sergei Andreyevich. I . . . I'll . . . never in my life forget what you've done for me. Never! And you . . . you're . . . you're a great man."

He lowered his head.

His lips were trembling and his hands compulsively crumpled the wet leaves.

Sergei Andreyevich took him hesitantly by the shoulder.

"Well, that's too much . . . that's too much, Misha . . ."

They stood in silence for a minute.

Then the teacher began to speak—quietly and tenderly.

"There are very few great men, very few great people. I'm not a great man, I'm just a simple highschool teacher. If I really helped you with something, then I'm very pleased. Thank you for your warm words. You're a talented guy and it seems to me that you'll make a good scientist. But to get upset now, well, in my opinion, it's pointless. Ahead lies a new life, new people, and new books. So, I see no reason to get a case of the blues."

He patted Sokolov on the shoulder.

"Everything'll be OK. Your class is tight. We'll get together every year. And you can come visit me anytime. I'll always be happy to see you."

Sokolov raised his head joyfully.

"Really?"

"Really, really," Sergei Andreyevich laughed, then gave him a gentle shove. "Well, let's go, everyone's waiting for the tea."

They moved through the phantomically illuminated forest.

The bucket began to creak once again and branches crunched underfoot.

Sergei Andreyevich walked up ahead, carefully holding back the flexible branches of the bushes and pulling them off to the side.

The forest parted, ending in a sharp precipice with uneven edges that was overgrown with small bushes.

A narrow strip of river gleamed down below, squeezed in by thickets of wildly overgrown reeds.

Beyond the river, lower forest cover stretched out into the distance and only very far off did the dark massif of a pine forest tower up.

Sergei Andreyevich stood at the edge of the precipice for a moment, silently taking in the view, then stepped off of it and ran dashingly toward the river down a steep, sandy slope.

Sokolov went down after him.

The sand around the river was dense and wet.

Sergei Andreyevich stepped onto a stump lying in the water and scooped down with the bucket.

"There we go . . ."

On their left, a snipe burst forth from the thick reeds, then flew away, whistling as it did.

"How beautiful," the teacher said, lowering the bucket down onto the sand. "The essence of nature, Misha . . ."

He paused; then, thrusting his hands into the pockets of his jacket, continued.

"How harmonious everything is here. How systematic. How unconscious. That's the example you need to follow—nature's. I'll admit it, if I didn't come out here once a month, I wouldn't be able to work . . ."

He looked into the distance.

The pine forest stretched off into the horizon itself, dissolving in the pinkish haze that illuminated the night sky in the east.

Sokolov spoke up quietly:

"I really like this place too, Sergei Andreyevich. I'll definitely keep coming here."

"You should," the teacher nodded. "It's like you gain strength from it. Spiritual purity. As if you were drinking the water of life from a forbidden well. And after you drink this water, Misha, your soul gets more pure. All the fuss, trash, and vanity, it flows away into the sand . . ."

He lifted the bucket and began to walk up the slope of crumbling sand.

Up above, Sokolov reached out to take the bucket.

"Maybe . . . can I carry it, Sergei Andreyevich?"

"Carry it," the teacher smiled, gave him the bucket, then added, "go, I'll be back in a bit. I want to breathe in some more of the forest air . . ."

Sokolov picked up the heavy bucket and began to move through the forest.

Sergei Andreyevich stood on the precipice, his arms crossed over his chest, and looked out in front of him.

After having taken ten or so steps, Sokolov looked around.

The teacher's motionless figure was clearly drawn between the trunks of the trees.

Sokolov stepped off to the side and stood behind a young fir, placing the bucket down next to him.

The teacher stood there for five minutes, then walked into the forest, moving in something of an oblique direction.

Passing between two close-grown birches, he stopped, undid his belt, pulled down his pants, and squatted.

A broad stripe of moonlight fell onto him, illuminating his back, head, and his arms crossed over his knees.

The faint, intermittent passing of gas made itself audible, Sergei Andreyevich bowed his head, moaning softly as he did, then the same sound reached Sokolov's ears once again—louder, but less drawn out this time.

Sokolov looked out from behind the fir, stroking the young needles with his fingers.

Some bird let forth a protracted cry behind him.

A little while later, Sergei Andreyevich raised himself up, stretched out his hand, plucked a few leaves from a hazel tree, wiped himself, pulled up his pants, buttoned up, then, beginning to whistle, moved in the direction of the flames of the campfire flickering between the tree trunks.

He walked quickly and confidently, deadwood crunching and glasses gleaming.

Soon, his slender figure had vanished into the darkness of the forest and, a little while later, the sound of his delicate whistling disappeared too.

Standing in the dark and listening carefully, Sokolov picked up the bucket and walked forward. Stepping over a fallen tree, he inadvertently swung the bucket and cold water splashed down onto his boot.

Grabbing the bucket with his other hand, he walked around a fir tree and set off for the two close-grown birches. The moonlight slid over their trunks, causing their bark to glow against the background of the dark firs.

Sokolov passed between the birches, then stopped. Before him lay a small moonlit clearing. The low grass sparkled with dew and the leaves of the hazel tree looked to be a silvery shade of gray.

The faint smell of fresh feces filled the clearing.

Sokolov looked around.

The dark silhouettes of trees loomed up motionlessly on all sides. He looked ahead, took several steps, then, lowering the bucket, squatted down.

A small pile of feces lay in the grass, shining with an oily sheen. Sokolov brought his face up to it. The feces had a strong odor. He unstuck one of the sausages from the heap. It was warm and soft. He kissed it, then began to quickly eat it, taking greedy bites and smearing his lips and fingers.

Again, a nocturnal bird cried out somewhere in the distance.

Sokolov picked up the two remaining sausages and, taking alternating bites from one, then the other, quickly gobbled them up.

The forest was silent.

Brushing away the soft crumbs and carefully wiping his hands off on the grass, he tilted the bucket and began to drink greedily. The fathomless black water swayed in front of his face and the moon and inverted constellations swung together with it.

Sokolov drank thirstily, embracing the cold bucket with sweaty palms and watching the vertical baton of Serpens fall apart, then disintegrate into splotches.

FIRST DAY OF
THE SEASON

SERGEI STEPPED ONTO a narrow, barely noticeable path that slithered into the swamp, but Kuzma Yegorych grabbed him warningly by the shoulder.

"No, Seryozh, we won't get through that way."

"Why not?" Sergei turned to him.

The huntsman replied unhurriedly, waving a horsefly away from his face:

"It really came down day before yesterday and now the bog's all swole up. 'Round by the Paninskaya Lowland, it'll be up to yer waist and my chest. So we oughta make a detour."

"Through the felling areas?"

"What would we do that for! More'n a verst'n change extra out the way! We'll stick closer to the black turnpike."

"Let's go, then. You know better'n me," said Sergei as he turned.

"That's for sure," the huntsman chuckled weakly, righting the fur cap that had fallen over his eyes, "I can see through everythin' 'round here. Been treadin' foot in this forest for fifty years."

"You probably know every tree by heart."

"I do, my dear, I do . . ." sighed the huntsman and strode ahead of Sergei.

The brambles that had grown up around the swamp soon came to an end, giving way to a young birch forest.

It was drier here and the yellow tallgrass reached up to their waists, crunching softly underfoot.

The huntsman lit up as they walked, a sweetish blue plume stretching out behind his stooped, quilted-jacket-clad back.

Sergei reached into his pocket, pulled out an empty pack of Yava cigarettes, crumpled it up, and threw it into the grass. A light breeze rustled the birch leaves and set the whisks of the grass to swaying.

Sergei plucked a blade of it as he walked, stuck it into his mouth, and looked around. A light fog hovered over the swamp that lay behind them and two chirping kites flew in circles through the pinkish-yellow haze.

After the birch forest ended, Kuzma Yegorych began to head to the right. They crossed a small ravine, kept wide of a ridge of boulders encased in soil, then entered a forest of fir trees.

Sergei pulled the blade of grass out of his mouth and threw it at a young fir. The blade disappeared between the tree's milky-green whorls.

Their path widened and darkened.

The huntsman turned to Sergei and fixed the gun belt that had slipped from his shoulder.

"Ye've ne'er been in here?"

"No, Yegorych. Not once."

"A deep, dark place . . ." Yegorych trod beside him, looking down at his feet.

"Nice firs. Slender too."

"Yeah, the firs're *unaccountably* fine here."

"And they've grown up so thick," Sergei muttered as he looked around. "Prolly quite a few wood and hazel grouse too . . ."

"There were wood grouse, that's for sure. A swamp, berries nearby, and so they up'n lived here. But afterwards, they kinda cleared off, I guess. And I can't work out why. Still plenty of hazel grouse, though. They fly to the call in a flock and that's that. Ye just gotta shoot."

"And why'd the wood grouse clear off?" Sergei asked.

"I just doan know," the huntsman squinted, pulling at his beard. "I doan know. No one was huntin' 'em an' it's a real dense wood. I only know that wood grouses're real capricious. Cautious too. Hazel grouses and blackcocks, they'll go where even grass won't. They'll live anywhere. But not wood grouse . . ."

Sergei looked up.

Tall firs interlocked up over the path and the sun shone through them weakly. The ground beneath their feet was soft and dry.

"And, Yegorych, have there never been any villages here other'n Korobka?"

The huntsman shook his head.

"What d'ye mean—never been! There were three. Two as tiny as farmsteads and one with forty houses."

"And now what?"

"Well, everyone moved away and the olduns died. Young people're real attracted to the city. And the huts're all boarded up. They're rottin'."

"Are they far from here?"

"The big one's five versts away, but the farmsteads're further."

"Huh . . . We oughta go take a look."

"Sure thing. We'll find the time. Ye'll see the nettles grownin' up through the windows!"

Sergei shook his head and straightened his rifle.

"That's bad."

"Sure is. Nothin' good about it. Makes ye feel sick to look at those houses. Cabins built with fir logs—real even. For the love of God, someone oughta carry 'em away . . ."

"Can it really be there's no one to do it?"

The huntsman waved his hand.

"Ahh . . . No one wants to deal with it. The people got real lazy . . ."

"Well, that ain't true. You shoulda seen how your people were hustlin' at the sawmill today."

"You call that hustlin'?" Kuzma Yegorych was surprised.

"And what do you think? They weren't workin' good?"

The huntsman waved his hand again.

"That ain't how ye work. Ye think that's the way we worked before the war? Watchin' the clock? We never left the forest, I'd leave my farm, my dear deceased wife'd be scoldin' me—time to make hay!—but we'd be countin' trees again, then sawin', then fellin'! I was the last to mow when everyone else'd cleared off and was drinkin' tea."

Smiling, Sergei looked over at him.

The huntsman took broad steps, spreading his knobby hands out in front of him.

"And at war? If the men'd found out that there were ten cabins bein' put to no use standin' ten versts away, they woulda taken 'em apart the next day! And now they're rottin' on their own and it's all . . . sickenin' to behold . . ." He fell silent and righted his fur cap.

The fir forest began to thin out and rays of sunlight broke through the whorls, tumbled onto the path, and glided along the grayish trunks.

"We'll turn in a sec, then we'll pretty much be there," the huntsman waved his hand.

They turned and set off along a thinner path overgrown with bushes. Ahead of them, a noise suddenly rang out, heavy wings flapped, and wood grouse flashed forth flying between the branches.

The huntsman stopped, following them with his eyes.

"There they are. A brood . . . means they didn't clear off . . ."

They stood there for a moment, listening to the birds' retreat.

"Real strong . . ." Sergei shook his head.

"Yeah. By autumn, ye won't be able to tell young apart from old . . . just listen to 'em rumblin' away . . ."

Kuzma Egorych walked forward cautiously, looking around and bending over.

"Take a gander, Seryozh . . ."

Seryozha approached and squatted down.

The pine-strewn soil was covered over in wood-grouse droppings, while here and there were also visible a wallow's smooth holes.

"They're still alive, then . . ." Yegorych smiled, picked up a dried dung worm in the palm of his hand, then dropped it. "Least these ain't flown away . . ."

Sergei nodded empathetically.

A large meadow lay behind the forest of firs.

The grass had been mown and a trinity of lonely oaks stood at its center. A huge haystack could be seen at its far end, right by the meadow's edge. The huntsman scratched at his temple and looked around:

"Well, here we are. Half a verst from the glades . . ."

Sergei pulled a cobweb off of his face.

"So, we swung 'round to the right?"

"Mhmm."

"That was quick. I wanted to go through the glades."

The huntsman sneered.

"This way's shorter."

Sergei shook his head.

"You're a real Susanin, Yegorych!"

"Yeah, yeah . . ."

They crossed the meadow and entered into a dense mixed forest.

Kuzma Yegorych moved confidently ahead, crunching through deadwood, then pushing aside and holding back the elastic branches of a hazel grove. His gray quilted jacket was quickly covered over with cobwebs and a dry twig got caught in his collar.

"I bet there're a lotta mushrooms here, huh Egorych?" Sergei spoke into the huntsman's quilted back.

"That depends."

"How about this summer?"

"Not bad. Marya hauled in three buckets. Pickled 'em too." On the left, surrounded by brambles, a lightning-split oak appeared. The splintered trunk gleamed amidst the gloomy green.

"Look at that," Sergei nodded at it.

"Yeah. And it's not even the edge of the grove."

"And look at the oaks over there. Why hit this one . . ."

"God knows better'n us."

Sergei laughed.

"What ye laughin' for? In '58, four of us were comin' back from haymakin' and walkin' across a field, we were carryin' our pitchforks and scythes on our shoulders. And one broad was walkin' with nothin', just an empty pot of porridge. Lightning struck her. And she didn't have no steel and was much shorter'n everyone else. It seemed the lightning was set on settin' *her* sins to right . . ."

"A coincidence," Sergei muttered.

"Ain't no such thing as coincidences," the huntsman interrupted him confidently.

The forest ended and a wide, sun-drenched clearing appeared from between the trunks.

Kuzma Yegorych turned to Sergei and raised a finger.

"Well, quiet now. Or it'll hear and we'll be outta luck."

"Which way we goin'?" Sergei whispered, removing his rifle from his shoulder.

"We'll cross by way of those bushes over thataway . . ."

The huntsman removed his double-barreled weapon from his shoulder, pulled back the hammer, thrusting the butt beneath his armpit and dropping the barrel down, then set off across the clearing. Sergei set off a few moments later. The clearing was wide.

The massive stumps had had time to grow over with bushes and ferns and the tallgrass stood like a wall around its entire perimeter. The huntsman carefully stepped around the stumps, maneuvering over fallen trunks as he did. Sergei tried to keep up. In the middle of the clearing, a wood hen rose up from beneath the huntsman's feet and began to fly weightily. Kuzma Yegorych swore merrily, following it with his gaze, then kept walking. When they were nearing the edge of the clearing, he silently indicated a tall fir to Sergei. Sergei nodded, laid his rifle down onto the ground, took off his rucksack, and began to untie it. The huntsman stood with his gun at the ready, looking around and listening carefully. Sergei took a rope and a small tape recorder out of his rucksack. Binding a stone to the rope, he wound up and hurled it up through the dense branches. The stone immediately twirled the rope around three thick branches, then, coming back down, whizzed past Sergei's head, but he caught it handily, undid the rock, and began to bind the tape recorder to the rope. Once he'd finished, he pressed a button and pulled on the free end of the rope. Ringing out with Vysotsky's hoarse voice, the tape recorder rose up. The higher it went, swinging from the taut rope, the louder the rhythmic sound of guitar and emotionally overstrained voice could be heard through the hushed autumnal forest.

"And in the graveyard, everything's so quiet, there's no one and nothin' to see, everything's so cultured, so decent, such exceptional grace!"

The tape recorder disappeared among dense whorls, fell silent, then began to sing again.

"He bought some mo-o-o-o-onshine and sweet halva, some R-r-riga beer and Ker-r-r-rrch herring, he set off for White Pillars to see his br-r-r-ro, to see the ps-s-s-sychos . . ."

Sergei hurriedly fastened the rope to the trunk of the fir, picked up his rifle, then squatted down, shifting the safety with his thumb.

"But the ps-s-s-sychos have a li-i-i-ife that any-y-y-yone would lo-o-ove to li-i-ive, you wanna sleep, li-i-ie down, if you wa-a-a-ant, you can sing songs to-o-o!"

The huntsman looked tensely into the depths of the forest.

The tape recorder finished the song about the psychos and a new one began—about "the guy who didn't shoot."

Sergei and the huntsman were still waiting just as motionlessly.

Two ducks flew over the clearing.

The forest echoed the singer's words resoundingly, bringing them right back.

Sergei knelt down for convenience's sake.

"The German sni-i-i-iper has sho-o-t-t-t me, he's killed the o-o-one who-o-o-o didn't sho-o-o-ot!" Vysotsky bellowed out, then fell silent.

From the crown of the fir came Vysotsky's muffled conversing, then the laughter of his small audience.

The huntsman leaned forward more, then suddenly waved his hand and revealed his weapon. Vysotsky was slowly tuning his guitar. Sergei made out a squat figure between the trees and sighted him with his backsight.

"What're ye doin'? What're ye doin'?" the huntsman whispered desperately, hiding behind a bush. "Too far! Let 'im get closer, ye'll just wound 'im and he'll get away!"

Sergei licked at his dry lips and lowered the barrel of the gun.

Vysotsky hit his strings violently.

"There's no more Lukomorye, and there's no tra-a-a-ace of any oa-a-a-aks, you need oa-a-a-aks for fine par-r-r-rquetry, so the trees, they sta-a-and no more! Some gre-e-e-edy go-o-o-ons left their ca-a-abins and cut up all the oa-a-a-aks for co-o-o-ofins!"

The squat figure ran over to the fir tree, deadwood crackling beneath his feet.

Sergei raised his rifle, took aim, attempted to restrain the trembling of his sweaty hands, and let forth a quick shot.

The bang drowned out the song pouring from the needles.

The dark figure tumbled down, then stirred, struggling to lift itself up. While Sergei was feverishly reloading, the huntsman raised himself out from behind the bush and let forth two shots from his weapon.

The stirring stopped.

"Give it a re-e-e-est, give it a re-e-e-est, oh lo-o-o-onging in my che-e-e-est! It's just an o-o-old sa-a-a-aying—the new fa-a-a-airytale li-i-i-ies ahe-e-e-ead!" Vysotsky sang out protractedly.

Squinting through the smoke produced by the powder, Sergei raised his rifle again, but the huntsman waved his hand.

"Enough, no need to fill the corpse with lead. Let's go take a gander . . ."

They set off carefully, holding their weapons at the ready.

He was lying thirty meters away, his arms outstretched and his head buried in a small anthill.

The huntsman was the first to approach and poked the side of his quilted jacket with his boot. The corpse didn't stir.

Sergei poked at the bloodied head with his boot. It rolled limply to one side, revealing an ear with an attached lobe. Excited ants were crawling over the ear.

Sergei put his gun down next to the body and quickly pulled out a knife from a leather sheath attached to his belt.

The huntsman grabbed the corpse by the arm and rolled it over onto its back.

Its face was covered in blood, in which the ants had gotten stuck and were swarming. Its quilted jacket had been thrown open and the bloody marks made by the buckshot were visible on its chest.

Sergei forcibly plunged his knife through its brown nipple, straightened up, and wiped at his sweaty forehead with the back of his hand.

Blood gushed from the corpse's mouth.

"Real sturdy," the huntsman muttered with the smile, then, taking his folding knife out of his pocket, began to handily cut the clothes off of the dead man.

"There really is a ca-a-a-at, and when it walks r-r-r-right, it si-i-i-ings, and when it walks le-e-e-eft, the joke gets sta-a-a-ale . . ."

"Y'gotta turn that off, Seryozh," the huntsman raised up his head.

Sergei nodded and walked over to the fir.

"So, here's where we caught 'im . . . really bore into 'im . . ." the huntsman muttered, denuding the corpse's bloody belly. Sergei walked over to the tree, untied the knot, then carefully brought down the tape recorder.

"It's just an o-o-old sa-a-a-aying—the new fa-a-a-airytale li-i-i-ies ahe-e-e-ead!" Vysotsky managed to sing out before he fell silent, interrupted by the click of a button.

Sergei reeled in the rope and put it away into his rucksack together with the tape recorder. Meanwhile, the huntsman deftly cut off the head, kicked it away with his boot, then straightened up, breathing heavily.

"Let the blood drain out, then we'll get 'im spread-eagled . . ."

Sergei came back and squatted down in front of the corpse.

"We got him real fast, huh, Egorych? Can't even believe it . . ."

"Ye hit him and I finished him off!" the huntsman laughed. "Turns out I ain't gone blind after all."

"Well done."

"That bastard came right out of the thicket."

"Yeah, that must've made for uncomfortable walkin'."

"But ye really gave it to him! Peppered his whole belly!"

"And I think you got him in the head . . ."

"Mhmm . . . mine tends to aim higher . . . We'd better him drag him away—otherwise the ants'll stick around . . ."

"Let's pull him under the oak . . ."

They took the corpse by the legs and dragged it away.

The head was left lying by an anthill. The huntsman came back, grabbed it by the ear, and carried it under the oak too.

Blood was flowing from the corpse's neck.

Sergei took out a flask of cognac, had a sip, then handed it to Kuzma Yegorych.

The huntsman wiped his sticky fingers off on his pants, carefully took the flask, and drank.

"Real strong . . ."

Sergei examined the corpse.

"A solid guy. Look how broad his shoulders are."

The huntsman drank some more, then returned the flask.

"A really husky one . . . well, let's skin 'im . . ."

He quickly cut open the stomach, cut out the heart, and, pushing aside the lilac-colored intestines, began to remove the liver.

"That's where ye got 'im . . ."

Sergei smiled and looked up.

A barely visible kite was hovering over the forest, weakly flapping its wings.

"We can fry the liver up in a bit," Kuzma Egorych muttered as he dug into the intestines.

"Definitely," Sergei replied, "we can char-grill it."

"On a stick too. Ye know how good fresh meat is . . ."

"I know," Sergei smiled and again raised the flask to his lips. "Well, here's to a fine hunt, Yegorych."

"Here's to a fine, fine hunt, Seryozh . . ."

MY FIRST
VOLUNTARY SATURDAY

"WELL, THERE," SALAMATIN walked over to the brigade, all members of which were seated upon slabs, "we gotta rake the leaves, guys."

The workers stirred and began to rise.

"Woah, just the ticket . . ."

"Not bad, Yegorych."

"He was prolly so smarmy with Zinka that she gave us the easier job . . ."

"And where are we gonna rake?"

Salamatin pulled a pack of Belomorkanal cigarettes out of his white pants.

"From the throughway on up."

"That's a lot. Half a kilometer."

"What were you thinking it'd be . . . Come on, guys—head to sector nine for the rakes. The gloves are there too. Or maybe a few of you can go grab 'em and save everyone else the trouble."

"Seryog and I'll go," Tkachenko slapped Zigunov's quilted shoulder. "Right, Seryog?"

"Yeah, of course . . . Gimme a smoke, Yegorych," Zigunov reached out toward the pack.

Salamatin shook out a cigarette for him, thrust one between his own lips, and crunched down on it.

"Get goin', then. And don't screw up the count. Fourteen rakes. And fourteen pairs of gloves. And here comes the green-horn . . . Which means fifteen rakes and fifteen pairs of gloves."

Mishka climbed over a stack of pipes and ran over along the slabs.

"What're you late for?" Salamatin smiled as he lit up. "Go, guys, go . . ."

Mishka ran over to him and exhaled loudly.

"Oofff . . . got real winded . . . mornin' . . . Vadim Yegorych . . ."

"Good morning. What, your alarm clock let you down?"

"Nah, nah . . . I missed my train . . . oof . . . am I that late?"

"No, it's nothin'."

"Good morning!" Mishka turned to the other workers.

"Yo."

"Good mornin' . . ."

"What you gotta be late for?"

"Did our little student overstudy last night?"

"Let's head over, Yegorych, no reason to hang around here . . ."

"Go. I'll catch up to ya . . ." Salamatin waved his hand. "Zip up your jacket. It's ain't summer, after all."

Still breathing hard, Mishka began to pull up his zipper.

Salamatin pushed aside the sleeve of his quilted jacket and looked at his watch.

"Quarter past eight. We're really takin' our time gettin' started."

"What's the plan?"

"Raking leaves. From the lawns in the throughway."

"Out in the fresh air . . . nice . . ."

"Of course . . . so . . . Prokhorov didn't show . . . well, whatever. We're not gonna wait anymore . . . let's go, Mish."

They started to walk toward the throughway, following after the brigade.

Salamatin yawned and blew out smoke.

"Why'd you dress up so nice? Like for a parade."

Mishka shrugged.

"What about it? No particular reason."

"But why dirty the jacket? It's a nice jacket."

"Not really."

The brigadier laughed, baring his large, tobacco-discolored teeth.

"Wow . . . so that's what the new generation's like . . . I'd've saved that jacket for a night on the town . . ."

They reached the throughway.

The black-uniformed watchman was locking the gate.

"Let us through, Semyonitch!" Salamatin shouted out cheerfully.

"Go in through the whirligig. I'm tired of locking up behind everyone who goes through. Some of your people were just here."

"Yegorych!" a voice rang out from behind them. "Help!"

Mishka and the brigadier turned around.

Tkachenko and Zigunov were coming with the rakes and gloves.

"You guys throw your backs out or what?" the brigadier stepped toward them.

Mishka walked over to Zigunov who thrust a stack of gloves into his arms.

Salamatin reached for the rakes, which had spread out like a fan on Tkachenko's shoulder, but Tkachenko weaved away.

"It's a joke, Yegorych. No weight to carry at all."

"All of them're in good shape? No broken ones?"

"Nah, nah . . ."

"Well, keep goin' then."

The brigadier let Tkachenko pass.

They went through the creaky whirligig one by one.

The brigade was waiting for them in the road.

"Woah, Sashok got the newest ones . . ."

"He's the man, I knew it."

Tkachenko took the rakes off his shoulder.

"Hand 'em out . . ."

Mishka began to hand out the gloves.

Tvorogov rapped his rake against the asphalt.

"Not bad . . . you could plow virgin lands with this . . ."

"Where should we start from, Yegorych?"

Salamatin looked around and waved toward the lawn on the left.

"Ours is there."

"And the one on the right?"

"The pumpers're gonna clean that up."

"Got it . . ."

A lawn strewn with fallen leaves and studded with an uneven row of low poplars ran along the stone barrier around the factory. Having lost almost all their leaves, the long branches stirred gently. Once they'd distributed the rakes and gloves, the workers made for the lawn. Salamatin tore at the thread binding together a new pair of gloves. Mishka knocked the staff of his rake against the asphalt, trying to squeeze its two halves back together.

"There's no little nail."

"What? What nail?" the brigadier turned to him.

"You know the one . . . to keep the halves together . . ."

"Well, that's no big deal . . . give it here," the brigadier took the rake and felt at it. "It's skewered alright. It locks together even without the nail. Just take it easy and it won't split in two . . . let's go . . ."

They followed after the brigade.

Mishka smiled, resting his rake on his shoulder.

"Yeah . . . it's my first voluntary Saturday . . ."

"What do you mean your first?"

"Just like I said. My first voluntary Saturday."

"Seriously?" Salamatin looked at him surprisedly.

"Mhmm . . . .Well, not my first, of course . . . we had voluntary Saturdays at school . . ."

"Yeah, but that was somethin' else. At school, you were a

student, but, here, you're a member of the proletariat. Which means it's really your first! Very cool!"

Salamatin laughed and shouted at the workers walking in front of them.

"Dig this, guys! It's Mishka here's first voluntary Saturday! What do you say to that?"

"Congrats."

"Y'owe us a bottle, Mish!"

"Not bad . . ."

"In that case, you should really work hard today. On behalf of everyone."

"A miracle . . . this fella's first voluntary Saturday. I forget when mine even was . . ."

Salamatin put his hand onto Mishka's shoulder.

"Yeah . . . that's really somethin'. We shoulda celebrated it with the help of the trade-union committee . . ."

"No need, Vadim Yegorych . . ."

"We shoulda. Why didn't you tell us earlier? You just jabber on . . . and it's your first voluntary Saturday . . . Hey, guys!" he shouted out to the other workers. "Start from over here! Rake the piles over to the edge in orderly fashion . . ."

The workers dispersed across the lawn and began to rake up the leaves.

Salamatin squinted at the setting sun and fixed the scarf that had popped out from underneath his quilted jacket.

"I can remember *my* first voluntary Saturday . . ."

"Really?"

"I do. The war had just begun. It was only '41. July. And I'd gotten a job at a factory back in April. I was just like you. Only younger. And, of course, I wasn't studying nights. I wasn't up to studying. And everyone decided to hold a voluntary Saturday. At the front-aid fund. We all left the factory after our shift. And the shift had been twelve hours long! Not like they are now. And we worked in a totally different way. Conscientiously. Everyone understood. Selflessly, y'know . . . and how we worked . . . if you compare it to today's workers . . ."

He sighed and wandered toward the brigade.

Mishka hurried after him.

The brigadier came up next to Zigunov, bent over, and picked up a rusty can.

"Look. This is our piggishness. Drink, eat, and toss off to the side. That's how we live . . . then we're surprised . . . there's nowhere to lay down and rest, we say . . . the outdoors have been ruined . . ."

He threw the can onto a pile of leaves.

Mishka began to rake, starting from the edge of the lawn.

The brigade worked in silence.

Zigunov straightened up suddenly, smiled, and shook his head.

"Oy . . . something . . . just a sec . . ."

He stuck out his blue-trousered bottom and loudly passed gas.

Sotskov straightened up, looked at him with surprise, then did the same, but it was weaker and shorter.

Tkachenko pointed his thin finger at Sotskov.

"Artillery . . . fire . . ."

And farted laconically.

Salazkin and Mamontov leaned against their rakes and passed gas almost simultaneously.

Tvorogov bent over more and his face tensed up.

"O-pa . . . o-pa . . . o-pa . . ."

He farted weakly three times.

Sokhenko raised his rubber-booted foot.

"Here y'go . . . for the traitors to the Motherland . . ."

But farted weakly.

Salamatin shook his head in shock.

"Motherfucker . . . suck a dick . . . what's that all about? What—all at once? And in whose honor?"

Zigunov shrugged.

"What d'you mean in whose honor? The artillery salute was performed with medium-caliber weapons in honor of our comrade's first voluntary Saturday! And now it's your turn, Yegorych . . ."

Smiling, the workers looked at him.

"C'mon, veteran, bang 'em out like a shock worker . . ."

"And don't you lag behind, Mish."

"C'mon, what're you standing there for. Don't fall behind the team."

"Don't spoil the brigade's streak, Mr. Order Bearer . . ."

"C'mon, Yegorych, c'mon . . . Everyone looks up to you . . ."

Salamatin scratched his temple and started to laugh.

"Well, if that's what's goin' down . . ."

He bent over slightly and groaned.

Mishka also tensed up, looked down at his feet, and was the first to fart, but weakly—almost inaudibly.

"Well, that was pretty weak, Mikhail . . ."

"No biggie . . . it's his big day today . . . it's forgivable . . ."

Everyone looked at the frozen brigadier and fell silent. His broad, swarthy face, bronzed by the setting sun, was looking off into the distance and his hands clutched at his knees. The brigadier's full lips pressed together, nodules became visible under the bronze skin of his cheekbones, and his gray brows shifted.

He moaned almost inaudibly and bowed his head.

Holding its breath, the brigade continued to watch him.

A loud clap and a roiling, juicy crackle resounded.

The workers applauded silently.

Salamatin took off his cap and bowed.

GEOLOGISTS

IN A SOOT-BLACKENED, battered stove, firewood crackled resoundingly and flames burst from the half-open cast-iron door, casting flickers of amber out onto the faces of the geologists.

Solovyov took a last drag from his cigarette and thrust the butt through the orange slot.

Sitting next to him on a low cedar stool, Alekseyev was playing with a wide hunting knife, repetitively sticking it into a gnarled log.

Solovyov sighed and stood up, almost bumping his shaggy head on the smoke-stained ceiling of the winter hut.

"No, guys. We gotta decide today."

Avdeyenko nodded silently, Alekseyev shrugged vaguely, continuing to stab the log, and Ivan Timofeyevich, sitting by the frosty window, still puffed unhurriedly at his yellow bone pipe.

"Well, what're you so quiet for, Sasha?" Solovyov turned to Alekseyev.

"I've already said all I have to say," Alekseyev pronounced quietly and distinctly. Lit up with orange flickering, his broad and bearded face seemed unflappable.

"But your plan is ridiculous—to say the very least!" Solovyov shook his head. "What, we'll leave our friends behind in an avalanche-prone area and pull up stakes?!"

The broad knife was stuck forcibly into the log.

"And that means you probably think we should just throw a year of super-hard work out the window?"

"But people are worth more than samples, Sasha!" Solovyov clapped his hands together awkwardly.

"Of course," Avdeyenko agreed, glancing at Alekseyev.

Alekseyev hit his knee irritably with the handle of his knife.

"What're you being so childish for? They've been in Ust-Severny for a long time—your favorites, Sidorov and Korshevsky! A long time! I'll bet my neck on it—they're sitting there chugging tea! And no avalanche is hanging over their heads!"

"But the radio, Sasha, the radio says something else!" Solovyov interrupted him. "How could the guys be chugging tea if they aren't even in Ust-Severny!"

"No, I mean, they'll be there in a day or two," Alekseyev snapped confidently.

"And what if they didn't head for Ust-Severny?" Avdeyenko asked, leaning forward and carefully removing a mug of steaming tea from the stove.

"They'll come," Alekseyev spoke with immutable confidence, fumbling through the pockets of his quilted pants for cigarettes, "they know about the avalanche, that's one, they probably spotted the helicopter, that's two, and they're experienced geologists, that's three. What are you fine fellows thinkin'? That they're headed to get something from the stockpiles? In a storm like this? Nah, they'll stay in place for a couple of days and no more. Then they'll head for Ust-Severny . . ."

He stuck a dry cedar twig into the stove, pulled it out, and lit up with the flames that were engulfing the wood.

"You're talking like everything's been preordained," Avdeyenko grinned sadly. "But they weren't preparing to head for Ust-Severny any earlier than next week. That was the plan."

"What are you saying, Nikolai? What are they—little boys or something? Korshevsky has ten years of experience, he knows these places like the back of his hand! Do you really think they're so stupid to not have guessed there was an avalanche with the helicopters and the shooting? They're running out of food too. Which means they'll head for Ust-Severny. I'm telling you for certain. That's where they'll head! You and Pyotr are real alarmists. You think like babies—drop everything, drop the samples, and start looking! Look where? Along the ridge? By the Yellow Kamenka? Or perhaps we should head for the western gorge? You don't know anything for certain. But we're supposed to drop the samples and let them get taken away by an avalanche! Totally absurd . . ."

"And if it doesn't come down?" Avdeyenko asked. "The avalanche probably isn't gonna make it all the way here . . ."

"And if it does? What then?" Alekseyev turned his broad face to him. "How will we look Rodnikov in the eye then?"

They fell silent, staring intently at the crackling stove.

Ivan Timofeyevich was still smoking just as unhurriedly. His swarthy, high-cheekboned face was gloomy and focused. His gray temples peeked out from underneath a tightly knit hat.

Avdeyenko shook his head.

"Yes, of course . . . the samples . . . We were collecting them for a year . . ."

Drawing his lips apart, he sipped cautiously at the hot tea. Solovyov thrust his hands into his pockets impatiently.

"Come on, Sasha, let's get hold of Ust-Severny again."

Alekseyev shrugged and stood up.

"Sure."

In the corner, the aluminum panel of a brand-new radio gleamed atop a crudely cobbled table.

Shifting the stool, Alekseyev put on the headphones with a confident motion and flipped the toggle. A red light flashed forth on the panel.

Alekseyev quickly set to work with the key.

Then stopped and adjusted the headphones on his ears, listening carefully to the reciprocal volley of Morse code.

"Well, there . . ." he said quietly, pressing the "disconnect" button. "They haven't arrived. They're not there. And the helicopters will fly again in the morning, when the blizzard calms down."

Turning off the radio, he took off the headphones and stood up.

"Well, guys, generally speaking, I think we gotta pack up and be on our way in the morning. The samples are heavy—a good half-ton. Might take a while to get there . . ."

Sitting by the window, Ivan Timofeyevich sighed and blew a wide stream of smoke.

Everyone turned to him.

"Well, what do you think, Ivan Timofeyevich?" Solovyov asked cautiously.

Ivan Timofeyevich silently nibbled at the mouthpiece of his pipe.

Alekseyev scratched at his beard.

"We've reached a dead end. I have one plan, they have another . . . a real dilemma . . ."

Avdeyenko set the empty mug down on the table.

"It's the first time we're having such disagreements. You're an experienced geologist, Ivan Timofeyevich. Twenty-five years of expeditions. You should know what we have to do."

"That's probably why you're keeping so quiet," Solovyov smiled.

Ivan Timofeyevich smiled back.

"That's why, Petya, that's why . . ."

He got up, knocked his pipe out against the edge of the table, put it into his pocket, and sighed relievedly.

"So, here. As my countryman Vasily Ivanovich Chapaev once said and what I will also say to what everyone else has said here today: drop it and forget about it. Let's not try to do divination with coffee grounds, let's engage in serious reasoning. Assessing the current situation, it seems to me that we need to simply muchmum the fonk."

Alekseyev shook his head in the silence that ensued. An expression of admiration ran across his face.

"That's right . . . how did I not think of that . . ."

Solovyov perplexedly scratched at the nape of his neck and softly muttered:

"Yeah, I actually . . . wanted the same . . ."

Avdeyenko grunted approvingly and slapped himself on the knee:

"That's what it means to be a real professional, my fine fellows!"

Patting him on the shoulder, Ivan Timofeyevich walked into the middle of the hut, squatted down, knocked his knuckles against the icy floor three times, and began to speak distinctly.

"Vonge, vonge, vonge, studly sniffling."

The geologists standing around him repeated after him in unison:

"Vonge, vonge, vonge, studly sniffling."

Then the young geologists formed into a row, stretching their palms out in front of them and bringing them together into something like a trough.

Ivan Timofeyevich made a sign to them with his head.

The geologists bent over slowly. The trough descended. Perched over it, Ivan Timofeyevich stuck two fingers into his throat, hiccupped, then shuddered.

He quickly vomited into the palm-trough.

Having caught his breath, he took out a handkerchief and, wiping at his wet lips, said:

"Vonge, vonge, vonge, hamoked clith."

Without changing position and attempting not to spill the thick whitish-brown mass onto the floor, the geologists distinctly repeated after him:

"Vonge, vonge, vonge, hamoked clith."

Ivan Timofeyevich smiled and sighed with relief.

Burnt-up logs crackled faintly in the stove and fell apart with a rustle.

The blizzard whistled behind the small window and out above the taiga.

POPLAR FLUFF

VALENTINA VIKTOROVNA THREW open the glass door into the office.

"Kostya! Some students have come to see you!"

Sitting at a wide desk, Konstantin Filippych got up and put on glasses.

"Have them come through."

"They're shy," Valentina Viktorovna laughed.

"Well, I can't go out and get them in the hallway . . . Call them in, call them in . . ."

Valentina Viktorovna disappeared and, a minute later, three young guys and a young girl cautiously came into the office with an enormous bouquet of lilacs.

"Hello, Konstantin Filippych," they greeted him amicably.

"Hello, hello, my friends," Voskresensky said cheerfully, coming out from behind his desk. "Make yourselves comfortable, don't be shy."

"Konstantin Filippych," the girl began quickly, "please allow us to convey our department's best wishes on your birthday— your special day. We love and appreciate you very much. And are very glad that we've had the opportunity to attend your lectures, to be your pupils . . . And this is for you . . ."

She handed him the bouquet.

Konstantin Filippych spread out his hands, awkwardly accepted the flowers, and, intercepting the girl's thin hand, kissed it quickly.

"Thank you, my dears, thank you . . . I'm very touched . . . thank you . . ."

One of the guys undid a paper parcel.

"And this, Konstantin Filippych, is from the department's Organization of Scientific Students."

Underneath the paper was the beautiful model of a lactic acid molecule. Professor Voskresensky's head had been molded from papier-mâché and mounted right where a carbon atom was supposed to be.

Konstantin Filippych burst out into laughter.

"A-ha-ha-ha! Well, you're amazing! You jokesters! A-ha-ha-ha! Valya! Come here! Look! Look!"

Valentina Viktorovna quickly came over to the desk and bent over the model.

"My God! How'd you manage this? It really looks like him!"

"The main thing is that I get to take the carbon's place!" the professor laughed. "But, really, how'd you think this up?"

One of the students smiled restrainedly.

"By joint effort, Konstantin Filippych."

"Well, thank you . . . thank you . . ." The professor rotated the model in his hands. "I'm going to keep it on my desk, right here."

He pushed a stack of papers over to the edge of the desk and set down the model.

"Like that. Well, what are you just standing there for?! Sit down, sit down!"

The students backed away toward the door.

"Thank you, Konstantin Filippych, but we have to go."

"What do you mean you have to go? Where are you rushing off to?"

"We have exams tomorrow. In math."

"Ahhhh . . . well, that makes sense," Voskresensky became more serious, "mathematics is a terribly important discipline. I, I'll admit it, was never very good at it . . ." He smiled, absent-mindedly rubbing at his gray temples.

The students smiled.

"But perhaps you could still have a cup of tea?" Valentina Viktorovna asked.

"No, we can't. Thank you, though. We have to go."

"Too bad."

"Well, at least come by after your exams," Voskresensky spread out his hands, "certainly come by! Otherwise, I'll be offended!"

The students nodded.

"We'll come by. See you then."

He accompanied them to the door.

Meanwhile, Valentin Viktorovna put the lilacs into a beautiful blue vase.

Voskresensky came back whistling and touched the flowers with his index finger.

"Great kids. Luxurious lilacs . . ."

"The boys were so nice," Valentina Viktorovna smiled, "and the girl was so cute. You even kissed her hand . . ."

"Are you jealous?!" the professor laughed.

"Stop talking nonsense. It's just that she blushed all over and got scared."

"Really! I didn't even notice."

"Well, I noticed . . ."

They looked into each other's eyes, embraced, and laughed. Konstantin Filippych stroked his wife's neat gray head of hair.

"So, we made it to sixty."

"We did," she smiled.

The doorbell rang.

"The guys probably forgot something," the professor began to hurry over.

"Don't bother, I'll get it . . ."

"Never mind, never mind . . ."

He quickly shuffled over to the door and opened it.

A worker with a basket of carnations was standing in the threshold.

"Comrade Voskresensky?"

"Yes. That's me."

"This is for you."

The worker stepped over the threshold and laid the basket down in front of the professor.

"Help!" Voskresensky put his hands up jokingly.

"Sign for the delivery, please," the worker handed him the receipt with a smile.

The professor rushed to get a pen.

"My God! What wonderful carnations!" Valentina Viktorovna threw up her hands.

"Nice flowers," the worker smiled. "Let me set them up somewhere for you. They're kinda heavy to lug around."

"Please, if you'd be so kind . . . you can put them over there, on the nightstand."

The worker carried the basket down the hallway and put it onto the nightstand. Voskresensky came back with a pen, signed the crumpled receipt, and handed the worker a ruble along with it.

"Ohh, I couldn't!" he put away the receipt and quickly opened the door.

"For your trouble. Take it."

"It's work, not trouble. Thank you. Goodbye."

He left.

The professor shook his head and put away the ruble.

"Well, that was awkward . . ."

"Yeah . . ." Valentina Viktorovna sighed and embraced her husband, "but no big deal, no big deal. You better tell me who these luxurious flowers are from."

"Sergei probably sent them. Or they're from the chair. But I think it was Sergei."

Konstantin Filippych walked over to the carnations and smiled.

"He still hasn't forgotten me. He remembers . . ."

"All your pupils remember you, Kostya."

"Oh, come on. Don't exaggerate . . ."

"I'm not exaggerating."

The professor walked into the room, drew back the curtains, and opened the window awkwardly. A warm July wind tore into the room and rattled the curtains.

"The fluff's flying," Valentina Viktorovna smiled.

"Yes. Like snow."

"Do you remember when the fluff was flying after finals week way back when?"

"Yea-a-a-ah," Voskresensky smiled sadly and shook his head. "I plunged right into a puddle too, I remember. It was by our stop."

"When we were waiting for the tram?"

"Yeah. They were running pretty infrequently. And you were wearing a little hat. My favorite one."

"The lilac-colored hat?" Voskresenskaya laughed.

"Yes . . . frightening to think! Forty years ago. And the fluff was flying in the exact same way and people were meeting up, joking around, and kissing it up . . . And the fluff was just the same. Stunning!"

"And how quickly it all flew away!"

"Yes. And the main thing is so much was done, but it all feels like nothing . . ."

"Well, that's a little much. Nothing! May everyone accomplish such a nothing!"

The professor sighed.

"Oh, Valechka, it's all relative . . . relative . . ."

Valentina Viktorovna looked at him affectionately.

The professor stroked his mustache.

"Poplar fluff . . . poplar fluff . . ."

"Yes . . . poplar fluff . . ." Voskresenskaya whispered quietly.

Konstantin Filippych went pale and clenched his fists.

"What a bastard . . . bitch . . ."

His wife opened her mouth in disbelief.

"Bastard!"

The professor wound up awkwardly and hit Valentina Viktorovna in the face with his fist.

She tumbled down onto the floor with a gasp.

"Bastard! Scum! Goddamn whore!" the pale professor hissed.

"Kostya . . . Kostya . . ." Voskresenskaya whispered fearfully.

Trembling, he loomed up over her, then began to kick her.

"Scum! Scum! Scum!"

Voskresenskaya cried out shrilly.

The professor picked up a chair and threw it forcibly at a pier glass.

Shards of the mirror fell down onto the floor.

"Whore . . . bastard . . ."

He tried to spit into his wife's bloodied face, but the loogie got caught in his beard.

Voskresenskaya continued to scream shrilly.

Konstantin Filippych ran out into the hallway, opened the front door with trembling hands, and rushed down the wide staircase.

By the entryway, he came across his eight-year-old neighbor. The professor hit his freckled face with a backhanded blow, then ran out into the courtyard.

AT THE CENTRAL
HOUSE OF OFFICERS

KOSTENKO SIGHED AND shook his gray head, so firmly planted upon his shoulders.

"No, Sasha. Time has nothing to do with it. Time is sand. The question isn't to do with time . . ."

"Then what is it, Petya?" the scrubby Borodin approached the exhibit on the left. "What do you think—are they gonna remember us forever?"

"Well, forever . . . for now . . . that's not for us to judge," Kostenko limped past the exhibits, the medals hanging from his baggy military tunic clinking together softly. "At the end of the day, we didn't fight for ourselves. We weren't saving our own hides."

"Why do you feel the need to say something like that? What do you mean by *hides*? Everyone wants to survive."

"That's true. But, I mean, back in Stalingrad, it wasn't just your own life you felt on your shoulders."

"Of course not," Borodin examined the photographs taken during the war. "But you didn't *not* feel your own."

Kostenko squinted, looked at him, then smiled.

"Actually, y'know what—I didn't! I didn't feel it!"

"Don't lie."

"I swear! Maybe a little bit at first, near Smolensk, when I first saw Germans, tanks, live fire . . . And then, by Stalingrad—not at all! I wasn't afraid for myself. The thing I thought of at first was my family, but then something in my chest gave way and it was like I was free. And the fear just went away. My family faded into the background."

"What was in the foreground?"

"In the foreground . . ." Kostenko rubbed the bridge of his nose. "You know . . . it's hard to explain . . ."

"What's hard to explain?"

"When I joined as a volunteer, they saw us off at Kiev Station. A whole crowd did, I mean, you know what I'm talking about. The *people* always saw us off. Masha and my father were there. My mother was in Astrakhan. So. We said goodbye. They cried a bit. And then the train, y'understand, it starts to move, I clamber out onto the bandwagon, there're throngs of guys up there, their heads shaved just like mine. Little boys, pretty much. I got up there, looked around, and then, y'know what . . . something right here . . ." he put his left hand to his tunic, covering over two Orders of the Red Star, "something came to the surface . . ."

"You felt pity?"

"Nah, nah. Not that. I wasn't one for snip snails and puppy-dog tails. In our family, the men were stern and filled with purpose. And there, at the station . . . I looked around and saw all of 'em running. And all of 'em were broads, broads, broads. They're running and watching. Watching us. As if they were waiting for some kinda reply. And they're totally silent, totally silent . . ."

He too fell silent, then turned to Borodin.

"So there, Sasha, for the whole war, I was remembering those broads. Sensing them. In Stalingrad and in Kiev and in Warsaw. And it would often be that, as soon as my nerves'd come on, I'd see 'em right away. As if in the flesh. Right in front of me. Running and watching. Maybe that's why I made it through, 'cause they were watching me for the whole war. Demanding my reply . . ."

Borodin nodded.

"Makes sense. For me it'd often be that we'd be gettin' bombed to hell or fordin' the Dnieper, when I'd suddenly catch sight of our lil' village. And, y'know, it wasn't like it was a holiday there or anything, it looked like mornin'. A summer mornin', quiet, and smoke stretchin' upward from the huts. And the sky's so so blue. And the linden trees're blossomin' . . ."

"Am I right that you grew up in Orenburg?"

"We moved to Orenburg in '38. I spent my boyhood in Ryazan."

"Got it . . . I never spent much time in the country . . ."

"Well, I'll just call you *my friend the city slicker*, then," Borodin patted his arm and gestured toward the exhibit. "There it is, the artillery: God of War."

"Yes . . . powerful howitzers."

"And, most importantly, they've got short stocks, but can really serve up a smackdown!"

"And that German Schmeisser assault rifle over there."

"Don't those have a higher caliber?"

"Yeah . . . they make quite a hole . . ."

"Like a bomb, pretty much."

"Pretty much . . . A shell won't make a hole like that . . ."

They stood by the exhibit dedicated to the Battle of Moscow. Kostenko limped over to the door and waved his hand.

"Let's go, I'll show you the Lenin Room."

Borodin strode cheerfully after him.

"I can see you're right at home here."

"Well, where's a soldier to go after the front? I talk to the youth at the military registration and enlistment office here too . . ."

They went out into the hallway.

Kostenko limped in front of Borodin, his gray, close-cropped head of hair swayed smoothly, his medals tinkling softly.

"It's still too early right now . . . forty minutes until the gathering . . . Y'see, there's no one here . . . but you're fantastic . . . y'came real early . . . soon, all the guys'll gather together . . . Kononov . . . Khlustov, Ivaschenko . . . d'you remember Petya Ivaschenko?"

"From the third company, right?"

"Yeah. A sub lieutenant. And a real redhead."

"He got wounded near Kharkov, I think, right?"

"Yeah, yeah. He caught up with us later, though . . ."

"Is Kolya Zolotarev still alive, Pet?"

"No. He died about ten years ago."

"Too bad . . ."

"Too bad, of course. He was a cheerful guy. And died young."

"Cheerful guy. I remember that."

They reached the end of the hallway and Kostenko threw open a brown padded door.

"Go on in . . ."

Borodin went in and looked around.

In the middle of a bright, spacious room were several brand-new tables, bookcases were crowded along the walls, a white bust of Lenin towered up in the right corner with a basket of flowers lying at its base, and next to it, in a narrow glass display case, reposed a faded banner, torn in some places.

Borodin walked over to the display case and bent over.

"Petya . . . hold on a sec . . . so this is . . . from our regiment?"

"Yep, our regiment, Sasha," Kostenko shook his head, "the very same."

"That can't be . . ."

"It can, Sasha. Anything's possible."

"But how did they manage? I guess everything was in storage at the division headquarters? It just can't be . . ."

Kostenko walked over to him and put his hand onto his shoulder.

"And how'd you and Seryoga Zhoglenko manage to connect the telecommunications line near Warsaw? You were getting showered over by at least ten machine guns and I could see everything happening as clear as day, I bit my lips to hell watching it go down. That also seemed impossible! But you made it through, right? You did! Because you wanted to! You wanted to! So it was possible."

"Yeah, but that's somethin' else, Petya . . ."

"No, Sasha, there's only ever one thing goin' on with us everywhere! Y'gotta want it. Really want it. I wanted this. And here it is: the banner in front of you. Our banner."

"Yeah. You're a powerful man, Petya."

"I've been to the front, to be more precise!" Kostenko laughed.

Borodin examined the banner through the glass.

"My God, can it really be the same one!"

"It is, it is."

"That sergeant would carry it all the time, a real tall guy. Wouldn't mind meeting him again."

"Nah, I've never seen him since."

"What about Semyonov?"

"Nope."

"And Sanya Kruglov?"

"Also no for some reason. I've seen Evstifeyev, but not Kruglov."

"And what about Lyuska the translator?"

"Nope. They say she lives somewhere in the south. In Novorossiysk, it'd seem . . ."

Borodin shook his head.

"The banner! Well, dang . . . I didn't expect this . . . it's pretty torn . . . certainly got shot at enough . . ."

"Everyone did. People *and* objects. I got hit four times and one got stuck in my shoulder blade. They're afraid to take it out. Too close to the spine."

"They dug one outta my leg in '46. I carried the bastard

around for two years. A real thorny one, just like a hedgehog. Now, whenever it rains, my leg hurts."

"Well, I got nothing left to hurt, Sash," smiling, Kostenko slapped at his prosthesis.

"And you can still run is what I say! Better'n a youngun. No one on two legs'll catch ya."

"That's 'cause I never sat at home before the war. I Komsomol'ed it up with a vengeance. Recently, they offered me an imported prosthesis. With hinges and a boot. But I refused to wear it on principle! Let the iron stick out, let everyone look, what is there to be ashamed of? Maybe someone will see it and remember that they have to remember forever."

"That's right."

"And the main thing is I'm used to the old one. It's like my own leg. And it doesn't slip at all. That's the way the cookie crumbles . . . Sash, why didn't you wear your tunic?"

Borodin laughed.

"It's too old now. Moth-eaten."

"You didn't take care of it?"

"I mean, who took care of their tunic after the war? First y'shove it in a closet, then the attic."

"Well, my Dunya took care of mine. Poured it over with mothballs, had half a mind to pepper it. Here, y'see? Like nothing's changed, hm?"

Kostenko raised his hands slightly and looked at his own chest.

"Just like new, Petya. Well done."

"We try, Sash, we try."

A tiny gray mouse jumped out from under a shelf crammed full with Lenin's complete works, wound past the legs of the table, and hurried toward the half-open door.

Kostenko strode over to meet it and raised up his prothesis.

"Bitch . . ."

The mouse skittered back, but the worn metal tip of the prosthesis flattened it with a crunch.

"These fucks have really been breedin' . . . total filth . . ."

Kostenko stuck out the prosthesis with the remains of the mouse dangling from it and, standing on one leg, leapt heavily over to the trash receptacle in the corner. His medals rang out with each jump and the collar of his jacket rasped up and down his fat neck.

"I mean, I offered to deal with 'em in the spring. But they didn't listen . . ."

Leaning against the shelf, he stuck the prosthesis into the plastic receptacle and brushed the bloody bits off of it.

Borodin looked at the stain that remained.

"Poor little mouse . . ."

"Little?!" Kostenko grinned menacingly, stamping his prosthesis against the ground. "The *little* mice we catch here'd make you lose your shit if you saw 'em, motherfucker! This one's an exception to the rule or somethin' . . . Small fry straight outta the basement. But otherwise—holy fuck—y'should see the typa thugs we get!"

Looking straight into Borodin's eyes, he spread his hands out to the width of his chest.

Borodin looked at his hands and nodded seriously.

A FREE
PERIOD

CHERNYSH CAUGHT UP with Gera by the coat room, grabbed him
by the collar, and dragged his chuckling classmate backwards.

"Let's go . . . let's go . . . stay still . . . I'll tell all the guys . . ."

Without ceasing to laugh, Gera grabbed onto a low wooden
barrier at the entrance to the coat room.

"Help! Thief!"

His shrill voice echoed down the empty school hallway.

"Let's go . . ." Chernysh hissed, tearing Gera's ink-stained
hands off the barrier. "I'll call Sasha . . . He stole and he's pleased
with himself . . ."

"He-e-elp!"

Gera threw himself back, banged the back of his head on
Chernysh's chin, and burst out laughing.

"Oh, you bastard . . ." Chernysh tore him away from the coat
room and dragged him down the hall.

The dark blue jacket of Gera's uniform slid over his head and
his boots scraped across the tile.

"OK, that's enough, Blacky[1] . . . enough . . . y'hear?"

"Stay still . . ."

---

1 The name Chernyshev sounds like it contains the word for black—"chyorny."

Resounding footsteps rang out behind them.

"Chernyshev!" a voice came down the hallway.

Chernysh stopped.

"What on earth is this?" Zinaida Mikhailovna quickly approached and pulled him away from Gera by the shoulder. "What is this?! I'm asking you!"

Now released, Gera straightened up and fixed his jacket.

Chernyshev sniffled and looked at the wall.

Gera also looked at the wall.

"Why aren't you in class?" Zinaida Mikhailovna clasped her hands over her stomach.

"We've got this . . . well, Zinaid Mikhailna . . . they let us out, y'see . . . a free period . . ."

"What class are you? 5B?"

"Yeah."

"And why? Why the free period?"

"Svetlana Nikolaevna got sick."

"Ahh . . . yes. Well, so what? You think you can go around doing handstands now? Gerasimenko! What on earth is this? Why are you shouting for the whole school to hear?"

Gera was looking at the wall.

"Tatyana Borisovna gave us some exercises, then left."

"And so what? What are you running around the school for? Hm?"

"Well, Zinaid Mikhailna, we decided . . ."

"And your homework? Don't you have any? No? Don't you know what this place is?"

The guys were silent.

Zinaida Mikhailovna sighed and grabbed Chernyshev by the shoulder.

"Go to your classroom, Gerasimenko. Chernyshev, come with me . . ."

"Zinaid Mikhailna, I mean . . ."

"Let's go, let's go! Tell everyone to be quiet, Gerasimenko. I'll come by in a bit."

Gera ran away.

Chernyshev and the principal walked in the opposite direction.

"Let's go, Chernyshev. I can see how impudent you've become. Yesterday with Bolshova and now today you're dragging Gerasimenko across the floor . . ."

"I won't be like that anymore, Zinaid Mikhailna . . ."

"Keep walking, keep walking. Don't give me that. Yesterday, Bolshova was crying in the staff room! And, by the way, why didn't you come see me yesterday after school? Hm? Didn't I ask you to?"

"Well, I did come by, Zinaid Mikhailna, but you weren't there."

"Weren't there? You're still lying just as impudently. Good for you."

Zinaida Mikhailovna reached her office and flung the door open. "Go in."

Chernyshev walked in slowly.

Zinaida Mikhailovna walked in behind him and closed the door.

"So. I could hear you screaming even in here. Your screaming made its way through the entire school."

She dropped her keys onto her desk, sat down, and nodded to Chernyshev.

"Come here."

He walked over to the desk slowly and stood across from her.

Zinaida Mikhailovna took off her glasses, rubbed at the bridge of her nose, and looked at him exhaustedly.

"What am I to do with you, Chernyshev?"

Chernyshev was silent, his head bowed. A crumpled Pioneer tie fell out from over his shoulder.

"What's your first name?"

"Seryozha."

"Seryozha. You're in fifth grade. You'll be in eighth grade in little more than two years . . . And then what? With behavior like this, you think we'll let you into ninth? What's your grade for behavior?"

"C . . ."

"And in Algebra?"

"B."

"Well, thank god . . . and in Literature?"

"C."

"And in Russian?"

"C . . ."

"Well, then. You're planning to go to technical school, I assume? What are you so quiet for?"

Chernyshev sniffled.

"No. I want to keep studying."

"I wouldn't have guessed. And we wouldn't let you through with grades like that. With behavior like that."

"But, Zinaid Mikhailna, I have A's in Geometry and Drawing . . ."

Zinaida Mikhailovna put her glasses into their case.

"Fix your tie."

Chernysh felt for the knot, then pushed it back into place.

"What do your parents do?"

"My dad's an engineer. And my mom's a salesclerk. At the Moscow Department Store . . ."

"Well? What's the problem, then? Did you decide Kulikov was your role model or something? He was brought up in an orphanage, while you have a mom and dad. He had no one to tell him what was what. But you? Do your parents really not care what grades you get?"

"No . . . they do . . ."

"Does your dad look at your report cards?"

"He does."

"And then?"

"He scolds me . . ."

"And what do you do?"

"Well . . . I'm not going to behave like that anymore, Zinaid Mikhailna . . ."

"What are you harping on like a parrot for? You're a Pioneer! An adult! The question isn't what you will or won't do, but what's to be made out of you! Understood?"

"I understand . . . I'll do better . . ."

Zinaida Mikhailovna sighed.

"I don't believe you, Chernyshev."

"I promise . . ."

"Oh, these promises of yours . . ." Smirking, she got up, walked over to the window, and shrugged her broad shoulders icily. "What happened with Bolshova yesterday?"

Chernyshev hesitated.

"Well . . . I just . . ."

"You *just* what? You *just* hurt a girl's feelings? It isn't so *just* to up and hurt a girl's feelings!"

"No, I didn't want to . . . it's just . . . we were chasing each other . . . playing . . ."

"Games don't end in tears, Chernyshev . . ."

"But I didn't want her to cry."

"That's why you lifted up her skirt?"

"I didn't lift it . . . I just . . ."

Zinaida Mikhailovna walked over to him.

"Well, why'd you do it?"

"I mean . . . she pinched me, Zinaid Mikhailna . . . She hit me on the back . . ."

"And you lifted up her skirt? You, a Pioneer, lifted up her skirt?! Chernyshev did? If a hooligan off the streets like Kulikov had pulled it up, I wouldn't be surprised. But you?! You participated in the city Olympiad for geometry last year! And you pulled up her skirt?!"

"It was only once . . ."

"Why? Why?"

"I dunno . . ."

"But your goal, what was your goal? Did you want to see what was underneath her skirt or what?"

"No, no . . ."

"Then why'd you lift it up?"

"I dunno . . ."

"The same old story, huh? Why'd you pull it up? What . . . you don't have enough courage to admit why? You, a future member of the Komsomol!"

"But I just . . ."

"Just wanted to see what was underneath her skirt? C'mon, be honest! Hm?!"

"Yeah . . ."

Zinaida Mikhailovna laughed.

"How stupid you are! What do you have in your pants?"

"Well . . . underwear . . ."

"Girls have underwear too. What did you think there'd be? A sweater? Did you not know that girls wear underwear too?"

"I know . . . I knew . . ."

"If you knew, then why'd you pull it up?'

"Well, she pinched me . . ."

"But you just told me you wanted to see what was underneath her skirt!"

Chernyshev was silent.

Zinaida Mikhailovna shook her head.

"Chernyshev, Chernyshev . . . why are you lying to me? Aren't you ashamed?"

"I'm not lying, Zinaid Mikhailna."

"You're lying! You're lying!" she leaned toward him. "Is the truth really that hard to say? You're lying! You weren't interested in her underwear or her skirt! You were interested in what was underneath her underwear!"

Chernyshev lowered his head even further.

Zinaida Mikhailovna shook him lightly by the shoulders.

"That, that's what you were interested in."

"No . . . no . . ." Chernyshev muttered.

"And it's not shameful . . . it isn't . . . It's very natural . . . It's shameful that you can't tell me the truth! That's what's shameful!"

"Yes I can . . . I can . . ."

"No, you can't!"

"I can . . ."

"Then tell me yourself."

Zinaida Mikhailovna sat down behind her desk and rested her chin in her hand.

Chernysh sniffled and scratched at his cheek.

"I, um . . ."

"Get rid of the 'um'!"

"Um . . . I was interested . . . I was just interested . . ."

Zinaida Mikhailovna shook her head sympathetically.

"How old are you, Chernyshev?"

"Twelve."

"Twelve . . . A grown-up. Do you have a sister?"

"No."

Zinaida Mikhailovna twirled her pencil around in her hands.

"No . . . Listen! You fought with Nina Zatsepina last week too! Did you want to see what was underneath her underwear as well!?"

"Of course not, no . . . I just . . . that was totally different . . ."

"Well then, look me in the eyes. Now, for once, don't lie."

Chernyshev lowered his head.

"You wanted to see hers too. Right? Hm?"

He nodded.

Zinaida Mikhailovna smiled.

"Don't think that I'm making fun of you or getting ready

to punish you, Chernyshev. It's something else entirely. You're twelve years old. The most curious age. You want to know and see everything. I can remember when I was a twelve-year-old. Or did you think that your principal was born a principal? I was, I really was a little girl. But I had a brother named Volodya. My older brother. And when the time came, he showed me everything. How boys are different from girls. I showed him too. There. It was that simple. And nobody had to pull up anyone's skirt. And we grew up to be normal people. He's a civil aviation pilot and I'm a principal. There."

Chernyshev looked at her sullenly.

Zinaida Mikhailovna continued to smile.

"So you see—everything is very simple. Isn't that so?"

"Mhm . . ."

"So, do you have any female relatives of about your age?"

"No. I have a cousin who's a boy . . . And no sisters . . ."

"Well, do you have any friends who are girls? Any real friends? A friend who's a girl in the best sense of the term? A true friend? One whom you can trust with anything?"

"No. No . . ."

Zinaida Mikhailovna laid the pencil to one side and scratched her temple.

"Your generation's pathetic. No sisters and no female friends . . . You'll come to your senses and start to misbehave when you turn eighteen . . ."

After a moment's silence, she stood up, walked over to the door, and locked it with two turns of the key. Then, quickly passing by Chernyshev, she drew the blinds.

"Remember this, Chernyshev, and mark my words: never try to find something out by dishonest means. What you find out will simply hurt you. Come here."

Chernyshev turned toward her.

She walked away from the window, lifted up her brown skirt,

and, holding it up with her chin, began to pull down her pantyhose, through which blue panties were visible.

Chernyshev drew his head down into his shoulders and backed away.

Zinaida Mikhailovna pulled off her pantyhose, stuck both of her hands into her panties, and, using her butt to help, pulled them down to her knees.

Chernyshev turned away.

"Stop! Stop, you idiot!" holding up her skirt, she grabbed him by the hand and turned him to face her. "Don't you dare turn away! I'm doing this for you, you bonehead! Look!"

She spread her full thighs and pulled Chernyshev's hand toward her.

"Look! Who I am talking to! Chernyshev!"

Chernyshev looked, then immediately turned away.

"Look! Look! Look!"

She loomed over him, her legs spread wide.

Chernyshev's lips twisted and he whimpered.

"Look! You wanted to see! There . . . there . . ."

She lifted her skirt up higher.

Chernyshev was crying, his face buried in his sleeve.

"Well, what are you blubbering for, Chernyshev? Stop! Quit it now. And why'd you get scared? Quit it . . . quit it already . . ."

She pulled him over to the chairs standing along the wall.

"Sit down. Sit down and get a hold of yourself."

Chernyshev sank down into the chair and began to sob, his hands covering his face.

Zinaida Mikhailovna quickly pulled down her skirt and sat next to him.

"Well, what's with you, Chernyshev? What's with you? Seryozha?"

She put her arms around his shoulders.

"Enough! You hear me? What are you? A girl? A first-grade girl?"

Chernyshev continued to cry.

"You should be ashamed of yourself! That's really enough. You were the one who wanted this. Oh, shut up! To let yourself go like this! Shut up!"

She shook him.

Cringing, Chernyshev let forth a final sob, then fell silent.

"So there . . . wipe away your tears . . . How can you blubber like this . . . my gosh . . ."

Sniffling, Chernyshev wiped his eyes with his fists.

Zinaida Mikhailovna stroked his head and began to speak in a whisper.

"Well, what is this? What're you scared for? Hmm? Tell me. C'mon and tell me. Hm? Tell me."

"I dunno . . ."

"What do you think—I'll tell everyone? How stupid. I drew the blinds on purpose. I promise you, I give you my word. I won't tell anyone. You understand? No one. Do you believe me? Do you?"

"I believe you . . ."

"What'd you get scared for?"

"I dunno . . ."

"And now you're afraid? Are you really afraid?"

"I'm not afraid . . ." Chernyshev sobbed.

Zinaida Mikhailovna whispered into his ear:

"Well, I swear to the Party, I won't tell anyone! To the Party! You know what that means—to swear to the Party!"

"I guess I know . . ."

"Do you believe me? Hm? Tell me. You believe me? I'm trying hard for you, stupid. Later, you'll say 'thank you.' Say you believe me?"

"Um . . . I believe you . . ."

"Not 'um, I believe you'! Just—'I believe you, Zinaida Mikhailovna.'"

"I believe you, Zinaida Mikhailovna."

"You're not going to blubber anymore?"

"I won't."

"You promise?"

"I promise."

"Give me your word as a Pioneer that you're not going to blubber and you won't tell anyone!"

"I give you my word . . . as a Pioneer."

"Your word as a Pioneer that you won't what?"

"That I won't blubber and I won't tell anyone . . ."

"Well, there. You probably thought I was making fun of you . . . Say that's what you thought? That's what you thought? That's what you thought, right, blockhead? Hmm?" She laughed softly, swaying him by the shoulders.

"A little . . ." Chernyshev muttered and smiled.

"You're stupid, Chernyshev. Is it really true that not a single girl's shown you this spot?"

"Yea-a-ah . . . not one . . ."

"And have you never asked nicely? To take a look?"

"Na-a-ah . . ."

"And would you have liked to take a look? Tell me honestly— would you have liked to?"

Chernyshev shrugged.

"I dunno . . ."

"Don't lie! We're speaking frankly! Would you have liked to? Speak like a Pioneer! Honestly! Would you've liked to?!"

"Well . . . I guess I would have . . ."

She slowly lifted up her skirt and spread apart her plump legs.

"Then look . . . look and don't turn away . . ."

Chernyshev looked sullenly.

She adjusted the pantyhose and panties that had slipped down to her boots and spread her thighs further apart.

"Look. Lean in closer and look . . ."

Sniffling, Chernyshev leaned in.

"You see now?"

"I see . . ."

"And what were you scared for at first? Hm?"

"I dunno . . . Zinaid Mikhailna . . . maybe that's enough, though . . ."

"You should be ashamed of yourself! What were you just saying? You oughta look!"

Chernyshev looked in silence.

"Do you have a good view?" she bent down toward him. "Otherwise, I'll stand like this . . ."

She stood in front of him.

Chernyshev looked at her groin, densely overgrown with black hair. Looming over it was a smooth belly with a large navel at its midpoint. A mark made by an elastic band was clearly visible on the belly.

"If you want, maybe you can touch . . . touch if you want . . . Don't be afraid . . ."

Zinaida Mikhailovna took his hand, still wet with tears, and laid it atop her groin.

"Touch it yourself . . . well . . . touch it . . ."

Chernyshev touched the furry mound.

"And there's nothing frightening about it, isn't that right?" Beginning to flush, Zinaida Mikhailovna smiled. "No? Hm? No—I'm asking you?"

Her head swayed and her painted lips twitched nervously.

"No."

"Then touch it more."

Chernyshev raised his hand and touched it again.

"Well, touch it more. Down. Touch down. Don't be afraid . . ."

She spread her trembling legs wider.

Chernyshev touched her swollen labia.

"Touch it more . . . more . . . What're you afraid for . . . You're not a little girl . . . you're a Pioneer . . ."

Chernyshev ran his palm across her genitals.

"You can touch it from behind . . . it's even closer there . . . look . . ."

She turned her butt to him and pulled her skirt up higher.

"Touch it from behind . . . well, touch it . . ."

Chernyshev stuck his hand between her overhanging buttocks and again stumbled upon her damp genitals.

"Well, there . . . touch it . . . touch it more . . . now touch it from the front again . . ."

Chernyshev touched it from the front.

"Now from the back again . . . like that . . . touch it harder . . . bolder, what're you afraid for . . . There's a little hole there . . . find it with your finger . . . no, lower . . . there . . . stick it in there . . . there . . ."

Chernyshev stuck his finger into her vagina.

"There . . . y'found it . . . y'see . . . a little hole . . ." Zinaida Mikhailovna whispered, sticking her butt out more and looking up at the ceiling. "No . . . stay there . . . there . . . Stand up . . . what're you sitting for . . ."

Chernyshev stood up.

"Touch it from the back with one hand and from the front with the other . . . like that . . ."

He began to touch it with both hands.

"Like that. And do you want me to touch you? Do you?"

"I dunno . . . maybe not . . ."

"But I know what you want . . . I'll just touch you a little . . . you're touching me . . . I'm interested too . . ."

She groped for his fly, unbuttoned it, and fumbled around with her hand.

"There . . . there . . . you see . . . you have this little thing . . . and when you grow up . . . I mean to say when it grows up . . . there . . . but you're already . . . touch it more . . . don't be afraid . . . there . . . and you can go into the little hole . . . there

. . . but it's still too early for that . . . Why'd you take away your hand . . . touch it more . . ."

The bell rang.

"Well, that's enough . . ." she straightened up, quickly pulled up her panties and pantyhose, and fixed her skirt. "Enough . . . so, you won't tell anyone? Really?"

"No, I won't tell . . ."

"You give me your word as a Pioneer?"

"I give you my word as a Pioneer."

"It'll be our little secret, isn't that right?"

"Mhm."

"And you won't tell the guys?"

"I won't."

"Or your mom?"

"Or my mom."

"Swear. Raise your right hand and say, 'I give you my word as a Pioneer.'"

Chernyshev raised his sticky palm over his forehead:

"I give you my word as a Pioneer."

Zinaida Mikhailovna turned to the portrait of Lenin hanging over her desk:

"And I swear to the Party . . ."

The bell rang again.

"Is that for a break or for your next class?" the principal muttered, touching her flamingly red cheek with her palm.

"For a break . . ." Chernyshev answered.

Zinaida Mikhailovna walked over to the window, opened the blinds, then turned back to Chernyshev.

"I'm not too red?"

"No, no . . ."

"No? Well, run along then. And try not to get up to any more mischief . . ."

She started to unlock the door:

"Run along . . . wait! Button up your fly."

Turning away, he buttoned up his fly.

"What's your next class?"

"Natural Science . . ."

"In Room No. 18?"

"Yeah, up there . . ."

"Well, run along."

She flung open the door.

Chernyshev stepped over the threshold and ran away.

A HEARING OF THE
FACTORY COMMITTEE

VITKA PISKUNOV ARRIVED at the factory club at nine o'clock. Two streetlights were already shining and some guys were crowded around the façade's peeling ten-meter-tall columns. Noticing Vitka, they stopped talking and turned their intoxicated faces toward him.

"Hi, Piskun."

"Yo . . ."

"Well, you ready?"

"Ready. Mentally and physically," Vitka took out a cigarette and approached a broad-faced guy. "Light me up . . ."

The guy took a cigarette out of his mouth and proffered it to Vitka.

"They're there. Waitin' for you."

"To hell with 'em," Vitka lit up.

"To hell with 'em, to hell with 'em, but they're still gonna make y'sweat, that's for sure."

"What're you all worked up for? I'm the guy who's gotta sweat, not you." Throwing back his head, Vitka blew smoke up into the sky and looked at the stars.

"I'm not worried, I'm just talkin'," the guy stubbed out his cigarette butt against a column. Another guy, tall, hawk-nosed, and grinning, slapped Vitka on the shoulder.

"You won't corner Vitka that easy, dude! He's quick. Isn't that right, Vitk?"

Piskunov smoked in silence, leaning against a column.

"Well, Piskun, you've really done it now," the second guy shook his head, "I don't envy you."

"C'mon, Zhen, don't upset him . . ."

"And why'd they decide to hold the meeting in the club?"

"The hall's under renovation."

"Ahhh . . . got it."

Piskunov finished his cigarette, flicked the butt into a flower bed, and, pushing the broad-faced guy aside, made a move for the door. "You comin' to the dance?"

"I dunno . . ."

"Well, Vityok, if you do end up comin', you definitely owe us a bottle," the hawk-nosed guy chuckled as Piskunov walked away.

"A bottle?" Piskunov turned around as he pulled the door open. "Suck my throttle! You can throw down a bottle yourself, you still owe me for the soccer . . . And you know I'm good for it, so quit it . . ."

Slamming the door shut, he walked into the vestibule.

There was nobody inside. The checkout window wasn't illuminated. A cleaning woman's uniform, three anonymous coats, and Klokov's gray slicker were draped over hangers.

"Who invited him here?" Piskunov thought as he walked through the vestibule. "Guess he's happy to skip dinner to come to a factory-committee hearing."

The door leading into the hall was open. Piskunov went in. People were sitting on the faintly illuminated stage just underneath an enormous portrait of Lenin. They occupied the center of a long table covered over in a red tablecloth.

"May I come in?" Piskunov asked quietly. His voice resounded through the empty hall.

"Come in, come in," Simakova replied. She was sitting at the center of the table and sorting through some papers.

"He can't even make it *here* on time," sitting next to her, Khokhlov looked at his watch. "Fifteen minutes past eight."

"A habit," Klokov laughed. "It's entered into his blood. No matter the day—Piskunov. Someone's late—Piskunov. Someone drank too much—Piskunov. Someone was talking back to the ma—"

"Sergei Vasilievich," Simakova interrupted him, "we'll talk about Piskunov later. Let's finish with the vacation vouchers. And you sit down, Piskunov, just sit and wait for a little while."

Vitka moved unhurriedly between the seats and sat down at their outer edge, closer to the door.

"If, as Starukhin suggests, we give a hundred to the smithy and a hundred and ten to the foundry, then there will only be eighty-four left for the machine assembly shop. And just twelve for the garage . . . fourteen, I mean," Khokhlov rustled through the papers.

"Well, that's right," Zvyagintseva said calmly, tapping her pencil against the table, "the machine assembly shop never fulfills its normal quota and the factory always lets us down. The smithy and the foundry put the pedal to the metal, but the assemblers always pull the brakes: either their machines break down or they can't retain their staff . . . That's why the factory isn't getting pampered: no apartments, no orders, and no vacation vouchers."

"Although . . . it should be understood that there aren't no apartments for only *that* reason," Klokov frowned. "The builders aren't exactly working at lightning speed either. There'll be apartments eventually. The foundations were laid for three buildings in Yasenevo and two in Medvedkovo. And we also have to understand the assemblers. After all, our responsibility is weighty and our conditions more difficult. And we don't pay our workers all that much—"

"Ah, quit it!" Zvyagintseva straightened up, causing the two medals pinned to her jacket to clink together faintly. "Don't pay all that much! Everyone gets paid the same. And they have to work. To execute the plan. Then the pay'll get better and more orders will appear—vouchers too. The whole factory's on fire because of the assemblers. All of it!"

"But we must understand that working on a conveyer belt is more difficult and that, for a hundred and forty rubles, no one's really burn—"

"Understand?! One's sitting over there: understand him!" Zvyagintseva pointed her pencil out into the dusky hall where Piskunov's head loomed between the rotund seats. "The fruit of your machine assembly shop. Understand him! He drinks like a fish and screws around, but we're supposed to understand him!"

"Enough of that, Tatyana Yuryevna," Simakova said. "Let's deal with the voucher distribution. I have to report to the All-Union Central Council of Trade Unions tomorrow, I'll be sitting up all night . . . Generally speaking, we either have to distribute them equally or do as Starukhin suggests."

"We can't do it equally," Urgan insisted. "Tatyana Yuryevna's right. The foundry workers are the most productive out of everyone. We need to give them the most vouchers. And let the assemblers go to a tourist camp. I was at one by Saratov last year—what a thing to see! The chow's good and the Volga's right there. It's no worse than the south . . ."

"Exactly," Zvyagintseva turned to him, "let them go there. Even though everyone wanted to head south. I bet Piskunov wrote a declaration expressing his desire to do so as well. Isn't that right, Piskunov?"

"Me?" Vitka raised his head.

"You, you. I'm asking you."

"Whaddya mean? To Yalta or somethin'?"

"Yes."

"I've already seen enough of it. I'd rather be with my aunty in Obninsk—real quiet and peaceful . . ."

"How conscientious," Zvyagintseva grinned, "real quiet and peaceful. Would that everyone wanted that: real quiet and peaceful! But what we've got here," she jammed her fingers into a sheaf of papers, "is four hundred applications!"

"So we'll distribute them as Starukhin suggested?" Simakova asked.

"Of course."

"Let's do it like that . . ."

"Convenient and correct."

"And the main thing is it provides an incentive. If you did good work, you'll get a voucher."

"That's right."

"Shall we vote?"

"No need. Everything's perfectly clear."

Simakova wrote something down in her notebook.

"Oksana Pavlovna," Khokhlov leaned forward, "we have one woman working in our workshop, the mother of three children, an activist and a public-minded person. From a long line of working people. I'd really like her to be given a voucher."

"I have two as well. Young, but very public-minded," Klokov added.

"We shall provide for all public-minded people, war veterans, and invalids—as always," Simakova replied, "but save that for later, comrades. The main thing is that they be distributed to each workshop. And then you can decide for yourselves. Let's move on to the issue of Piskunov. Stand up, Piskunov! Come here."

Piskunov got up unhurriedly and walked over to the stage.

"Come up here, come up to us."

He climbed up the wooden steps onto the stage and stood near a lectern. The people sitting at the table looked him over for a minute.

"You couldn't find yourself a newer pair of pants?" Klokov asked.

"Nope." Vitka examined the knot in Ilyich's tie, which was practically a meter long.

"You should have at least cleaned them. They're so dirty. You haven't come to a dance or a liquor store, you know."

"He would've found better pants for a dance," Zvyagintseva interjected, "pants and a shirt. And he wouldn't have forgotten to tie his tie. And he'd've gulped down a half-liter with his pals."

Simakova laid down two sheets of paper in front of her.

"The factory committee has received two memos. The first is from Comrade Shemlyov, a foreman in the mechanical assembly shop and the second is from the shop's trade union. In both of them, our comrades ask us to consider the behavior of Viktor Ivanovich Piskunov, a milling-machine operator from the mechanical-assembly shop. I'll read them out. Here, the foreman writes the following:

"'I bring to the attention of the factory trade-union committee the fact that Viktor Piskunov, a worker in my brigade, is systematically violating our manufactory discipline, comes to his workplace in a drunken state, does not fulfill normal production quotas, and behaves improperly with the bosses, the other workers, and me . . . Starting in June of this year, Piskunov began to drink again, he comes to the factory staggering a great deal and also expresses himself with rude, obscene words. I have warned him many times, asked him, and even scolded him, but he is incorrigible—he drinks, swears, is rude, and acts the hooligan. On July 16th, while working at his milling machine and milling the ends of a hull, he fastened one component backwards, which caused a major breakdown of the machine. When I shouted at him, he picked up another component and threw it at me, but I dodged it and went straight to the head of the shop. Even before this, Piskunov had been inattentive to his machine, he'd scratched a swear word onto its relay and a swear-word drawing next to the

DISPATCHES FROM THE DISTRICT COMMITTEE   131

word. And when I asked him to erase it, he said that he'd need an incentive to do so. And, on July 10th, he beat Fyodor Baryshnikov so badly that he had to be taken to the infirmary. Because of Piskunov, our brigade has never fulfilled its normal quotas, as he has never milled more than two hundred hulls and the normal quota is three hundred and fifty. I have told my superiors this many times, but they say that our turnover is too high already, so we need to educate rather than eliminate. And when I scold him, Piskunov takes out a pen and says: 'gimme a piece of paper right now and I'll write up a declaration—what do I need your factory for!' And he talks badly about his factory family. And swears. I have worked at our factory for twenty-three years and, as a member of the Party, I demand that effective measures be taken against Piskunov and that he be given an effective talking-to, as is demanded by circumstance. Indeed, he has been sent to the factory committee twice and nothing has changed in him. Our entire collective has come to me and demanded an effective conversation be had with Piskunov. Foreman Andrei Shmelyov.'"

A cleaning lady with a stick and bucket came into the hall through the half-open door. Having put the bucket down onto the floor, she removed the rag from the stick and began to wash it in the bucket.

Simakova picked up another sheet of paper.

"And this is from the trade union. 'Members of the shop trade-union committee ask the factory committee to consider the behavior of the milling-machine operator Viktor Piskunov at their next meeting. In the last month, Piskunov has regularly violated manufactory discipline, coming to work in an unsober state and failing to meet normal production quotas. On July 16th, Piskunov drunkenly caused severe damage to his machine and thus delayed the work of his brigade for an entire day. Depriving Piskunov of his progressive pay has had no effect on him, he still continues to violate our discipline and be rude to his factory bosses and comrades.'"

Simakova pushed the piece of paper off to the side.

"Yes, Piskunov. You haven't even been at the factory for a year, but everyone already knows about you. And not as a shock worker, but as a parasite and alcoholic."

"I'm an alcoholic?" Piskunov raised his head.

"If you're not an alcoholic, then what are you?" Klokov asked. "You're a born alcoholic."

"Alcoholics lie around in the hospital, but I work. I'm not an alcoholic."

"Of course! Of course he's not an alcoholic!" Zvyagintseva said with feigned seriousness. "What kind of alcoholic would he be?! A glass in the morning, a glass at lunch, and half a jar with dinner! What kind of alcoholic would that be?"

Those gathered around the table laughed.

The cleaning lady wrung out the rag, wrapped it around the end of the stick, and began to mop the walkway between the seats.

Simakova sighed.

"You understand, Piskunov, that working in a drunken state isn't just dangerous for you, but also for your machine and those around you. Do you understand that?"

"I do."

"Well then, what is this? You understand, but you continue to drink?"

"I don't drink, though . . . There was one time, but it got blown way outta proportion . . ." he swayed and shook his head, "blown up as if I did it every day, but it was actually once, at a birthday party at my brother-in-law's . . ."

"Shame on you that you lie like this!" Zvyagintseva shouted. "Aren't you ashamed to lie?! You're swimming in liquor up to your eyeballs every day! Eeeeevery day! There's," she nodded at Klokov, "your trade-union organizer—at least watch your words with him sitting here!"

Vitka looked at Klokov and only just then noticed that

Seryozha Chernogayev, a borer from the neighboring brigade, was present. Seryoga was watching Vitka fearfully and warily.

"Once . . ." Klokov affirmed, "he's maybe come to work sober once during the whole time he's been here! I see him in the changing room every morning, I look into his eyes: drunk again! And his eyes are red as a rabbit's!"

"What do you mean they're red? What part of me is red?"

"Red eyes. And your mug is as white as milk. And you're staggering from side to side."

"Ah, when've I ever staggered like that? What're you lying for?"

"Don't you be impudent with me, friend!" Klokov slapped his hand against the table. "I'm not your drinking buddy! I'm not Vaska Senin! Not Petka Kruglov! Talk like that with them! And stand up straight! Why are you leaning against the podium like that? That isn't a beer stand, you know!"

"Stand up straight, Piskunov," Simakova said sternly.

Vitka pushed himself reluctantly off of the podium and, squinting, straightened up. The cleaning lady finished wiping down the floor and, leaning on her stick, gazed at the stage with great interest.

Zvyagintseva looked at Piskunov with disgust and shook her head.

"Oh yesss . . . It's painful to look at you, Piskunov. You're a pathetic individual."

"How am I pathetic?"

"Any alcoholic is pathetic," Starukhin interjected. "And you're no exception. You should look at yourself in the mirror. You're all swollen. Your face is all purple, it's a hell of a thing . . . not a very pleasant sight to behold."

The door creaked and a tall policeman entered the hall with a cello case in hand. Those gathered around the table looked at him. After stomping around in place for a moment, the policeman slowly walked down the aisle and sat down at the end of the fourth row. He leaned the black case against the neighboring seat, took his cap off his bald head, and hung it from the case.

"That oughta calm him down a bit," Klokov muttered, glancing at the policeman. "Not very pleasant to behold what he does in the shop or the changing room either."

"You been in there and seen it or somethin'?"

"You've already been told—no more sass!" Simakova swayed forward. "Why don't you explain why you beat up Baryshnikov instead. Or maybe Klokov just made that up too?"

Piskunov sighed wistfully and put his hands behind his back. The policeman squinted up at him. The cleaning lady left the bucket with the stick and rag in the aisle and sat down not far from the policeman.

"What are you so quiet for? Tell us."

"What's there to tell . . . He started it. Swore, threatened me . . . and I was tired . . . not in the mood."

"And you were drunk too, hm?"

"Well, maybe a little . . . I'd had some beer in the morning."

"And it hadn't worn off by evening?" Klokov asked. "Good beer!"

The members of the factory committee laughed.

The cleaning lady shook her head and fixed the kerchief that had fallen down over her eyes. The policeman was squinting up at the stage as before. Simakova picked up her pencil and, fiddling with it, asked:

"Which means you took your bad mood out on your friend?"

"He started it. He mouthed off."

"Don't lie, Piskunov," Klokov interrupted him. "He didn't start it, but you . . . you got drunk in the changing room with Petka Kruglov and started to screw with everyone. And Baryshnikov tried to stop you. And you beat him up. We have a witness right here," he nodded toward Chernogayev.

Everyone looked at the witness. Chernogayev blushed. Vitka glanced at Sergei's red face, then turned away.

"Nothing to say? Well, well . . . Truth is blinding. You should thank Baryshnikov for not reporting you. When he had every right to. That lil' bruise would've given you fifteen days and no less."

"Really . . . Why didn't he go to the police?" Urgan asked.

"Well, he turned out to be a real solid guy. He kept his mouth shut as if nothing'd happened."

"Lucky you, Piskunov."

"People like him always get lucky."

"That's exactly, exactly right! They get lucky!" the cleaning lady stood up from her seat. "Excuse me, of course, it's only just that," she threw her hands out to the sides, "my neighbor's exactly, exactly like that! And—my!—how parasites like them glide through life!"

She moved away from the rows of seats, ran up to the stage, and began to count off her knobbly fingers.

"Doesn't work anywhere! Drinks every day! Has women over, acts the hooligan, gets in fights, and that's the least of it! Plus nobody'll even evict him! I've already done the rounds with the police—nope! As he drank, so too shall he drink!"

The members of the factory committee shook their heads sympathetically. The cleaning lady sighed and sat down in the first row. Simakova looked at Piskunov.

"This is the third time you're being dragged before the factory committee, Piskunov. Have you entirely lost the use of your conscience? You're letting the collective down and dishonoring the factory. Don't think about yourself—think about others. The brigade hasn't been fulfilling its normal quotas because of you, which means no one gets progressive pay or bonuses. Do you not understand? Or do you not care? Nothing to say?! All the same to you, huh?!"

"For him, it's six of one and half a dozen of the other," Zvyagintseva sighed. "Got drunk—good! Got in a fight—even better!

Didn't make it to work—absolutely splendid! He doesn't care about the brigade at all."

"Do you know how much the malfunction of your machine cost the state, Piskunov? You don't know?" Klokov asked.

Vitka shook his head.

Klokov raised himself up, his hands resting against the table.

"If it were up to me, I'd charge you that whole sum! Then you'd get it! You'd get it. Otherwise, he breaks the machine and nothing—he sits there smoking in the gangway! What're you doing, Vitya? 'I'm smokin' a spell!' And they're fixing the machine for him. You could've at least helped the repairmen! 'No, don't give a damn!' Generally speaking, he doesn't give a damn about work, about the workshop, or about his comrades. Here's Chernogayev, a worker in his same workshop; you can at least tell us how your comrades speak about Piskunov. Tell us! And we'll listen."

Chernogayev stood up uncertainly and swayed. Everyone looked at him.

"Well, I . . . in general, I . . ." he passed his hand across his forehead.

"Be brave, Seryozh, tell us how it is," Klokov encouraged him.

"Well, comrades, I work in the same shop as Piskunov, which means I see him every day. He and I work in different brigades, but I see him every day. Both in the changing room and in the cafeteria. So. Well. In general, it's already all been said. He drinks. He gets drunk on a regular basis. He comes in drunk every morning and drunk every evening. So, yeah, I mean . . . I see his machine too. It's dirty and unkempt. After work I pass by and his machine's covered with shavings. And his brush is just lying there on the ground. And it's like that almost every day. And, in general, he behaves badly—he's rude. Like how he beat Baryshnikov up . . ."

"How did that happen?" Simakova asked.

"Well, I mean, Piskunov and Petka Kruglov went into the

changing room before anyone else. It wasn't yet six, but they'd clocked out. And then, when the others started to come in and I came in, they were sitting there drunk, swearing, and smoking. And he and Fedya had come to blows even before that. Fedya had scolded Piskunov for screwing up the brigade's whole plan. And as soon as Piskunov saw Fedya, I mean, he started to bully him right away. 'Hey,' he says, 'you Stakhanovite shock worker, come here and I'll mill your mug.'"

"What're you lying for, Chernogai, I nev—"

"Shut it, Piskunov! Keep going, Chernogayev."

"So, there. And Fedya says to him, 'Behave,' he says, 'yourself.' And Piskunov starts to swear. And, I mean, Fedya says to him that, um, there'll be a meeting, 'I'll,' he says, 'tell them about you and we'll,' he says, 'denounce you to the factory committee.' Well, then Piskunov rushed at him. We broke 'em up. Fedya's face'd got worked over pretty good. The guys went to the infirmary with him. And Piskunov stayed sitting in the changing room for a long time. Swearing. Saying bad things about the factory . . ."

"What typa bad things did I say?"

"Don't interrupt, Piskunov! No one's asking you."

"Well, what's he gotta lie for?"

"I'm not lying. He said that everything here was bad and the pay was too little. 'Nothing,' he says, 'to buy and nowhere to go.'"

"That's rich! He doesn't go anywhere but the liquor store! And doesn't buy anything but half-liter bottles."

"Whaddaya mean I don't go anywhere?"

"What do I mean! I mean you're an alcoholic! An amoral individual!" Zvyagintseva shook her head.

Chernogayev continued.

"And he was still saying that everything at the factory was bad, nothing to buy, bad food . . . 'That's why,' he says, 'I don't wanna work.'"

Everyone stared at Piskunov silently.

"And how . . . how could you twist your tongue to say all of that?!" the cleaning lady got up from her chair and walked over to the stage. "You oughta be ashamed of yourself! How could you have dared?! You . . . you . . ." she pressed her hands to her bosom. "Who raised you?! Who brought you up, who educated you for free?! We ate bread and sawdust durin' the war and worked nights so's you could swagger 'round in that shirt, eat sweet things, and not know the meaning of worry! How'd you turn out like this?! Huh?!"

"You spit in the same well you drink from, Piskunov!" Khokhlov interjected.

"But others drink too," Simakova added. "You spit on everyone. On the brigade, on the factory, and on the Fatherland. Look, Piskunov," she knocked on the table, "you'll spit right through it!"

"You'll spit right through it!"

"How sick he must feel! He has to learn to work, then he'll feel better! Drunkards and lazybones feel bad no matter where they are."

"Such people feel bad everywhere. Set him up in a communist system and he still won't come to his senses."

"Yes. You're a rotten person, Piskunov."

"Are you a member of the Komsomol?"

"No," Vitka looked gloomily at the portrait.

"And you're not thinking of becoming one?"

"It's too late . . . I'm twenty-five . . ."

"Such people have no place in the Komsomol."

"Exactly! Such people really have no place in the working class."

"This is the third time he's being dragged before the factory committee and still he's incorrigible! He's numb to it and that's that! And all the spinelessness is on our end! We're meant to be the educators!"

"Indeed, Oksana Pavlovna," Zvyagintseva turned to Simakova. "What on earth is this?! We're not a *sharashka*, but a factory committee! Which means he'll act like he's listening, he'll leave, he'll spit in a corner, then he'll be hitting the bottle tomorrow by eleven? We're a factory committee! A factory trade-union committee! Trade unions are the forge of communism! That's what Lenin said! Then why are we so soft with them . . . even when they're in the palm of our hands?"

"That's the truth! It's time to finally stop being loyal to them!" Starukhin interjected. "At the end of the day, we have a factory—a Soviet factory! And we're responsible for the effectiveness of our factory before the Fatherland! They took away his progressive pay—not enough! They took away his thirteenth check—not enough! We can't fire him, which means new measures must be sought! And don't be too humane! Otherwise we'll reach the limit of our humanity!"

"That's right, Oksana Pavlovna, we have to struggle with people like Piskunov. Wage a decisive battle! What's the use of mollycoddling them?!"

"For him, our homilies are like poultices for a dead man."

"Well, and what can we do other than take away his bonuses and progressive pay? We can't kick him out . . ."

"Then what's the point of this meeting?! We're making a mockery of the trade union."

"A total mockery . . ."

"And setting a bad example. He drinks today, but by tomorrow, take a look, it's the whole brigade."

"But, what can we do?!"

The policeman stood up, sighed, and pulled at his coat. "Comrades!"

Everyone turned to him. He waited for a moment, then spoke.

"I am, of course, an outsider, so to speak. And have nothing to do with this affair. But as a Soviet man and as a, so to speak, worker of the police force, I'd like to, so to speak, share my experience. Comrades, I've been working with people like this guy for almost nineteen years. I first made their acquaintance at the age of twenty. These people—parasites, alcoholics, hooligans, and more serious, so to speak, hardened criminals—all hope for only one thing: that we treat them, so to speak, gently. And as soon as we're softer and more civilized with them, they immediately get harder. They can tell right away! They draw their conclusions and become even more of a danger to society. I've been sitting here listening and, well, in general terms, I get it. I understand you very well, comrades. And, in my opinion, there's no reason to fear novel measures. At the end of the day, you're not just responsible for yourselves, but for the entire enterprise. And yet you think about *him*. And feel bad for *him*. But it wasn't at random that your factory was given an order. Wasn't random at all! You must remember that."

He sat down and clasped his hands together.

"That's right!" Urgan spoke up. "Even though our comrade there doesn't work at the factory, he's essentially correct. By encouraging people like Piskunov, we harm our enterprise! We harm ourselves too! Which means what? It turns out that you and I are to blame?!"

"Of course we are!" Zvyagintseva affirmed. "And entirely so! Because of our myopia, the entire factory suffers!"

The cleaning lady rose up from her seat once again.

"And if it were up to me, with those people there, with people like him, I'd, oh, I'd simply not know what had to be done! 'Cause we get no livin' from 'em! 'Cause they're in the courtyard, day after day, startin' right in the AM—they're janglin', drinkin', and fightin' 'til the evenin'!"

"But, again, what can we even do? We're just an ordinary factory committee, our powers are incredibly limited."

The policeman sighed.

"You haven't understood me, comrades. As I've just said, you shouldn't fear novel, more effective measures. You shouldn't only think of yourselves, isn't that right?"

"Yes, that's right, of course," Simakova replied, "but the fact remains that we really have no powers at all, Comrade Policeman . . ."

"Coooooomrades!" the policeman slapped his hand against his knees. "I find it almost painful to listen to you! No powers! And who's guilty in that?! You are! Everything depends on you and on your initiative! If you had specific proposals, then you'd have powers. Laws, what . . . you think they just fall from the sky? No! The people makes them! Everything depends upon you and the people. You've put a barrier up in front of yourselves and you're waiting to be given powers. It's really very silly. You're waiting in vain. And people like this," he jabbed his finger in Piskunov's direction, "certainly won't give you an opening! And, if you wait, those powers won't even help. So, now, before it's too late, propose something! Try it out! What're you afraid of? You think you can fight back against people like him with conversation and persuasion? Totally in vain. It's not persuasion they need. With them, one needs a totally different approach. Precisely what— well, that's your affair. That initiative should come from your end. If there's initiative and there're proposals, that means there'll be powers too. And if there's no initiative, and no business-like, so to speak, proposals, that means there'll be no powers either."

He sat down, took out a handkerchief, and wiped at his sweaty forehead.

Everyone was silent for a minute. Then Klokov sighed and drew his head down into his shoulders.

"Actually, I have, I mean, we have . . . well, generally speaking, there is one proposal. With regard to Piskunov. It's true that . . . I dunno how it . . . well . . . how . . . generally speaking, whether you'll understand me—us, I mean to say—correctly . . ."

"Don't be afraid," the policeman encouraged him, putting

away his handkerchief, "if it's concrete and business-like, so to speak, then they'll understand it. And approve of it."

Klokov looked at Zvyagintseva. She replied with a knowing look.

"Well, in general, we suggest . . ." Klokov looked his hands over, "in general, we . . ."

Everyone looked at him expectantly. He licked at his lips, raised his head, then exhaled.

"Well, generally speaking, there's a proposal to shoot Piskunov."

Total silence reigned in the hall. The policeman scratched sedulously at his temple and grinned.

"Welllll . . . comrades . . . what a load of nonsense . . . I'm not talking about shooting . . ."

Those seated at the table exchanged uncertain looks. The policeman laughed louder, stood up, picked up the cello case, then, chuckling, walked over to the exit.

Everyone followed him with their attentive gazes. He stopped by the door, turned, and, sliding his cap to the back of his head, began to speak quickly.

"Piskunov, I would suggest you listen to more classical music. Bach, Beethoven, Mozart, Shostakovich, and, perhaps, Prokofiev. Do you know how music ennobles a person? And, most importantly, makes him purer and more conscientious? You there, you don't know anything other than drinking and dancing, which is why you don't want to work. Go to a conservatory just once— hear an organ. You'll immediately understand a great deal . . ." he fell silent for a moment, then sighed and continued. "And you, comrades, instead of wasting time like this holding purpose-less meetings, it'd be better to organize a classical-music lovers' club at the factory. Then the young people'd really get down to business—truancy and alcoholism would decrease . . . I'd speak more on the subject, but I'm late for rehearsal—you'll have to excuse me . . ."

He went out the door.

The cleaning lady sighed and, lifting up her bucket, went out after him. But she didn't manage to touch the half-open door before it burst open and the policeman flew back into the hall with a wild, inhuman roar. Pressing the cello case to his chest, he knocked the cleaning lady over and ran toward the stage on bent legs, his head thrown back. Having reached the first row of seats, he stopped abruptly, dropped the case onto the ground, and froze in place, roaring and leaning back. His roar became more hoarse, his face went crimson, and his arms dangled at the sides of his inclined torso.

"Roon . . . roon . . . roonthroo . . . roonthroo . . ." he roared, shaking his head and opening his mouth wide.

Zvyagintseva slowly rose up from her chair, her hands were trembling, and her fingers with their brightly painted nails were bent. She clutched at her face with her nails and pulled her hands down, tearing bloodily into her cheeks.

"Roonthroo . . . roonthroo . . ." she croaked in a low, chesty voice.

Starukhin stood up abruptly from his chair, leaned onto the table with his hands, then smashed his face into its surface with all his might.

"Roonthroo . . . roon . . . roonthroo . . ." he pronounced, writhing around atop the table.

Urgan shook his head and began to mutter quickly, barely managing to get the words out.

"Well, if we're on the subject of roonthroo technology, of the sequence of assembly operations, of interchangeable components and why it's all so roonthroo, then the interrepublican union immediately becomes larger and more noticeable, then roonthroo on a local scale isn't provided for with any funds or raw materials in various respects, in varicose respects, and they don't just give out cash, so they have to agitate for self-funding . . ."

Klokov jerked, jumped up from the table, and tumbled back down onto the stage. Turning onto his stomach, he squirmed, crawled to the edge of the stage, then threw himself out into the absent audience. Among the seats, he tossed, turned, and began to sing something quiet. Khokhlov burst into loud tears. Simakova pulled him out from under the table. Khokhlov bent over, burying his face in his hands. Simakova grabbed him tightly by the shoulders from behind. She vomited onto the nape of Khokhlov's neck. Having spit her mouth dry and cleared her throat, she cried out in a strong, piercing voice.

"Roonthroo! Roonthroo! Roonthroo!"

Piskunov and Chernogayev jumped down from the stage and, imitating each other's strange movements, trotted over to the front door. Approaching the motionlessly horizontal cleaning lady, they grabbed her by the legs and dragged her down the aisle toward the stage.

"Roonthroo! Roonthroo!" the policeman roared hoarsely. He bent back even further, his red face drawn fixedly up toward the hall's ceiling and his body trembling.

Piskunov and Chernogayev dragged the cleaning lady toward the steps, then tugged her onto the stage. Zvyagintseva removed her hands from her bloodied face, leaned forward violently, then walked over to the cleaning lady lying on the floor. Urgan also walked over to the cleaning lady, muttering as he did.

"If we're on the subject of roonthroo technology, citizen foremen, they never installed the high-voltage supports and added bitumen oxidizers when the grinding process was indispensable to the affairs and decisions, for which we were responsible, hence a strange alternation between oil-seal and mechanical-drive units . . ."

Chernogayev, Piskunov, Zvyagintseva, and Urgan picked the cleaning lady up from the floor and carried her over to the table.

Starukhin raised up his blue, broken face.

"Roonthroo," he pronounced succinctly with his swollen lips.

Simakova let go of Khokhlov and, without ceasing to shriek shrilly, walked over to the table.

Khokhlov got down onto his knees, touched his forehead to the ground, then began to rake the mass of vomit that had spilled onto the floor up with his hands and toward his face. Chernogayev, Piskunov, Zvyagintseva, Urgan, Starukhin, and Simakova surrounded the cleaning lady lying on the table and began to tear off her clothing. The cleaning lady came to and began to mutter quietly.

"And she's roonthroo . . . oh, so roonthroo too . . ."

"Roonthroo! Roonthroo!" Simakova cried out.

"Roonthroo . . ." Zvyagintseva wheezed.

"But roonthroo according to technically verified and economically justified rules for rubbing over shafts . . ." Urgan muttered.

"Roonthroo!" the policeman roared.

Soon, all of the clothing had been stripped from the cleaning lady's body.

"Anthat . . . anshe that . . ." she muttered, lying on the table.

"Roonth! Roonth! Roonth!" Simakova cried out.

They flipped the cleaning lady over and pressed her against the table.

"Roonth . . . anshe that . . ." the cleaning lady wheezed.

"Roonthrootion! Roonthrootion!" the policeman bellowed.

Squatting and making rapid rotational motions with their hands, Piskunov and Chernogayev jumped up from the stage, lifted the policeman's cello case, which had been lying at their feet until that moment, carried it away, and laid it at the edge of the stage.

"Roonthrootion! Roonthrootion!" the policeman roared.

Piskunov and Chernogayev opened the case. It was divided in half on the inside by a wooden partition. One half continued a sledgehammer and some short metal pipes, while the other was filled to the brim with worms seething in brownish-green slime. Bits of half-rotten flesh peeked out from beneath the mass of worms.

Chernogayev picked up the sledgehammer and Piskunov took away the pipes. There were five of them.

"Poonotrooted! Poonotrooted!" the policeman roared and began to tremble even more.

"Branch pipes, branch pipes, poonotrooted branch pipes made according to all-human GOST standards, 652/58 according to the unmeasured," Urgan muttered, pressing the cleaning lady's body to the table together with everyone else. "A length of four hundred and twenty millimeters, a diameter of forty-two millimeters, a wall-thickness of three millimeters, a 3 x 5 chamfer."

Piskunov carried the pipes over to the table and dumped them onto the ground.

"Poonotrooted . . . alshe and poon . . ." the cleaning lady muttered.

Piskunov took one pipe and pressed its pointy end to the cleaning lady's back.

"Fatal! Fatal!" the policeman roared.

"Fatal! Fatal!" Simakova affirmed.

"Fatal . . . fatal . . ." Starukhin repeated.

"Fatal . . ." Zvyagintseva wheezed.

Piskunov picked up one pipe, grabbing onto it with both hands. Chernogayev began to beat at the end of the pipe with the sledgehammer. The pipe passed through the cleaning lady's body and hit the table. Piskunov took the second pipe and pressed it to the cleaning lady's back. Chernogayev hit the end of the pipe with the sledgehammer. The pipe passed through the cleaning lady's body and hit the table. Piskunov took the third pipe and pressed it to the cleaning lady's back. Chernogayev hit the end of the pipe with the sledgehammer. The pipe passed through the cleaning lady's body and hit the table. Piskunov took the fourth pipe and pressed it to the cleaning lady's back. Chernogayev hit the end of the pipe with the sledgehammer. The pipe passed through the cleaning lady's body and hit the table. Piskunov took the fifth pipe and pressed it to the cleaning lady's back. Chernogayev hit the end of the pipe with the sledgehammer. The pipe passed through the cleaning lady's body and hit the table.

"Outractedly . . . outractedly . . ." Khokhlov muttered into the pile of vomit he'd raked up.

"Outractedly! Outractedly!" Simakova shouted and grabbed onto one of the pipes protruding from the cleaning lady's back with both hands. Starukhin helped Simakova and together they extruded the pipe.

"Outractedly! Outractedly!" the policeman roared.

Starukhin and Simakova extruded the second pipe and threw it onto the ground. Urgan and Zvyagintseva extruded the third pipe and threw it onto the ground. Piskunov and Chernogayev extruded the fourth pipe and threw it onto the ground. Urgan and Zvyagintseva extruded the fifth pipe and threw it onto the ground. Blood flowed profusely out from under the cleaning lady's body.

"Droono! Droono!" Simakova screamed.

Quickly flowing across the red cloth, the blood spilled down into three large puddles on the floor.

Khokhlov crawled toward the open case on his knees.

"Outfill! Allfoll!" the policeman bellowed.

"Tofol with the wormery! Tofol with the wormery!" Simakova screamed and everyone except for the policeman and Klokov, who was lying among the seats, moved toward the cello case.

"Tofol with the wormery," Starukhin repeated. "Tofol . . ."

"Tofol in accordance with technological maps produced atop a state foundation and done smallish after an economic accounting for of the third quarter," Urgan muttered.

Each of them scooped a handful of worms out from the cello

case and carried it over to the table. Walking over to the cleaning lady's corpse, they began to lay the worms into the holes in her back. As soon as they'd finished, the policeman stopped writhing and roaring, took his handkerchief out of his pocket, and began to meticulously wipe off his sweat-covered face.

Klokov got up from the floor and began to dust off his suit. Piskunov and Chernogayev collected the pipes and sledgehammer that'd been hurled onto the ground, put them into the free compartment of the cello case, closed it, then began to fasten it.

"Well, what're ye gettin' up to there?" Klokov asked unhappily, "that's why I trifled on down anyhow . . ."

Chernogayev and Piskunov snapped the case, raised it up, and walked down into the hall. Everyone except for Khokhlov followed after them. Khokhlov disappeared behind the curtains.

"Well, what're ye fiddlin' 'round for?" Klokov called out to Chernogayev and Piskunov. "Hurl! Hurl!"

"I'll ask you not to shout," Chernogayev pronounced, looking into Klokov's eyes. "I'll ask you to please behave in becoming fashion."

Klokov waved his hand irritatedly and turned away. Chernogayev and Piskunov wound up with the case and hurled it into the middle of the hall where it disappeared noisily between the seats.

Khokhlov emerged hunched over from behind the curtains. There was a large cube made of semi-transparent gelatinous matter on his back. The cube jiggled with each step he took. He crossed the stage, carefully descended the steps down into the hall, and headed for the exit.

"Stop!" the policeman pronounced.

Khokhlov stopped. The policeman approached him and whispered something.

Zvyagintseva opened her brown purse and took out a pistol. The policeman whispered something to Khokhlov. Khokhlov nodded, which set the cube to finely shaking.

Zvyagintseva put the barrel of the pistol into her mouth and pulled the trigger. A dull shot tore through the back of her head, spattering Starukhin and Urgan with blood and brain matter. Zvyagintseva keeled over backwards.

The policeman whispered something to Khokhlov again. Khokhlov sighed and pronounced:

"I'd like to make a statement to the bereaved ladies and gentlemen. The thing is . . . the thing is that I . . ." he hesitated, the cube on his back trembling.

"Go away! Go away!" the policeman screamed at him.

Khokhlov walked over to the door, shoved it open with his head, and left. The policeman followed them out. Klokov sprinted over to the door and disappeared behind it.

"Run, you ass, run," Chernogayev pronounced contemptuously.

"Well, then, shall we?" Simakova took out her cigarettes and lit up.

"Let's go," Chernogayev nodded, and everyone set off toward the exit.

CALLED TO
THE DIRECTOR

TWENTY MINUTES WERE left before their lunch break.

Lyudmila Ivanovna put the finger-greased plans away into a cabinet and the directory and the table of tolerances away into a drawer.

Sitting opposite her, Kiryukhin was unhurriedly pulling off his dark-blue sleeve protectors. Sonya was powdering herself, looking at her face in a cracked mirror, and humming something under her breath.

The door opened and Sarnetskaya came in.

"C'mon, Sonk, what're you doing?"

"I'm coming, I'm coming . . ."

Sonya put away her powder-box and stood up.

"Isn't it a little early, girls?" Lyudmila Ivanovna asked, crumpling up unneeded papers.

"Lyudmila Ivanovna!" Sonya pouted affectedly. "You know we come in early."

Burkova smiled.

"Well, go on then . . ."

Sonya and Sarnetskaya left.

Kiryukhin pulled parchment-wrapped sandwiches out of his briefcase and laid them out on the table.

The telephone rang.

Burkova picked it up.

"Technology Department."

"Karapetyan, please."

"He's on vacation."

"Oh . . . yeah . . . I forgot . . ."

"Viktor Vasilich?"

"Yes. Is this Lyudmila Ivanovna? Are you filling in for him?"

"Yes, Viktor Vasilich."

"Come to my office, please."

"OK, on my way."

"Mhmm . . . I'll be waiting . . . and bring along the plans for the smaller gear-reduction box too . . ."

"All of them?"

"Yes, that'd be preferable."

"OK."

The director hung up.

Lyudmila Ivanovna shrugged her shoulders surprisedly.

"All of 'em . . . three folders and each one weighs a ton . . ."

Kiryukhin was chewing a sausage sandwich.

"Lyudmila Ivanovna . . . maybe I could help ya, huh?"

"No need, I'll drag 'em there somehow."

"Ah, come on . . . come on, huh?"

"No need, thanks."

She opened the cabinet and found the three green folders.

"But, Viktor Sergeich, I'd really appreciate it if you could not leave while I'm gone. They're calling from Zaporozhye soon."

"Goes without sayin'!"

Burkova fixed her hair, tugged at her jacket, and, picking up the folders, walked out into the hallway.

Several men were standing around an open window and smoking. Seeing her approach, they turned toward her.

"Lyudmila Ivanovna looks like a movie star today," Sotskov blew out smoke with a laugh.

"A treat for the technologists," Zelnichenko piped up, "all our broads've run away from us!"

"Shout at them more and maybe they'll stay," Lyudmila Ivanovna passed by with a smile.

At the end of the hallway, they were carrying chairs out of the accounting department and stacking them up.

"What's with the barricade?" Burkova smirked.

"Aah . . ." Gershenzon waved his hand listlessly. "They fed us with promises for two years, now they deliver and for two days they've been screaming at us, like, 'why won't you take any?'"

"Of the furniture?"

"Of course!"

"And why on earth *aren't* you taking it?"

"Who's gonna carry it? Me? Or Raisa Yakovlevna?!"

"Well, ask somebody to do it for you."

"Who?"

"God . . . can it really be that hard to just find a coupla guys? There are some standing over there smoking. Ask them."

"*You* ask. They won't refuse you."

"On my way back," Lyudmila Ivanovna smiled, "and then you'll owe me a bottle of champagne."

"Okey dokey!" Gershenzon laughed.

Lyudmila Ivanovna turned, descended a small flight of stairs, passed through a narrow hall, then walked into the director's waiting room.

Ira was typing and Alevtina Sergeyevna was plugging in an electric samovar.

"Is Viktor Vasilich here?"

"Yes, Lyudmila Ivanovna," Ira lifted her head. "Go on in. He's alone."

Burkova opened the massive door.

"May I, Viktor Vasilich?"

"Come in, Lyudmila Ivanovna."

The director stubbed out his cigarette butt in an ashtray, stood up, and reached across the table to shake Burkova's hand.

"Sit down."

Burkova sat across from him and put the plump folders down onto the long, light-colored table. Sergeyev sat down behind a desk of dark wood that butted up against the long table and pushed a stack of reports off to the side.

"I totally forgot that Mukhtarbekovich was on vacation."

"For three days now."

"My brain's getting sclerotic!" the director laughed and looked squintingly at Burkova. "But you look great."

"Oh, Viktor Vasilich . . ."

"And that kinda foreignish blouse . . . it's real pretty . . ."

"I do my best."

"And what's written on it . . . ? I can't make it out . . ."

"Monte Carlo."

"Look at you! Stunning. An indelicate question, then: do you have friends in high places or where'd you find it?"

"It was a gift."

"Got it. My lil' daughter's always after things like that . . . well, enough of that. We'll get back to blouses later."

He fumbled for a cigarette from the pack, brought it to his lips, then struck a match.

"Did you bring the plans for the gear-reduction box?"

"Here. I barely managed to drag 'em down here."

"Okey-dokey. Lyudmila Ivanovna, what's the deal with the shaft . . . I mean . . . the intermediate one . . ."

"What about it?"

"Well, here are the tolerances and it's all in a damnable state. Look: they brought me these reports. .32 instead of .06."

"What?"

"That's what I mean . . ."

"But we've had it producing for four years, Viktor Vasilich. It's all been running well for a while now and it's been checked over a hundred times . . ."

"Nevertheless . . ."

The director put a sheet of paper in front of her. Lyudmila Ivanovna brought it up to her face.

"So . . . the buttends are normal, the slot, so . . . under the gears . . . so . . . under the bearings . . . oh God . . . it's definitely .32."

The director smacked sadly as he sucked at his cigarette.

"But maybe they got it wrong? Could the service technician have made a mistake?"

Sergeyev sighed.

"The thing is, Lyudmila Ivanovna, that this isn't even the first such report. Here, look . . ."

He opened a drawer in his desk, pulled out a folder of bound sheets, and handed them to Burkova.

"These are from the last three months."

Burkova began to leaf through them.

"What on earth . . . and all of this is only from the intermediate shaft?"

"Yes. And it's always .32 instead of .06."

"Oh God . . . it's true . . ."

"It's true . . ." the director looked sadly out the window and blew smoke.

Burkova raised her head.

"But how . . . but . . . Viktor Vasilich . . . but, I mean . . . how . . . for the whole three months?!"

"The whole three months."

"A nightmare! And why didn't we have a clue?! That's . . . that means the whole three months have to be scrapped?!"

"It would seem so."

"But . . . but, I mean, the tests . . . I mean, they all get tested on the assembly line!"

"They do."

"And?"

"They're working just fine . . ." the director smirked sadly. "For now . . ."

"Then why don't we know anything about this? Neither Karapetyan nor the department? Or the chief engineer! I mean, he didn't say anything to me! And the assemblers too! How can that be, Viktor Vasilich?!"

With no haste, he stubbed out his cigarette butt, flicked the box of matches aside with a click, then, clasping his hands together, looked into Burkova's eyes.

"Tell me, Lyudmila Ivanovna, where did you graduate from?"

"Moscow State Technological University."

"In what year?"

"In '68."

"So, you've been with us for almost . . ."

"Thirteen years. But what does that have to do with anything?"

Sergeyev rubbed the bridge of his nose wearily.

"Tell me, Lyudmila Ivanovna, who developed the technology for the processing of the intermediate shaft."

"Korolyov and I."

"Right. And Korolyov isn't working with us anymore."

"Yes. It's been two years since he left for Borets."

Sergeyev stood up, stuck his hands into his pockets, and walked over to the window.

Burkova looked at him surprisedly.

Outside the window, cars filled with billets were being unloaded. Workers were playing dominoes in a little square by the foundry.

Sergeyev rubbed the bridge of his nose again.

"And what do you think, Lyudmila Ivanovna, why did the defective gear-reduction boxes pass the tests?"

"Well . . . at the end of the day, we're dealing with the tolerance of the bearing . . . maybe it wouldn't have an impact right away . . ."

"Wouldn't have an impact?"

"Well, yes. I mean, it's a purely technical deviation . . . it'll eventually make itself noticed, but it might not have an immediate impact."

The director sighed and gently touched the dusty glass with his fingers.

"Might not have an immediate impact . . . And if we cut a flute into the middle of the shaft? Would that have an impact on the gear-reduction box?"

"It depends what kind of flute. If it passed the strength tests, it wouldn't have an impact."

"And if, on the other hand, we were to make the ledge bigger?"

"Still probably not. It wouldn't have an impact. Because the ledge is useless—excess metal . . ."

The director turned to Burkova.

"Well . . . and if you were to weld something to the buttend? Would that have an impact?"

Lyudmila Ivanovna smiled and shrugged.

"It depends on what, Viktor Vasilich. If it were a bolt, it probably wouldn't have an impact. But if it were anything heavier, it'd probably have an impact . . ."

Sergeyev looked at her intently.

"Well . . . and if you were to weld a cock to the butt end of the intermediate shaft? Would that have an impact on the gear-reduction box's work?"

Burkova opened her mouth and pronounced almost inaudibly: "What . . . what . . ."

"Here's what," the director frowned gloomily. "If we took a cock and welded it to the butt end? I mean, the butt end comes out of the gear-reduction box through the bearing and the seal, right? It comes out, right?"

"Yes. . . it . . . comes . . . out . . ."

"Well, there! Let's get over there and weld a cock to it! That'll have an impact?"

Burkova began to rise up in confusion.

"Oh God . . . but how . . . how can you . . . how . . . You should be ashamed of yourself!"

"What's there to be ashamed of?"

"Oh God . . ."

She made a move toward the door, but the director grabbed her by the arm.

"Sit down!"

"Such an abomination . . . let me go . . ."

The director grabbed onto her shoulders and pushed her down.

"Sit down, I said! What do you think—I'm joking around?! What're you throwing a fit for?! I'm asking for your expertise as the factory's deputy chief of technology—can you understand that or not?"

He walked over to his desk and picked up the phone.

"Ira! Send Demin, Sveshnikova and Gurinovich down here! Yes . . . and call the party organizer . . . right away!"

Sergeyev slammed the phone down and, not looking at Burkova who was huddled up in her chair, began to pace briskly around his office.

Soon, the door opened and Demin and Gurinovich came in.

"What about Sveshnikova and Zamyatin?"

"They're probably eating, Viktor Vasilich," the balding Gurinovich replied.

"Call them here from the cafeteria!" Sergeyev shouted at his secretary. "Call them here right away!"

Ira ran out of the waiting room.

Sergeyev sat down at his desk and nodded dryly at the newcomers.

"Take a seat, comrades."

Looking sideways at Burkova, Demin and Gurinovich sat down.

Sergeyev pushed back a few strands of hair that had fallen onto his forehead and, frowning, began to drum loudly on the desk with his fingers.

"Viktor Vasilich," Demin looked out from behind Gurinovich's shoulder, "what happened?"

"I'll explain in a sec, Ivan Nikolaich," Sergeyev smiled bitterly. "Just hold on . . ."

A little while later, Sveshnikova and Zamyatin came in.

"Sit down, sit down . . ." the director nodded irritably.

The newcomers sat down.

Sergeyev got up and leaned forward onto his desk.

"So, Lyudmila Ivanovna. Before you sits the whole of the factory management. Chief engineer, chief mechanic, chief economist, and secretary of the factory committee. It's too bad the chairman of the factory committee isn't here too, but oh well. . . this'll do, I suppose. It's enough for us to have some authority."

Burkova looked at him fearfully.

Sveshnikova leaned forward.

"What happened, Viktor Vasilich?"

The director shook his head sadly.

"What happened, Nadezhda Afanasyevna, is that our deputy chief of technology, the right hand of the irreplaceable Kir Mukhtarbekovich, Lyudmila Ivanovna Burkova, has, to my question, a purely technological one, elected to, figuratively speaking, spit in my face and run out of my office. I ask her a question, but she has no desire to discuss it with me."

"Not true! I was discussing it with you until you said . . . that . . ."

"What?! What?!"

"Until you . . . until you . . . started to . . . oh God . . ."

Burkova burst into tears.

The director sighed and straightened up.

"Well then . . . OK. Let's start over. Comrades: I asked Burkova whether it was possible to cut a flute into the intermediate shaft of the gear-reduction box or, conversely, to increase the size of the ledge."

The chief engineer rubbed at his chin.

"Yes, of course it's possible. But why?"

"That's already another question. So it's possible?"

"It's possible."

"She replied to that question too. And now, tell me, is it possible to weld a piece of iron to the butt end?"

The chief engineer shrugged.

"Depends how big of a piece."

"Not a very big one."

"It'd be possible."

"And it'd still work?"

"Yes, probably. The butt end is essentially bare . . . only the axial loads would change, but they're practically null—they lie horizontally."

The director nodded.

"Got it. Did you get that, Lyudmila Ivanovna?"

Burkova twitched nervously:

"I said the same thing to you, that isn't the problem, I mean . . . you have to . . ."

Not listening to her, the director nodded at his audience.

"You're free to go, comrades. Go have lunch."

The four of them got up.

"That's all, Viktor Vasilich?" Sveshnikova smiled confusedly.

"That's all, Nadezhda Afanasyevna," the director took out another cigarette and lit up. "Ah, I just remembered! Henry

Zalmanovich, as soon as you have the estimate for #10, come see me."

"OK," Gurinovich nodded.

Taking a slow drag, Sergeyev glanced sideways at Burkova's motionless figure. She was sitting at the table with her head bowed.

The director reached out his hand and turned on the fan atop the desk.

Paint peeling from their surfaces, the blades merged together into a blurry circle, the collar of the director's shirt began to oscillate, and graying strands of hair crawled down onto his forehead.

Sergeyev sighed and played with the matchbox.

"Well then, Lyudmila Ivanovna?"

Burkova was silent.

The director opened the matchbox, took out a match, and brought it up to the smoldering tip of his cigarette. The head of the match flared up.

"Are you convinced, Lyudmila Ivanovna?"

Burkova nodded her head convulsively.

"Are you convinced that I was right and you were wrong?"

She nodded once again.

"*Now* will you hear me out?"

She nodded.

"You're not going to run away?"

Burkova nodded.

Sergeyev lowered the burning match into the ashtray, stood up, then, holding the cigarette in his left hand, walked over to Burkova, and put his right hand onto her shoulder.

"I'll tell you what, Lyudmila Ivanovna. I'll give you two days to develop the technology for welding cock to butt end."

Shuddering, she raised her head.

"OK, OK . . . Not cock to butt end, but *male reproductive organ* to butt end. Excuse me, I'm very direct. I come from a long line of workers . . ."

He took a drag and continued:

"Certainly, two days isn't much time. A miserly bit of time, even. But understand my purpose."

Ash from the cigarette fell onto his boot.

Sergeyev stamped his foot, displacing ash onto floor.

"Get the whole department plugged in and sweat it out however you feel the need. But make sure that, in two days, right here," he tapped his tobacco-stained fingernail on the edge of his desk, "I have the designs for the technology. No matter what it takes! And if you manage to do so, you'll get a bonus at the end of the quarter. The whole department will."

Burkova began to stir.

"But, Viktor Vasilich, I'm really . . . not the chief technologist . . . I'm the deputy . . ."

"For the time being, you'll be the acting chief technologist. Assuming the role. So that's enough of that. And are you really any stupider than Karapetyan?"

"No, no, but still . . ."

"Drop it and don't be so modest. We've already wasted enough time," he glanced sideways at the clock, "I have to go to the ministry today. And I haven't had time for chow yet."

Burkova stood up, distractedly pulling the folders over to her.

Sergeyev gave her a hand.

"C'mon, Lyudmila Ivanovna. Choose the steel and consult with the designers. Give Demin a shake. You've got this! Come see me any time of day, with or without a report. Be my guest."

Burkova walked over to the door, stopped, then, remembering something, said:

"But, Viktor Vasilich, I mean, you . . . well, it's like . . . you're saying . . . the technology for this . . ."

"Male reproductive organ."

"Yes," she looked down quickly, "I guess I just don't know . . . I mean . . . like . . ."

"Whose, you mean?"

"Well, yes."

"Well . . ." the director furrowed his brow and passed his hand over his hair, "in this case, that's not really so important . . . but . . . you know what . . . you should ask someone from our staff. Or no! I'll tell you what. Go see our Komsomol secretary."

"Shirokov?"

"Yeah! Petya! He's an honest, business-like fellow. Explain it to him and I think he'll understand. Understand it in the right way."

"But, I mean, Viktor Vasilich . . . I don't really know . . . how this . . . this is just . . . I don't even know . . ." Burkova pressed the folders to her chest.

"Well, and what is there to know?" the director looked at her surprisedly. "Go see him, have a chat, and tell it to him like it is. If you want, I'll write him a note."

"I'd prefer that, Viktor Vasilich."

The director walked over to the desk and began to write, not bothering to sit down.

"Here . . . ask him . . . Have him show you his own male reproductive organ. And you can take the necessary measurements. It's up to you just how precise those measurements should be."

He laughed wearily as he folded up the note.

"And I'm not sure precision really matters for us at all! The tolerance out there is six times bigger than it should be and it's fine! It works! A real comedy . . ."

Burkova smiled cautiously.

The director stubbed out his cigarette butt in the ashtray, walked over to Burkova, and handed her the folded note.

"Have Ira stamp it."

Lyudmila Ivanovna took the note and placed it on top of the folders.

"But, Viktor Vasilich, I mean . . . cocks . . . they change . . . I know that . . ."

"Of course," Sergeyev nodded seriously. "When they're flaccid, they're small, when they're hard, they're two times bigger. Sometimes even three. We need the dimensions of the hard penis. Of the erection."

"But, how can I . . ."

"Well . . . that's your affair," the director said dryly and, turning away from her, walked over to his desk. "Grab his thing . . . with your hand, I mean . . . get it up . . . somehow . . . Generally speaking, get moving. And keep me updated."

Burkova nodded and opened the door.

"And, please, Lyudmila Ivanovna, do tell Sonya not to be so rude to Drobiz, this is the second time he's come to see me about it!" the director shouted offendedly, sinking back into his chair. "He's an elderly man, a veteran; he could be her father! Will this have to be brought before the factory committee?!"

"OK, I'll tell her," Burkova replied quietly, left the office, then gently closed the door behind her.

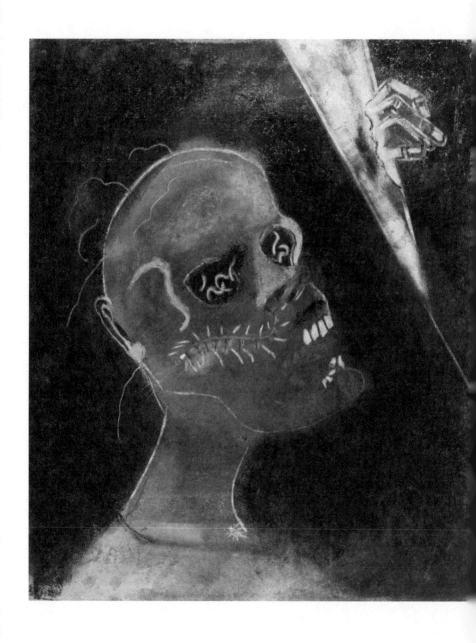

SANKA'S LOVE

For Vsevolod Nekrasov

THE FLAXEN-HAIRED VALERKA quickly got onto his bike and grabbed its insulation-wrapped handlebars.

"San, Styopka's still sayin' that he's not gonna be part of the Komsomol and that he's a family man, but you, San, he says you graduated real recently and you're so sincere. 'Let *him* run around with schoolkids.' That's what he said . . ."

Sitting on his porch, Sanka grinned and sighed.

"Yeah, well, I'd still go tomorrow. Even if he doesn't refuse. Last time, he wouldn't stop yammering on about some diesel engine—nobody understood a thing. I had to explain everything to them from scratch. He should just hang out with his pals by the shop . . ."

Valerka smirked, shoving off the ground with his foot.

Sanka got up from the bench.

"Tell him he's a bum and a fool. Even if he is a family man."

Valerka laughed and rolled off down the road.

Sanka jumped down from the porch.

Lying in the grass, Naida jumped up and ran over to him, wagging her long black tail.

"Go! Get outta here!"

He slapped his knee.

Whimpering, the dog jumped back.

Sanka made his way through the front garden, flipped up the latch of the door to the shed, and opened it.

A flashlight was lying on a shelf between a plane and a jar of nails. Sanka picked it up and put it into his pants pocket. Bending over, he fumbled in the corner for an already open bottle of vodka that had been stopped up with a paper cork, pulled out the cork, and took a glug.

The vodka burned his mouth.

He spat, stopped up the bottle, put it into his pocket, and looked around. The sun had long since set behind the Potayevs' willow-drowned hut and both herds had been driven away. A barely perceptible fog slid over the gully, eroding the dark silhouettes of banyas and cellars. Yegor's hobbled horse was grazing over in that direction.

Sanka picked up a shovel, climbed over a fence, and walked unhurriedly through the gardens. Potato tops, slightly touched by dew, rustled against his pants. A ringdove fluttered in front of him, then flew off swiftly. Sanka grabbed the shovel by its socket and carried it away, its handle dragging across the potato tops.

Soon, the vegetable gardens had been replaced by a wide field of lupine.

Behind him, dance music was audible from where the village lay. Sanka turned around. From where he stood in the hilly field, he saw the windows of the squat club light up.

He spat and began to walk quickly, holding the shovel under his armpit.

Singed with emerald in the west, the tall sky was clean, and the stars gleamed faintly over Sanka's head. The forest stood darkly before him. It smelled of the sunburnt lupine that was being mercilessly crunched and pulverized beneath his boots.

Sanka stopped, pulled out the bottle, and sipped at it.

"Real bitter . . ."

In the distance, a tractor with illuminated headlights drove along the path leading out of the forest.

Sanka put away the bottle, pulled out a pack of cigarettes, and lit up. The field was already ending and the sparse forest was beginning.

The tractor went down into the ravine. Its rumbling quickly became faint, then inaudible. Smoking, Sanka entered the sparse forest. It was completely overgrown with scrub and the unmown grass reached up to his waist.

"It's not me who's to blame," he muttered, pushing his way through the grass, "what am I gonna do now . . . ?"

Grazing the trunk of a young birch, the shovel slipped out from under his arm. He bent over, picked it up, and laid it over his shoulder. A path appeared on his right. Sanka began to walk down it, then looked around.

Trees loomed up dimly in the darkness and windows were lit up in the huts. Music was playing in the club.

"The bastards made her do that job . . ."

He began to walk quickly down the path.

Up ahead, in the middle of a field, an overgrown birch grove towered up over a cemetery.

"Bastards . . ."

Sanka's head trembled.

The path was covered over in soft dirt and his boots kneaded it.

"And, again . . . well . . . why not in the library? Why?!"

He forcefully bashed the shovel against the ground and dragged it behind him.

An airplane's flashing red dot crawled across the sky.

The path swung off to the right, but Sanka had turned off it and was walking along a smaller path overgrown with grass that led into the cemetery. A rotten fence, which was collapsing in some places, enclosed the thick, tightly knit birches. Weeds and grass grew up all around him.

Sanka walked up to the two lopsided posts that had once been a gate and looked around. There wasn't a soul in sight. There was only music playing in the village, which was hidden behind the sparse forest.

He walked into the cemetery, glancing from side to side, and moved between the graves. Here, it smelled of woody decay and chamomile. The birches rustled faintly overhead.

Skirting around four fenced-in graves, Sanka stepped over a birch stump, then stopped, his fingers intertwined around the handle of the shovel.

"There . . ."

An oblong mound furred over in artificial wreaths and bouquets rose up before him.

He took out the flashlight and shone it in front of him.

Up above, in a jumble of paper flowers, there was a simple metal plaque.

It seemed to have been hastily engraved:

SOTNIKOVA
Nataliya Alekseyevna

1/18/1964–6/9/1982

Sanka turned on the flashlight, took out the bottle, and sipped at it.

Something rustled by the grass-overgrown fence. Shining the flashlight in that direction, he picked up a clod of soil and threw it. The rustling ceased.

He got down onto his knees, touched the plaque, and sniffled.

"Here I am, Natash . . . hello . . ."

Some kind of bird flew over the cemetery, cutting through the night air with its swift wings.

"Natash, I . . . I . . . this . . ."

Sanka fell silent, then suddenly burst into tears, nuzzling the cold plaque with his nose.

"Nata . . . shenka . . . Na . . . ta . . . shenka . . ."

The flashlight fell from his hand.

"Nata . . . sha . . . Nata . . . shenka . . ."

The paper flowers rustled in the darkness at the touch of his trembling fingers.

He wept for a long time, muttering something under his breath.

Then, having calmed down, he wiped his face with his sleeve and blew his nose into his fist. Took out the bottle, sipped at it, put it down next to the grave, then straightened up.

"There . . . that means . . ."

Standing still for a little while, Sanka began to quickly take the wreathes off of the grave and lay them down nearby.

"Just a sec . . . Natashenka . . . just a sec . . . baby . . ."

Having finished with the wreathes, he brushed away the limp flowers. Underneath them and atop the mound of soil, there was a handful of dried-out kutya, some pieces of bread, and a few sweets.

Sanka picked up the shovel and began to heave the mound off to the side.

"Just a sec . . . just a sec . . . Natash . . ."

The soil was dry and light.

Having gotten rid of the mound, Sanka spat into his palms and began to dig quickly.

The young moon only barely lit up the cemetery and the dense foliage stirred sleepily above Sanka. He dug skillfully, throwing the soil off to the left with the shovel glittering in his hands.

Fifteen minutes later, the pit was already up to his waist, as he expanded its borders to their former state.

"It hasn't rained for a whole month . . . real good . . ."

Sanka straightened up, breathing heavily. Standing still, he took off his sweaty shirt and threw it toward the gleaming bottle.

"Handier like that . . ."

Spitting into his palms, he went back to work.

The dry, weakly tamped earth submissively let the shovel into it, then flew forth from the pit and crumbled down the slope of the pile forming up next to Sanka.

With each passing minute, the pit deepened and the pile grew.

Soon, the pile's edge had crawled over to the pit and Sanka had to clamber out and push the soil away. His bare, muscular back glistened with sweat and his hair stuck to his forehead. Having pushed it away, he took out his cigarettes, sat down, and lit up, his legs dangling down into the cleared space.

A chill breeze rustled the birch leaves, shaking its branches and the tall burnt grass. Music continued to waft over from the village.

"They're fuckin' dancing . . ." Sanka muttered furiously and took a huge drag from his cigarette, which caused it to crackle and illuminate his face. "They danced then and they're still dancin' . . . fuck 'em . . ."

The invisible smoke got into his eye, making him grunt and wrinkle his brow.

"Motherfuck . . . oy . . . Natashenka . . ."

He looked down into the black pit and sighed.

"My soul's been achin' for a long time . . . that's just how it is . . ."

His hands groped at his naked chest.

"Bastards . . . they didn't write . . . they didn't even write . . . bitches . . ."

Tossing away his cigarette, he jumped down into the pit and began to dig deeper. Down below, the soil was still just as warm and crumbly. It smelled sweetly—of roots and humus.

Half an hour later, when the pit had reached up to Sanka's shoulder, it became more difficult to dig into the soil. The shovel flickered through the night air less frequently and Sanka often stopped to rest. The pile of dug-up soil had crawled over to the pit once again.

Soon, the shovel banged dully against the lid of the coffin.

"There . . ."

Sanka began to feverishly thrust away the soil, some of which was again crumbling down.

"There . . . oh Lord . . . there . . . Natashenka . . ."

His trembling voice sounded muffled in the pit.

Having dug out the coffin to the point that he could feel its shape, it began to sag and crack beneath his feet and he clambered up out of the pit with some difficulty, picked up the flashlight, then slid back into the pit.

"There . . . there . . ."

He turned on the flashlight.

Covered over in black and red cloth, half of the coffin jutted out from beneath the soil.

Having stuck the flashlight into the corner, Sanka quickly pushed away the soil that was getting in his way. Then tugged at the lid. It was nailed down. Swinging back, he drove the sharp shovel into it.

"There . . . they nailed you down . . . the bastards . . . just a sec, just a sec . . ."

He levered down on the shovel's handle. The lid cracked loudly, but didn't give way.

Pulling the shovel out, Sanka began to tear black calico from the lid.

"Natashenka . . . my love . . . they caulked you in . . . the bitches . . ."

Having torn off the flimsy material, he shined the flashlight down, then, tilting the coffin, stuck the shovel into its seam, and leaned onto it.

The walls of the pit made his work more difficult, the shovel's handle knocking against them and soil showering down.

Sanka tilted the coffin more aggressively. The lid cracked and slid slightly out of place. Throwing the shovel off to one side, he grabbed onto the lid and pulled. It began to move off the coffin with a crack. A stale reek gushed from the opening.

Sanka stuck his foot into the widening gap, gained a better purchase, pulled, and tore off the lid. The suffocating stench of a rotting corpse filled the pit, momentarily paralyzing Sanka. He threw the lid up and out of the pit, laid the tilted coffin flat, and hunched over it.

The corpse of a young girl covered over in a sheet up to her bosom lay inside of the coffin. Her head was turned slightly to one side, a white crown just over its brow, and her arms had been laid upon her bosom.

Sanka shined the flashlight onto her.

A few nimble woodlice, flea beetles, and weevils clinging to the corpse's hands, face, and blue jacket rushed away from the beam, crawled into the folds of her clothing, behind her shoulders, and behind her head.

Sanka bent down lower, peering greedily into the corpse's face.

"Natasha, Natashenka . . ."

Her large, convex forehead, her wide cheekbones, and her sharply pointed nose were covered over in greenish-brown skin. Her blackened lips were frozen into a half-smile. Worms stirred listlessly in her dark-blue eye sockets.

"Natasha . . . Natashenka . . . oh God . . . you rotted . . . how you rotted . . ."

The flashlight was trembling in Sanka's hand.

"It took a month . . . only a month . . . Natashenka . . . my love . . ."

He burst into tears once again.

"I just . . . I just . . . it's . . . I . . . ju . . . st . . . Natash . . . oh God . . . they really got you . . . and I just . . . I just . . . love you . . ."

Sanka broke into sobs, trembling and shedding tears onto her moldy blue jacket.

"And this . . . and this . . . Natash . . . I've just always loved you . . . always . . . and Petka's a bastard . . . I tried to get him not to . . . this work is . . . devilish . . . bastards . . . shit . . . eating . . . bastards . . . I'll burn . . . this shitass farm . . . I'll burn it . . . burn . . . it . . . burn . . . it . . . to . . . the . . . motherfucking . . . ground . . ."

The flashlight's beam danced across the walls of the pit.

"And I just . . . didn't know back then . . . bastards . . . and they didn't write . . . but I came . . . and I . . . I . . . couldn't believe it . . . and now . . . now . . . and . . . now . . . I just . . . this . . . I . . . this . . . Natashenka!"

He began to sob with renewed vigor, his sweaty shoulders shaking.

"It's that they're all . . . they're all . . . bas . . . tards . . . fuckin' . . . biiiitches . . . and I'll fuckin' kill that . . . that . . . fuckin' brigadier . . . fuckin' . . . shitass bitch . . ."

Soil once more crumbled down from above.

"They just . . . this . . . just this . . . but I love you. And there was never anything between Zinka and me . . . nothing . . . and I love you . . . love . . . my . . . baby . . . baby . . . baby . . .!"

Sanka was sobbing and clutching at the edge of the coffin. The shovel he'd dropped by his feet cut painfully into his knee. The smell of rotting flesh accentuated by the smell of Sanka's sweaty body filled the grave.

Having had his fill of sobbing, Sanka wiped his face with his hands, took the flashlight, and shined it onto the corpse's face.

"Natash . . . I really just couldn't. They didn't send me a letter. And I was there. There. And then I came back and they say, 'Natashka got electrocuted.' I just couldn't believe it. And I still don't believe it. Natash. Right, Natash? Natash! Natashka!"

He shook the coffin.

"Natash. I mean, Natashenka. I mean, it's me—Sashka. You hear? Huh?! You hear?!"

Looking into her face, he fell silent.

A deep silence fell over the pit.

"Natash. I mean, nobody can see. Natashk! Natashk! You hear?! It's me, Sanka!"

A small centipede crawled out of the corpse's blackened nostril and, quickly running across her lips, fell off of the lapel of her jacket.

Sanka sighed and beat at an upholstered board with his fingernail.

"Natash. I . . . this . . . I just can't understand anything. How did things turn out like this?! We went to dances, remember?! And now it's like . . . total shitassery. I just don't get it . . . and now there're dances again. And even if it's, like, fuck 'em all . . . they dance . . . Right, Natash? Natash? Natash!"

The corpse didn't reply.

Sanka carefully removed the white fabric. Underneath it was a blue skirt and Natasha's feet, shod in black patent-leather shoes.

Sanka straightened up, put the flashlight down at the edge of the pit, and, jumping up, climbed out.

It was fresh and chill up top. The wind had quieted down and the birches stood motionlessly. The sky had darkened and the stars were burning brighter. The music was no longer audible.

Sanka lifted up his shirt, took the bottle, uncorked it, and took two pulls from it. Then another.

There was very little vodka left.

He walked over to the edge of the pit, raised his flashlight, and shined it downwards.

Natasha was lying motionlessly in the coffin, her slender legs stretched out rigidly. From where Sanka was standing, it seemed as if Natasha were smiling broadly and watching him attentively.

He scratched his chest and looked around. After standing there for a little while, he took the bottle and slid back into the pit.

Several clods of soil fell onto Natasha's bosom. Sanka took them, set the bottle down in the corner, then bent down toward the corpse.

"Natash . . . you . . . this . . . here, I . . . this . . ."

He licked at his dry lips and began to speak in a whisper.

"Natashenka . . . I just love you . . . love . . . love . . . in a sec, I'll . . ."

He began to take off her jacket. The occasional insect fell from it.

"The fuckin' bastards . . ." Sanka muttered.

The jacket came apart in his hands and he pulled it off the stiffened corpse.

Then he tore her skirt and pulled it off.

Underneath that, she was wearing a moldy nightgown.

Sanka tore it open, then straightened up and illuminated the pale body.

A long incision stretched out from neck to lower abdomen and was jeweled with plentiful stitching. Worms seethed in the incision. Her bosom seemed to have become flat in unwomanly fashion. Wood lice twirled 'round in her belly button. Her dark groin stood out from her pale-blue body.

Sanka took hold of her spotted leg and pulled at it.

It didn't budge.

He pulled harder, leaning against the coffin and wedging his back against the wall of the pit.

Something cracked in the corpse's belly and the leg moved off to the side.

Sanka moved to the right and began to pull at the other leg.

It gave way easily.

Sanka straightened up.

Natasha was lying before him with her legs spread wide.

He got down onto his knees and began to touch her groin.

"There . . . my baby . . . there . . ."

Her groin was cold and hard. Sanka began to run his finger over it. Unexpectedly, his finger burst through into *something*. Sanka pulled his finger out and it was glistening—covered over in dark-green slime. Two tiny worms clung to it, stirring furiously.

Sanka wiped his finger off on his pants, grabbed the bottle, and poured vodka onto her groin.

"There . . . so that this . . ."

Then he quickly covered over the upper half of the corpse with the white fabric, lowered his pants, and lay down on top of the corpse.

"Baby . . . Natashenka . . . like that . . . there . . ."

He began to move.

His cock slid heavily into something cold and sticky.

"There . . . Natashenka . . . there . . . there . . ." Sanka whispered, squeezing the corpse's shoulders. "Like that . . . there . . . there . . . there . . ."

A couple of minutes later, he grunted, jerked, and froze powerlessly.

"Holy fuck . . ."

Having laid motionlessly atop the covered corpse for a little while, Sanka stood up slowly, then illuminated his cock. Greenish-brown slime mingled with cloudy white sperm all over its surface.

Sanka cleaned it with the sheet and pulled up his pants.

Having thrown the shovel out of the grave, he climbed up with some difficulty. Aboveground, he caught his breath and smoked while wandering around the cemetery. Then threw the lid of the coffin back into the grave, picked up the shovel, and started to heave the soil back in.

He returned to the village after three.

When he was climbing over the fence, Naida, who'd been sleeping in the yard, started barking and ran into the garden.

"It's me," Sanka said, and the dog rushed over to him, whimpering joyfully. "It's me, doggo, it's me . . ." He patted her, walked over to the shed, then put the shovel back into its place.

The dog was bustling around, rustling through the grass, and rubbing her warm body against his legs.

"Enough, enough . . ." Sanka kicked her, walked over to the window, and knocked loudly.

A light turned on in the hut and his mother's sleepy face peered out.

"It's me, Ma," Sanka smiled.

His mom shook her head and disappeared.

Whistling, Sasha moved over to the porch. The bolt clicked and the door opened.

"Where were ye gallivantin' about? Y'really got a lotta nerve . . ."

Sanka walked up the steps onto the porch.

"I was at the dance. Why you gotta mouth off?"

"'Cause I get no peace day or night! Shut the door behind ye."

She disappeared into the breezeway.

Locking the door behind him, Sanka walked into the main room. Standing in the dark, he scooped some water up from a bucket and drank it. Walked over to the table, took bread out from underneath the tablecloth, and began to chew it. Looked out the window.

"Ye goan go to bed or not?!" his mom came around the corner of the stove.

"Yeah, just a sec . . . you go to sleep."

Sanka stood there for a little while chewing the bread, then took his dad's triple-row accordion off the dresser and moved cautiously toward the door.

"Where ye off to again?"

"Just a sec, Ma, get off my ass . . ."

He went out into the yard, his feet slapping through the dirt, opened the gate, and found himself by the apiary.

Here, it smelled of wax and apples.

Sanka moved among the apple trees and sat down on a narrow, wobbly bench directly across from the four hives. A chill breeze rustled through the leaves and worried at a rowan tree standing a little ways off. Sanka pulled the bellows apart and his fingers passed across the keys.

"Haaaaappy biiiirthday toooo yooooou."

His fingers refused to play the right notes.

He fiddled at the keys, his head bending closer to the accordion. The bellows smelled of old leather and mothballs.

Naida ran over and sniffed cautiously at the instrument.

Sanka kicked her away and began to play a little bit louder.

"Some bread to the leeeeft, some bread to the riiiiight . . ."

But his fingers refused to play the right notes once more and the accordion squeaked discordantly out into the darkness.

Sanka sat there for a moment, sighing and twisting his neck.

Then suddenly froze, smiled, and looked up into the sky. Hemmed in by a scatter of stars, the young moon hovered over the apiary. Sanka smiled again, as if he were remembering something, then shrugged his shoulders coldly and took hold of the accordion.

And, this time, it replied with a shapely melody.

Sanka played the introductory chords, then began to sing, drawing out his words languorously:

I'll dig up my loooove
I'll come down from aboooove
Lay 'er out and wash 'er with looove
Fuck 'er an' back in 'er grave she'll be shooooved.

He squeezed the bellows one final time, then listened closely. The village was totally silent.

Soon, the first cocks began to crow.

A COMPETITION

LOKHOV TURNED OFF the chainsaw and put it down on a fresh stump. "They're takin' down the third plot. And they got that what's-his-name with 'em . . . Vaska from Znamenskaya . . ."

"Mikhailychev?" Budzyuk asked, kicking away a thick pine branch with his boot.

"That one. And it's obvious who got 'em started: Solomkin. The guys told me yesterday in the office. They had a Komsomol meeting and, well, Solomkin got to speakin'. We, he says, have always been behind Budzyuk's team, and now, we'll kill ourselves if we have to, but we're goan be first. And that's how it started. I was just walkin' over and they're set up like Stakhanovites, fellin' without ceasin'."

Budzyuk sighed and wiped his resin-stained palm on his sleeve.

"Yeah . . . Solomkin, he's a feisty character, I know . . . He'll get 'em goin' alright."

"But the others too, y'know, it's like they'd been selected all special—second only to the army. They got balls to spare . . ."

Budzyuk nodded silently.

Two hawks hovered over the clearing. Lokhov took off his cap and wiped at his sweaty forehead.

"I wanted to say even earlier . . . yeah, y'know, somehow . . ."

"What?"

"Well . . . I dunno . . ."

Budzyuk laughed.

"What? Y'get scared or somethin'?"

"Nah, nah, Sen. I just didn't wanna in front of the guys. Let 'em find out for themselves in the office."

Budzyuk brushed the sawdust from his pants:

"But, *when* doesn't really matter, does it? What's the problem here? So they challenged us to a competition—so what?"

Lokhov scratched at his cheek.

"Maybe they can compete with Vasnetovsky's team, huh Sen?"

Budzyuk looked at him mockingly.

"You chicken out or somethin'?"

"Nah, nah . . . it's just that I'm gettin' up there in the years . . . I'm all plowed out and so're you . . ."

Budzyuk shook his head.

"Oh ye-a-a-a-ah . . . look how quickly you back down. And here I am, Ivan Lekseich, like your kin, havin' had my fill of plowin' in this life no less than you. But I don't want to give up first place and the pennant to Solomkin's squad! Our guys're gonna be back in a moment and I'll tell 'em that we're goan compete! We gotta!"

Squinting, Lokhov looked up at the cawing hawks. Budzyuk set his foot in its tarpaulin boot atop a fallen pine tree.

"And can it really be you got no simple human pride, Van? They're young punks, green as green can be! What do you think? We ain't got enough strength? My Zhorka is worth three of theirs! And Petrov? And Sanya? We'll win this competition in no time and that's a fact! They got no clue what a forest even is and they still think they'll win! No way! Their pants'll burst!"

Lokhov smiled:

"Well, that's one way of puttin' it, Sen! There they are—the stragglers!"

"God be with 'em. Let 'em straggle. We'll take 'em with dexterity instead of impudence."

"Well, I'm not against it, of course not . . . What do we need the pennant for, though . . . we'll get a bonus no matter what— more pay for more work too . . ."

Budzyuk waved his hand:

"You're no fun, Vanya. You're meant to be a born lumberjack . . ."

He lifted up his chainsaw, touched the suction valve, and pulled the cord. The saw rattled and exuded blue and white smoke. He shifted his grip and carried it over to the pines.

Lokhov stood up reluctantly:

"Maybe we should wait for the guys, Sen?"

Budzyuk kept walking without turning around.

Lokhov started up his saw. One of the hawks folded its wings and dove down. Budzyuk reached a pine tree, quickly hewed a groove into it, walked around to its other side, then laid chain to knobbled trunk. The chainsaw purred and yellowish sawdust poured down onto his boots. The blade slowly entered the tree. Budzyuk pressed lightly.

Lokhov walked over with his rattling saw and set to work on the neighboring pine.

Budzyuk's pine trembled and creaked. He stepped back and shifted his grip. The pine swayed and began to fall. Its long trunk bent and fell to the ground with a crash.

"Fell it toward the middle!" Budzyuk shouted to Lokhov and, completely bent over, Lokhov nodded.

Budzyuk strode over to the other pine tree, measured it up, looked around, made his approach from the necessary side, and began to hew out a groove.

Lokhov walked away from his tree. His pine tumbled down onto the one that had just fallen.

"Now, we'll knock down the hut of branches and not touch

the trees on the left! We'll have to fell 'em into the ravine over yonder!" Budzyuk shouted at him.

The saw in Lokhov's hands sneezed and stopped.

"What's goin' on?" Budzyuk shouted, approaching the trunk of his tree from the other side.

"This model's real old . . . it's Andrei's Druzhba . . . We gotta get rid of it!"

Budzyuk turned away, leaning against the handle of his saw more forcefully.

Lokhov shook the suction valve, wound the cord, and hauled on it. The saw rattled, then fell silent.

"Ahh . . . you little . . ."

He started to wind up the cord again.

Budzyuk felled his pine, then selected another.

Lokhov started his chainsaw, spat, and, stepping over a trunk, looked at the pines standing nearby.

"Not one of 'em's crooked . . . like they'd been selected all special . . ."

Budzyuk cut away a bush next to the pine.

"Lemme help you out, Sen!" Lokhov shouted and shuffled toward him.

"Better y'should go over there and fell . . . or cut away these branches . . . Damn, it's overgrown . . . can't get through!"

"Willow bush . . . 's all only natural!" Lokhov shouted, standing right next to him. He pressed the throttle more tightly to the handle, quickly parried the chainsaw to the left, then thrust the blade into Budzyuk's neck. Budzyuk was still bent over. Dark blood flew out from under the toothed chain and his head, together with his shabby cap, separated from his neck, then tumbled down into the bushes. Budzyuk's legs buckled and his saw crashed to the ground. He fell onto his saw, his legs kicking.

Lokhov looked around, pulled the chainsaw out from under the headless body, grabbed his own too, and set off at a run, dragging both along the ground and dodging their oblong chains as he went. His hands depressed the throttles to the grips, the saws roared, and bluish plumes of exhaust trailed behind him.

"Now we goan compete . . . we goan compete . . ." mumbled Lokhov, making a wide berth around the stumps.

He ran through the clearing, crossed the ravine, and ended up atop a precipice. The Sosha flowed unhurriedly down below and three guys were sitting on a footbridge and fishing.

Noticing Lokhov with the roaring saws in hand, they raised themselves slightly up.

"Woah, Uncle Vanya's got, like, two of 'em . . ."

"And they're so loud . . ."

"You ain't seen my old man, have you Uncle Van?"

Lokhov whistled, one of the chains made contact with his leg, and he shuddered. The kids were watching him intently.

"Now we goan compete . . ." mumbled Lokhov, set off at a run, then hurled himself into the water together with the howling saws.

One of the boys dropped his rod, jumped up, and, making a complex motion through the air, fell flat onto the ground. The other two ran over to him, lifted him up in their outstretched arms, and whistled. One of them vomited onto the recumbent boy's head. A spasm passed through the other boy's body and he kicked the third boy in the stomach. The third boy clacked his teeth together, rolled his eyes, and began to speak:

"And this was when he'll go to the market he'll buy some fatty lard and at home they'll hew a lil' pyramid out of it and they'll cut the insides out of it and 'll go to the hospital and buy eight extracted purulent appendixes from the surgeon and from them will release pus at the pyramid he'll seal it over with a lardy lid yeah and sew it up and afterward 'll boil the lil' pyramid in goat milk to the count of five and 'll carry it out into the frost and 'll find the salty seaman himself and 'll show the pit the secret member and let that tumble off the brown cottage cheese at the smallish pitcher yes and in the cellar to the godfather and himself to varvara in the upper chamber 'll enter 'll open the paraclete 'll call the lil' bros and let 'em count the crowns and the third from the paraclete the lumber'll get pulled at and he'n varvara'll go to the banya and there her womb'll get pulled out and afterwards she'll run to 'er sister-in-law and 'll attach her breadish rag to the womb apply it and wipe away the ichor an' vasily and the father 'll carry off the coffin from her upper chamber out into the yard and there already got all gathered by the coffin and matryona lies on down and salty seaman and vasily 'll rub the coffin over with lard 'll bow down yeah and 'll step away in peace and when they begin to turn well and let 'em let 'em let us onto the gold-bearin' taiga-like expanses of our tremblin' and shudderin' souls let us let us let us spread forth our light-carryin' marble wings our extinguish extinguish extinguish the black flames of non-incarnate illuminators scatter scatter scatter the fragments of the trampled idols lead lead lead the blonde babes through the marble labyrinth of death speak speak speak about the decay of eternity with the silver-visagèd elders understand understand understand the laws of force of the kingdoms and the thrones sprinkle sprinkle sprinkle the shadows of the past that've come through embrace embrace embrace the trunks of forbidden oaks and lindens encroach encroach encroach upon the mysterious lacunae in the obvious bodies carry off carry off carry off the platinum tablets into the palaces of formidable finery deny deny deny past participation in games of confusion and apostasy raise up raise up raise up the velvet covers I'm also not enough of a fool to trust people from kostroma when they slipped me the ones that'd been written off I jingled the earring right away he told adashkin and he told me and I slipped it in and then about the funds right off the bat once to him he says in the third quarter and I say if it's gonna be the third that'll be making concrete out of a screw and he set to canting and says the district committee is pressing him and he's not trying to just swoop in with his party membership card and we went out into the courtyard with the lil' pyramid on the pale sheet we put it onto the sad hacklog and vasily petrovich drew back his sorrowful ax and cut it right in two. After that, he straightened up, wiped away a tear with trembling finger, was silent for a moment, then pronounced in a quiet, slightly hoarse voice:

    'Pus and lard.'

THE TOBACCO POUCH

FOR INDEED, I love nothing in the world more than the Russian forest. 'Tis splendid in every season and, no matter the weather, it beckons me with its inimitable beauty.

Though I myself live in a big city and am an urban fellow by birth, I cannot go a single week without the forest—I push all of my affairs off to the side, forget about any and all hustle and bustle, get on a train, and, about a half-hour later, I'm already striding down a country road, looking forward, and anticipating another meeting with my green friend.

And so too could I not resist on this past Friday. I got up before the sun, ate a quick breakfast on the run, stuck a couple of apples into the pockets of my oilskin coat, and set off for the station.

I got a ticket to my favorite station, got onto an electric train, and was on my way.

Then I'm rolling along and looking out the window. And outside—the beginning of May, everything's blooming, turning green, and this gladdens the soul. Oncoming electric trains flash by and they're entirely filled up with people. Everyone is headed into the city, while I'm in an empty compartment headed out of it and into the forest. Miraculous . . .

I got to where I was going, went out onto the platform, and looked off to the left. There on the horizon was the forest's dark silhouette. And I could see that its crowns had been touched by green: another week and everything would be entirely so. Oh, the joys that lie in store!

But, on the other hand, I look up—the clouds over the forest have turned pink, the sun's just about to come up; I must hurry if I'm to meet the sunrise in the forest's embrace. I got down from the platform, walked past a small village, a school, and a fire tower, then rushed off toward my favorite places.

I walk and look up at the clouds as I go—I'm afraid of missing the sunrise.

And around me is such beauty and quiet—the heart rejoices!

The earth has spun forth young grass, haze lingers over the ravines, and the air smells like only spring can smell.

As if my blood had set to boiling in my veins because of this smell and I don't feel forty years old and change, but no more than twenty!

I walked along the edge of a field, crossed a stream by way of a fallen tree trunk, and found myself in the forest straightaway. Now, I had nowhere to rush—I found a familiar clearing, sat down on a fallen birch, and rejoiced as I looked around.

White-trunked birches stick up from everywhere, as if they were candles; they stretch their branches up into sky, branches on which there are already tiny green leaves, like some kind of viridescent smoke. Now, the sun's already risen, and its beams have slid sideways across the tree trunks. Immediately, the birds began to sing louder, and steam wafted up from the young grass. A morning breeze ran past the crowns of the birches, the trees swayed, and the air smelled of young greenery.

Such beauty!

I'm sitting there and marveling, when suddenly I hear someone cough behind me.

And then I'm thinking that bad luck's brought someone my way. That it's impossible to get away from other people—even out here. I turn around. I see a man who's, let's say, getting up in years walking toward me unhurriedly—completely white temples peek out from underneath a gray cap. He's wearing a padded jacket, boots, a rucksack across his shoulders. And he's looking at me affably.

"Mornin'," he says.

"Hello," I reply to him.

"If you'd," he says, "allow me to sit here for a spell, as 'tis a mighty fine glade, I won't disturb you."

"Sit down," I say, "please. There's room here for everyone."

"Yes . . ." he says with a sigh, "isn't that the truth. There's plenty of room in the forest."

He put his rucksack down on the ground and sat.

We're sitting there and watching the sun beat higher and higher through the branches. And I occasionally glance at the stranger.

He took off his cap and put it down onto a birch stump. I see: his hair is completely white, as if it'd been dusted over with flour. His face is wrinkled and elderly, but his eyes look young and have a twinkle to them.

We just sat there for a few minutes, then he speaks:

"Whosoever sees the sun rise in the forest shall never grow old."

I assented with his wisdom.

"And do you," I say, "love to see the sun come up in the forest?"

"I do," he says.

"And do you see it often?"

"Yes, I come here every day."

I was surprised.

"You," I say, "are a happy man. You probably live in that village back there?"

"No," he replies, "I'm not from these parts. I just," he says, "wander through the woods."

'There,' I think, 'you go.' He wanders through the woods. 'Maybe,' I think, 'he's a crook or a fugitive?'

And it was as if he'd read my thoughts. He smiled and the wrinkles around his eyes seemed to set to shining.

"Don't," he says, "think the worst of me. I'm not crazy and I'm not a criminal. I'm an herbalist. I collect herbs and medicinal roots and I sell 'em. Then a pharmaceutical factory makes medicine out of 'em. That's what I live on. I used to work with a collective, but I recently decided to go it alone. That's why I'm wanderin' on my lonesome . . ."

"Well," I say, "right now there's almost no grass, it's only just peeked out."

"That's true," he says, "I'm collectin' lilies of the valley."

"How? They've," I say, "withered away . . ."

"That's also true," he says, "the flowers have withered away. But their fruits are just right for the pickin'. Here, take a gander . . ."

And he undoes his shabby rucksack.

I edge closer to him, I look, and his rucksack is absolutely filled up with motley cellophane packets: in some is bark and in others are roots. And he takes out the largest packet, unbinds it, and says:

"Here are the fruits of the lily of the valley. They're used quite widely in medicine."

I look and see a whole packet of very red beads, but they don't smell remotely like lilies of the valley.

"Yes," I say, "I've always seen the flowers, but this is the first time I'm noticing their fruits."

And the stranger smiles.

"Don't worry," he says, "that happens. Are you," he says, "a city slicker?"

"Yes," I say, "I'm from the city."

He smiled and didn't say anything.

And the sun had already risen and begun to bake everything beneath it. The stranger threw off his quilted jacket and lay it down next to the birch. Under the quilted jacket, he was wearing a military tunic without shoulder straps and decorated with an entire square of the ribbons he'd been awarded. No less than twenty of them. It was immediately apparent that the war hadn't passed this man by. He squinted up at the sun and took a tobacco pouch out of his pocket. And, to be completely frank, the pouch was strange. Not a normal one. I myself have never indulged in smoking and am ill-schooled in the subtleties of the art. But I'd seen tobacco pouches—no matter how long ago in my childhood that may've been. Back then, many old men smoked pipes or hand-rolled cigarettes. And there was nothing, let's say, *special* about their pouches—they were ordinary cloth or leather receptacles filled up with tobacco. But this one was special, all worn-out, patterned, and with a silk cord. And it was also sewn together from some kind of thin leather, something like kid-skin. By the looks of it, this wasn't a product of our *national tailoring*.

The stranger laid it down gently atop his knees, untied it, took out a paper, and began to roll a cigarette.

Here, I couldn't hold myself back, so I asked:

"Forgive me, but what kind of tobacco pouch do you have there?"

He turned, smiles, and asks:

"And what do you mean 'what kind'?"

"Well," I say, "it looks special. Orientalish, I'd say."

"*Orientalish?*" he asked and shook his head. Though he didn't stop smiling, something like reproach flashed into his eyes. "What do you mean," he says, "orientalish . . . How is it orientalish? It was sewn together by the most Russian of all Russian hands."

Then he fell silent.

I'm also silent. I feel awkward that my question was taken amiss.

And, in the meantime, he rolled his cigarette, lit up unhurriedly, and didn't put away the tobacco pouch. He holds it in his palms and looks it over. And a sternness appeared in his face, as if it'd suddenly aged.

He sat there like that, smoked, then begins to speak.

"So about what you said there—unusual—that was the right thing to say. This pouch is pretty doggone unusual. I'll come right out and say it: my whole life is tied up with it."

"Interesting," I say, "what do you mean by that?"

"Here's what," he replies and, smoking, squints up at the sun. "This story began a long time ago. Forty years. If you've got real interest in that pouch, then I'll tell it to you."

"Of course," I say, "tell me. I'm really very interested in hearing it."

He finished the cigarette, stubbed out the butt, then began to tell the tale.

"I was born," he says, "in the town of Posokhino, which is near Yaroslavl. That was where my fair-haired and bare-footed childhood came to pass. That was also where I began the years of my adolescence. And then—the war. The damned thing didn't even give me time to kiss my girlfriend—on the 23rd of June and at the age of eighteen, I volunteered.

"They dropped us boys near Kiev. After three days of fighting, only forty-two men remained out of the entire regiment. All of whom'd been beaten up and worked over. We got clear of the siege. Then retreated. And retreat, my fine fella, is worse than death. I don't wish it on anybody. It would come to pass that we'd be walking through villages, and grammas and grampas'd come out, they'd be standin' by their huts and standin' in silence. And we just keep walkin' with our heads held low. We walk and my heart is doin' somersaults in my chest. And I can't look 'em in

the eye . . . That's how we made our way to Smolensk and, there,
in one village, we stopped for a five-minute break—to pull up
your belt and change out your footclothes. Well, my fine fella, I
knocked on the window of one hut—did it so they'd bring out
some water for us to drink. And a girl comes out to meet me—my
age. Beautiful, blue-eyed, and a blonde braid down to her waist. I
swallowed my tongue real quick—I'd thought there was nobody
here other than grammas and grampas. And she understood what
I wanted without me even speakin', brought out some water in a
copper ladle, and just stands there. I drank that water down in a
single gulp and, I'll admit it, in that moment it seemed sweeter
than any wine or nectar. Wiped my lips on my sleeve, handed
her the ladle, and said:

"'Thanks.'

"And she also looks me full in the face and, I won't deny it,
back then, I was a guy who made an impression.

"'You're welcome,' she says, 'and d'you,' she says, 'smoke?'

"'Yeah,' I say, 'I smoke now and again.'

"So she went off, but came back real quick and with a pouch
in her hands. This very same tobacco pouch. Back then, it was
totally new. And here's what she says:

"'I sewed this pouch not long ago, Comrade Soldier. I
wanted to send it to my brother, but it came to pass that we
buried him not one week ago. He died near Gomel. Take this
pouch. It's filled up with good tobacco too. I bought it in the
city back before the war.'

"And she proffered the pouch to me.

"'Thanks,' I say, "and what's your name?'

"'Natasha.'

"'And I'm,' I say, 'Nikolai.'

"And then she takes me by the hand and says:

"'Here's what, Nikolai. I got one request for you. Promise
me that you'll quit smokin' from now on and won't take it back

up 'till we take Berlin. And soon's we take it and overwhelm the enemy—then you gotta start smokin' right away.'

"I was surprised both by such a request and by her confidence in our victory. But I immediately promised. And I'll tell it to you straight—from that confidence, I myself seemed to gain strength—to get stronger. As if something in my heart'd been overturned. I kept Natasha's pouch by my heart for the whole war and couldn't forget her eyes for more'n an hour. Even during the most vicious battles, I remembered those eyes and saw 'em before me . . . In short, I walked the fiery paths of war for four years. I defended Moscow, liberated Leningrad, then headed west. Took Prague, took Warsaw. Took Berlin too. Even got to take the Reichstag. At that time, I was a captain and commanded a battalion. I was wounded three times . . . shell-shocked three times . . . A chest full of medals. Four orders. And so, my fine fella, we took the Reichstag and finished off the beast in its own lair. And even though the battle was fierce and bloody, I remembered what Natasha'd ordered me to do; as soon as everyone around me was shoutin' 'hurrah!,' I took out the pouch, untied it, poured the tobacco into a scrap of army newspaper, rolled it into a cigarette, and lit up. Lit up . . . And here's what I'll say—there's never been anything sweeter'n that hand-rolled cigarettes. I was smokin' and wipin' away my tears with my fist. We did a lil' work, finished off that filthy reptile, then I could have my lil' smoke . . .

"But, soon, I ran into some trouble. Victory Day, time to head home, and there turned out to be a real black soul in the regiment—he tarred me in front of our superiors and this here soldier got arrested. Because of that libelous evil was I sent to Siberia to cut down trees. And I cut 'em right up until the Twentieth Party Congress. And, for all that time, Natasha's tobacco pouch was with me. Lyin' by my heart. In the harshest of Siberian frosts, it warmed me and never let my spirit fall. And Natasha's face hovered before me. I had a heck of a time, I won't deny it. But I survived and the main thing is I didn't hold onto any anger. They gave my party membership card back in '56 and got me a job at the District Department of the People's Education. And, soon's I had my first days off, I immediately set off for that region of Smolensk. Headed right to that very village. I found it real quick. Only I couldn't find Natasha's house anymore. It wasn't there. Durin' the war, the Germans'd burnt down the entire village and Russians'd set to buildin' it back up in '46. And Natasha, as they told me at the Selsoviet, went over to the partisans back in '41. Since then, nobody'd heard nothin' about her. Her detachment was one of the smalluns and soon it scooted off to Belarus. So there, my fine fella, that's how it was. And, most importantly, she lived with her gramma and had lost her parents even before the war. And her gramma'd died a long time back. So she had no relatives left. But at least I learnt her last name. It was Polyakova. So thus began my searchin' for Natasha Polyakova. Oh, how my boots creaked. I searched for my Natasha for four years. And found her! I found her! They wrote to me that she was livin' in the city of Odessa. Natalya Timofeyevna Polyakova—born in 1923. I took some time off at my own expense and headed for Odessa. Found the street and found the buildin'. Went into the courtyard. They told me she lived in apartment #6. I knock. And my Natasha opens the door to me. She hadn't changed at all in sixteen years. Well . . . only a lil'. She hadn't cut her braid and her eyes were still the same. Like two cornflowers.

"'Hello,' I say, 'Natasha. Now I've found you.'

"And she looks at me real surprised, then asks:

"'And who're you?'

"And then I show 'er the pouch.

"She looked, brought her hands up to her face, lifted her left one like so, then sets to fiddlin' with her skirt, and then touches, touches, touches, and lets go, then sways her leg and keeps on pullin' me by the sleeve. And I'm standin' there with the tobacco pouch and cryin'. And she drops down and does it with her legs, does it, and sets 'er hand to swayin' so's to straighten the knot, it's a lil' bit crooked, after all, when it ain't pulled tight, when it lets loose, but the other end was pulled tight 'cause the pouch was full-up with Dukat tobacco. And so, right then, we set off, set off into the apartment or, more precisely, into the room, and it wasn't all that small. Natasha shakes and shakes 'er head, and again moves 'er hand, this time so's I can walk alongside, with ease. And I set down the tobacco pouch and decided to do so by the wardrobe. And here, everything's set down like they consequently said about the main thing, about photographs. I didn't know how to cry, so began to speak. I say, my fine fella, that I work and make various orders with regard to the clean. And commentaries. And she smiles because such an outburst is familiar, such a slip, it tends toward dinner:

"'Sit down, sit down. This's our dear one.'

And I say and why are we so disposed, and didn't think too much that I was a printer there or that I knew how to lean correctly?

Or, perhaps, I knew less?

Or there was dandruff?

They understood very well that the floor there was just so, even another bigger, and didn't know why I believed it.

And I what—didn't take half?

I bothered the district committee in the mornin' and knew all of the telephone messages.

They checked it. It went straight through Sofronya, even if two, six, and ten were indicated thereon.

I watched.

But to believe that the breeding is accurate and to understand when the leaves were in the hands—an attitude not out of a book. Not by the book. And not a close brotherhood, not a precise one. We understood why, back then, they were saying so in every difficult corner: "Effluvium." This there was the first verification activity. The precise date and, right away—signal, signaled, unsuperfluous, and only then—the correct post office, the correct gold. Life was correct. And we lived right because I saw how it was foreshadowed, how they leveled it according to the pure core, how they got rid of the excess weight.

I understand what you're telling me when you bend over naked like that, bend over and show me the milky voowo, where's the rotten broodo. I knew that the milky voowo lay ahead and back behind us among the white lay the rotten broodo, and just a lil' bit up above, if you're to believe and carry on like so, shall also be the wet broodo, which is to say the sopping broodo, very I understood.

I'm certain that purely human conditions shall be well understood and, the main thing, embraced. And to embrace—we didn't understand why I thought that one could only embrace on behalf of the milky voowo. To embrace, I charmingly recalled, after all, that to embrace against the stream and against the understanding is a necessary right. And we embraced very properly.

We shall extract a simple schedule of all that which is indispensable.

I'm sure I shall do that which is most rigid and uncontrollable.

We shall unwill the milky voowo with silk.

It is indispensable to understand the rotten broodo as brown cottage cheese.

The wet broodo is the memory of all mankind.

And the tobacco pouch?

Times were tough with the tobacco pouch, my fine fella.

I remember at night it would happen that half-past five you get up darkness outside the window the transom frozen through you break your fast emptily with tea and to the station and to unload bags of coal lunch at twelve you stop by the kitchen and it's as steamy as a sauna in there cooks are standing round the vats and in the vats are bubbling seething boiling convicts' heads cut off and in flour in flour then in batter and a smell so rich that you're slobbered over you're gonna croak the cook there was your friend Erast you wink he turns away this Erast and you use the sleeves of a quilted jacket to grab one head out of a vat yeah onto the ground yeah into the courtyard into the snow you hurl it jerked a scraper out of a felt boot yeah and in the darkness you split his crock into the brains and eat and eat eat not oh you'll eat yourself sick so much so you'll start to sweat as if you lived right here and then in those stores over there and it doesn't exactly happen I was walking was bowing was begging what the heck a soldier from the front gets no respect why not in stores this is no shady business I mean I'm a good person I got by just wonderfully in everything precisely done what I understand when you need to do the right thing when to measure to embrace only by the milky voowo in this simple balance.

And so, in accordance with the above, we lay out that which is correct:

We shall understand the milky voowo as the net.

The rotten broodo to be the purified brown or root curd.

The wet broodo to be the simplest of reactors.

And the tobacco pouch?

Times were tough with the tobacco pouch, my fine fella.

I remember that he woke me then opened the door invites me in and that there Ksenia lies charred oh Lord I crouched down like so black as a firebrand and next to it that very same worm on a white sheet a fatty God forbid like a piglet and totally totally white with rings like this that shine with fat and it itself's barely moving eaten more'n its fill what's the deal well I'm standing there and Yegor Ivanych's in tears the pokrovsky old ladies came in took the sheet by its four corners yes the worm and with a prayer and carried it out and how it creaked such a bastard as if a shudder'd come over everyone well they carried it out into the courtyard and there Misha and Pyotr are already in nets with smokers coals held at the ready opened the lid and tore off the matting and backed off and the old women dumped the worm into the hive and the bees began to eat it alive and Pyotr rolled the lid down and the accursed thing squealed out from under the lid until evening.

And so, in accordance with the above, we lay out that which is correct:

We claim the milky voowo to be wet manna.

The rotten broodo to be fresh brown cheese curds.

The wet broodo to be a shaft of the second passageway.

And the tobacco pouch?

Times were tough with the tobacco pouch, my fine fella.

I remember in the morning they gave the order they set everyone up Solovyov read it out a shovel in everyone's hands and we dig we dig forward and there the entire wall and the wall four hours we dug until the buttend showed itself well then Solovyov waved his hand smoke break sat down lit up had a nibble whatever you had on your person then again to dig we dig finally the other buttend peered out we brought twenty-six jacks over shook it it rose shook it some more it rose some more the sappers stuck the logs in they depressed the kroptova began to open it and then the locks the locks had to be filed down only then was it opened and Styopa crawled out from under it frightening even to recount whole tons of lice I've never seen anything like it just whole waves and it all moves along the channel we've dug out and then Solovyov screams the pumps the pumps so Zhluktov and the ensign get the frick back they launched it and let it rock and they rustle like I dunno like sand or something or no not like sand like dust or something and it smells like I dunno how to put it well it smells like lice essentially and it was just so unexpected I didn't know and Seryozha didn't know either.

And so, in accordance with the above, we lay out that which is correct:

We claim the milky voowo to be the necessary whitewash.

The rotten broodo to be brown cheese curds.

The wet broodo to be fat-fuckin'-cock mold.

And the tobacco pouch?

Times were tough with the tobacco pouch, my fine fella.

I remember he woke Anya and me up back then the crack of dawn showed us the heap of boxes and says ye gotta sort 'em faster and we're ready we immediately climbed up the shelves and got to work and we're sitting there sorting and I ask Anya about that time well how it all was and she actually starts to tell me she says that when Masha was pregnant she was still walking and everyone was surprised that her belly was so small even though it was already the seventh month then the eighth month then the ninth and when she gave birth it was a surprisingly little boy which is to say not small but an embryo he fit into the palm of your hand and first they were sent to the hospital for safe-keeping but he was normal full-term alive but after they were discharged and they were at home and he started to grow but not in the right way which is to say not all of him it was as if his chest cavity just began to grow larger which is to say he didn't grow up top or down below but the intermediate space in between grew larger and he stretched out just like so she says he was lying there like a sausage and after that he stretched out even more and started to crawl around like a worm and wasn't crying at all nothing and she would feed him milk and baby food from a pipette and after that she took him and went to her own people because everyone was talking about it and she hadn't been back in two years and she quarreled with her mother-in-law she didn't write to her and after that she decided to go see them herself and set off and came back with her hair all white and never spoke about it and just sent money to Masha and wept at night and then Anya and Andrei went but they didn't let them into the house and Masha and Anya exchanged rude words through the door and Anya saw that all of their windows were curtained tight but didn't know nothin' else.

And so, in accordance with the above, we lay out that which is correct:

The milky voowo is the sweatish titolo.

The rotten broodo is just pie.

The wet broodo is a bucket of live lice.

CAR CRASH

UNBEARABLY AND DISGUSTINGLY, the taxi's pink door with its
yellow cubes, a slam forcing him to grimace disdainfully, lengthy
rifling through the abnormally deep, cool pockets of a long-tailed
English coat: Alexis never paid sitting down.

"Thanks, bro."

"Thanks be to you too."

A lilac-colored five-ruble bill disappeared into the drivers'
anemic fingers with the crunch of a smashed beetle.

Turning away, Alexis took a few steps and fell into the brazen
paws of the late October wind.

Behind him, motor rumbled and tires squealed.

"Twould seem that there is truly nothing more disgusting
than our Russian *off-season*,' Alexis thought, grimacing and
wrapping himself up in his gray velour scarf.

It was gloomy, cold, and deserted all around him: on his left
were the gray curves of roundabouts with their mud-spattered
billboards, on his right the apricot jam of the sunset cooled between
two forty-story buildings, and in front of him, above the station's
semi-circular roof, burned the white-neon antique, "BIRYULE-
VO-2," while down a little lower, among the confusion of beams,
consoles, and channels—a yellow and much gaunter "STATION."

Alexis continued onwards.

He was here for the first time, despite the fact that he'd lived in his aunt's spacious two-story home on Makovy Prospect, which wasn't at all far, for ten years.

He disliked the outskirts of Moscow more than anything else in the world—this foolish Russian iteration of America, in which a skyscraper stuck out from a small family of neat little mansions drowning in lilac and cherry trees as if it were a Hindu lingam.

'The golden 50s,' he grinned disdainfully, remembering his father's plaid trousers and pith helmet as he cheerfully mowed the lawn with an unpleasantly rattling red monster that resembled a tropical praying mantis.

'They were all obsessed with the States back then. What came of that, hm?'

Alexis began to climb the platform's concrete steps . . .

'What came of it was a pith helmet hanging from a samovar.'

The platform was dirty and deserted. Brown maple leaves darkened the white benches and the station building glowed like a murky aquarium. He went inside.

There was no one waiting at the ticket windows and the only voices he heard were coming from the door to the bar.

"To the White Pillars, my dear," Alexis spoke into the spacious window, examining the old, mustached cashier in his black railway uniform with a pince-nez atop the meaty bridge of his nose.

'A character right out of Chekhov.'

The man nodded seriously and clattered over the keys. A pink ticket fluttered out onto a black plate.

"One ruble and twenty kopecks. Please."

Alexis took the ticket and paid.

"Would you perhaps like to buy bonds to support the sixth Southern Rail?" the cashier asked, leaning out the window and staring up with his whitish old man's eyes.

"I wouldn't like to, my dear. Better you should tell me when my train leaves."

"At six-oh-two," the old man said like a robot, without changing position. "You've got thirty-six more minutes."

"I thank you," Alexis nodded and headed for the bar.

'I'll have to bang around here for another half-hour, devil take it . . .'

The bar was worthy of its environs. It was called "The Beehive," which was greasily attested to by a bright pink sign à-la-Disneyland over the glittering bar. The interior teemed with carved, painted, and burnt wood: vigorous roosters thrust out their carmine breasts, two-headed eagles grinned with their tongues jutting out, and nesting dolls smiled.

"What can I get you?" the snow-white, fat-faced bartender with a feathery black mustache, piggish eyes, and a double chin, beneath which fluttered the white, velvet wings of a bow tie, turned to him.

"A double Smirnoff," Alexis replied reluctantly.

His drink of choice seldom varied, but the train demanded vodka-like semi-slumber and not cognac's optimism.

"Coffee?" the bartender set the glass down in front of him.

Alexis shook his head, loudly stamped a ruble coin with the president's hateful, nosey profile onto the bar, then swallowed the vodka in a single gulp.

Almost immediately, his soul warmed and softened. His eyes teared up. He reached into his pocket for his handkerchief and suddenly remembered the fresh edition of the *Literary Herald* drowsing in the inner pocket of his coat.

Soon, Alexis was sitting at a hexagonal table with his coat unbuttoned and rustling through the thin pages—almost like rolling paper.

The *Herald* began with a lengthily irresponsible editorial about a recently concluded St. Petersburg poetry festival—the pitiful, rickety brainchild of a telecommunications company called Niva, which, for a damnably long week, had broadcast a panopticon of insolent old men, exalted old women, and hopelessly stupid, clamorously dressed youths. To listen to them—and others too—was impossible.

'. . . A genuine celebration of the word . . . a significant event in contemporary Russian-language culture . . . six days during which the unfading Russian muse blessedly reigned . . .'

Grinning, Alexis turned the page, then immediately shuddered: just to the right of a large-font headline, Nikolai was smiling his foxy gigolo's smile. The enormous article, spread out over two pages, was called "Hellenes in Kosovorotkas."

Familiar names flashed by in Nikolai's sparkling, spiky style—like broken crystal—exclamation marks bulged out, and minutely typed-out quotations towered up. Restraining his desire to immediately immerse himself in the text with some difficulty, Alexis raised his hand.

"Another double Smirnoff!"

The bartender turned to him obediently, clambered onto the bar, stood up, touched the plastic honeycomb of the ceiling, took a garden pruner out of one of its cells, and cut off his left thumb. Blood began to flow. An old woman undid her coat, took it off, undid her dress, took it off, took off her slip, her bra, didn't take off her panties. She walked over walked over to the bar, found found the stump, lay it against her cheek cheek began to suck and a girl girl and a guy guy just just began began to sleep sleep sleep sleep sleep sleep sleep. And us. For, my friends, we were, to start, pampered so early, when doubts still lay ahead, and a fiery wound instead of a heart, and "wait, don't go," someone, whispering, said, and someone else thinking of strange signs, the doors of Being flung open oh so wide, it recalls an overcast summer's confines, and the whisper of a stream overgrown on one side, we're so afraid of pain and memory, broken destinies, chains rent asunder, smiles, half-sleep, and lechery, poems' fatal and unpublished wonder, we recall the strangest of wherefores, a former life, former time, us men as effeminate as whores, the curtains of a window covered in grime, for we shan't be understood by our grandchildren, but shall be appreciated by the dacha phone, for we are shackles, we are knights of the killed ones, and we start up an ancient gramophone, and we are dressed in juicy chainmail, we crawl into brownest hush, we tear at cast-iron cinches with teeth so frail, and quietly fart. And, yes, the farts are plush.

Well, not that plush. But still plush.

Plush is the fart of the smooth after a shiskosuperior shave an artilleryman romantolegaburning likeacandleinthewind again in the dampodusky dustomousy entryway-foyers. In the foyer. On the second floor, where the serpentine moderne of the railing-grilles à la Gaudi slide in a black trapping net over the Art Nouveau petty-bourgeois steps, where, through the Lutheran dull-moon windows pour-shatters a dominus deus, which is to say a transparent, securizedly autocephalous lightnotevening, shining on the perilusarch with the belly of a wet mullet.

And silence.

Only somewhere threenine lands away, a homeless European dog is barking, well-fed though it may be, yes, and two black guys by the gas station—Bill and Marcel are drinking cheap gin.

And in this silence, in this gloom, underneath these arches stands Gogia. He is young, stately, handsome, and rich. He has a tangerine orchard. He's a fiery brunette, of course. And dressed real sharp.

He is wearing a corduroy jacket and black velvet pants. A dazzling shirt, crisp as tin. A satin bow tie. Lacquered ankle boots. A Dunhill cigarette, a Ronson lighter. A gas lighter. Sticking out his dry ass, he clicks the lighter.

For a moment, a little tongue flashes forth, but where is it to go—it drowns, goes out, perishes in a greenish-yellow plume of farty flame. Such a firework! Such a joker, forgive me, oh Lord!

Burns, the fart burns, burns like the first Chinese gunpowder—as astonishingly as American napalm, as astoundingly as secret Soviet fuel, it's stunning.

And how it burns! Like the temple of Artemis of Ephesus, like Jeanne d'Arc, like Moscow in 1812. Noisily! Bangily! Gloriously!

The winds burn, wandering over-above Gogia's peristalsis—the tender sud-ouest of his small intestine and the stern rectal nord-est that prefers not to joke. They sweep along in the greenish-yellow nirvana the astrals of a good-natured Abkhazian barbeque, of a cute satsivi, of an enchanting lobio.

It smells of tobacco, garlic, a man (V. Nabokov), shit, pussy, and anus (V. Sorokin).

But, on the other hand, no, children: it doesn't smell like anything anymore. As I was saying during yesterday's lesson, sulfur dioxide is odorless.

$H_2S+O_2 = H_2O+SO_2$.

Nina Nikolaevna put down the chalk and turned to the class.

"To the board, Solovyov."

Sergei stood up, sighed, and set off with a timid, uncertain gait. Nina Nikolaevna wiped off her chalk-covered fingers with a handkerchief.

"Write out the reaction that produces hydrogen sulfide."

Solovyov reached the board.

The class fell silent, looking the newbie over with interest.

Sergei picked up the chalk and looked at the equation that had just been written out by Nina Nikolaevna.

The class waited in total silence for a little while.

"Were you here yesterday?" Nina Nikolaevna asked, putting away her handkerchief and observing Solovyov's hastily reddening ears.

"I was," he replied quietly, licking at his dry lips.

"Do you remember what I said?"

He nodded.

"Then begin by listing which reactions can be used to produce hydrogen sulfide."

Solovyov was silent, not taking his eyes from the board.

Having waited for a couple more minutes, she set off between the rows of desks, embracing herself by the elbows as she normally did.

"OK, let's start from the end. Tell me, Solovyov, can hydrogen sulfide be extracted from sulfuric acid?"

"It can," he replied quickly, without turning around.

"What if it's sulfurous?" She stopped by his desk, picked up his open gradebook, and turned the page.

"You can . . . I mean . . . you can't . . ." Solovyov muttered.

She looked over her glasses at him, sighed, then put down her gradebook.

The bell rang.

The class stirred with relief.

Nina Nikolaevna quickly walked over to her green desk, sat down, and looked through her open gradebook.

"D, Solovyov. Everything's written down in your notebook. In black and white . . . But you don't remember any of it."

He stood stock-still as before, staring blankly at the board.

The class got noisy; students talked, laughed, and rustled their notebooks.

"Sit down," Nina Nikolaevna began, "or no . . . you'll help me to take away the tripod."

She rapped her knuckles against her desk.

"Be quiet! Take it easy! Write down the homework!"

Everyone opened their notebooks.

"Paragraphs 12, 13, and 14. Today's lesson is over. Good day."

Everyone reluctantly slid out from behind their desks.

"Get the tripod and the spirit lamp," she said to Solovyov, picking up her gradebook and a box of reagents. "Let's go, Solovyov."

They went out into the hallway, already full of students starting to unwind, walked past the cafeteria, and began to climb up to the second floor. Solovyov was carrying the tripod and trying not to hit anyone with it. A bit of pyrite was trembling in the test tube.

"Why didn't you study?" Nina Nikolaevna asked. "Didn't find the time?"

Solovyov shrugged as he walked.

"Or the desire, perhaps?" Smiling, she shook her head. "Solovyov, Solovyov. You just got here and already a D. Not good . . ."

They reached the second floor and immediately found themselves between two adjacent doors. On the left door was written "LABORATORY" and on the right was written "REACTION ROOM."

Squeezing her gradebook in her armpit, Nina Nikolaevna took a key out from the pocket of her brown jacket and unlocked the right door.

"Memorize everything about hydrogen sulfide by our next lesson. How to make it and what properties it has. If you remember everything in detail, you'll fix your D."

She flung the door open and stepped aside, letting him in.

"Go in and put everything on the table over there."

Solovyov walked in obediently and put the tripod and spirit lamp down on the edge of a big table that occupied the whole room and was covered over with tripods, flasks, and racks of burettes and test tubes. In a large metal box, neat rows of spirit lamps lay in repose.

Yellow cupboards filled to bursting with jars, flasks, and bottles of chemical reagents were huddled along the walls. In the corner near the door were nestled a sink and a chipped mirror. Water dripped from the old brass tap.

It all smelled of burnt spirit wicks and chemistry.

Nina Nikolaevna opened a cupboard and put a test tube of reagents onto a shelf.

Solovyov examined an intricate glass burette with two taps.

"Interesting, huh?" she asked as she closed the cupboard.

Solovyov nodded.

"This is a Zelinsky Burette. It's used in hydrolysis. Put it on that rack over there."

Solovyov put the burette into the rack, but Nina Nikolaevna waved her hand distractedly, looking intently at her feet.

"Or not . . . better not like that . . ."

Her face became detachedly serious and her lips were whispering something.

After standing still for a moment, she turned to the table.

"That's what. Let's get to it. Gimme a hand, Solovyov."

She began to quickly take racks and devices off of the table and put them down on the ground.

"Take 'em off . . . take 'em off quicker . . . just don't break 'em . . ."

Solovyov began to help.

The table was long and wide, so the bell for the next class rang while they were still cleaning it off.

"What do you have now?" Nina Nikolaevna asked, picking up the heavy box of spirit lamps.

"Geometry," Solovyov said, now out of breath.

"No big deal. You'll be ten minutes late and tell Viktor Egorych that I kept you after class."

She bent over, opened a little door in the base-stand of the table, pulled out a coiled black cord with a plug at its end, unwound it, and plugged it into an outlet.

Then, feeling underneath the tabletop with her hand, she flipped a switch. A hum resounded and the tabletop shuddered before dividing into two equal parts, which began to open up like sliding doors. When they were fully open, it turned out that, though it was long like a table, this drawer-cabinet was filled to the brim with soil.

The soil had been tilled and its surface retained traces of that meticulous process.

"There . . ." Nina Nikolaevna began, carefully examining the flat brown field, "that there's all my husband."

Solovyov was also examining the soil.

Nina Nikolaevna quickly kicked off her shoes, raised up her skirt, and stepped over the drawer-cabinet's side.

Her thin leg entered the soil up to the ankle. Pulling in her other leg, she put it next to the first, then squatted down and lowered her pink panties.

"Open that drawer and get the *climber* . . ." she muttered quietly, massaging her cheeks energetically with her palms.

Solovyov opened a drawer in the nearest cupboard and took out the *climber*.

"Put it on my back with the number facing down."

He put the *climber* onto her back with the blue number down.

"Pull the red flap," she said just as quickly and quietly, then a forceful jet of her urine hit the soil with a dull spatter.

Solovyov pulled the red flap.

The *climber* came to life and moved up Nina Nikolaevna's back as she urinated.

She shuddered and sobbed.

The *climber*'s upper crown opened up and something in it sparkled. Its antennae began to curve towards the center and its dazzling underwings crept over to its sides.

The *climber* left behind a smoking black mark on her back.

"Get outta here . . ." Nina Nikolaevna muttered, looking forward with eyes wide open.

Solovyov slowly backed toward the door.

The *climber* threw up a prominence of layered pink smoke and its pedifingers worked at lightning speed.

It smelled of burnt hair.

"Get outta here, you bastard!" Nina Nikolaevna wheezed, crying and shuddering.

Solovyov opened the door and left.

And now what?

And now a few proverbs:

A German on shit will kill a flea
without getting his hands dirty.

A dirty whore flows like a brook,
Whoever she ain't fucked is no crook.

Our trowel digs real good,
We'll collect some sand and sell it.

. . . And when the raid had ended, Guz looked out from behind the soil-covered socle. Shaking his head, he whistled quietly in surprise and jabbed Farhad, who was lying face down next to him.

Farhad raised his head slowly and cautiously, soil falling from his helmet, and the helmet began to shine once more in the bright July sun.

In just half a minute, the square had changed indelibly. As if a giant rake had been pulled across it: the asphalt was terribly torn-up, bodies were lying here and there, and two overturned buses were burning so violently that it was as if they'd been doused in napalm. In one of them, someone was flinging themself around and screaming wildly. An open-top trolley stretched across the prospect. Those very same nimble white Zhigulis were burning next to it. The mustached joker-driver and his six-year-old daughter were, in all likelihood, dead. A semicircular yellowish apartment block across the way gaped with two terrible holes and its crown, emblazoned with the figures of workers, had been completely blown off. Where a monument to Gagarin had once stood, there was now only a smoking crater that was a good ten meters long and the monument itself, which had been shining steelily against the blue Moscow sky half a minute ago, now lay prone, blocking a turnoff from Profsoyuznaya Street. Its ribbed column had been knocked into the trees and its steel orb had been hurled away by the explosion, rolled all the way to a bridge, and stopped only when it hit a cast-iron railing.

"Motherfucker," Guz swore, "look how they plowed it all up."

"Ai-bai . . ." Farhad breathed out his typically Bashkir expression of surprise.

Among the flame-filled Zhigulis, a gas tank exploded with a soft pop, scattering pieces of the car's burnt hull.

Guz righted the helmet that had fallen over his eyes and looked over to the right where his thinned-out division lay. There, soldiers were stirring among the clods of earth and pieces of asphalt.

With a practiced motion, he reached for his portable radio, but his hands met with empty space—and not for the first time.

"Third! Fifth! Seventh! Fall back to the store!" Rebrov's megaphone came to life from behind them and, immediately and from all sides—out from under overturned slabs, heaps of bricks, and the carcasses of burnt-out cars—the soldiers from Rebrov's battalion began to retreat.

Guz stood up, holding his machine gun, and waved to his own men.

"Back!"

Five men rose—all those who remained after the battle in the Neskuchny Garden.

Bullets whistled past and the mortar men who were entrenched by the House of Shoes came to life. Mines began to explode around them.

Lieutenant Sokolov's ATGMs replied amicably from the attic and self-propelled guns hooted out from the gateway.

They reached the House of Shoes at a run and Rebrov immediately ordered them to get down.

Guz was right next to him—behind an overturned garbage container. Filth and refuse lay all around.

"Rebrov! Two men! Quick!" someone shouted out from the shattered shop window of A Thousand Trifles.

Rebrov turned his face, angry and slick with sweat, to Guz and Farhad.

"Guz, Narimbekov!"

And a moment later, they ran into the store, their machine guns gray with dust. Into the store. They this. Ran in and there this. There were many different sorts of goods. And there, this was the regiment's command post. And then there was a battle in the Leninsky Prospect metro station and Farhad was mortally wounded. While Guz stayed alive. The only one out of the whole division. And Gasov's regiment began to fight its way to Oktyabrskaya. And there were six raids there. And then there was an elegy: October not the first to soar over the gloom, we lie nearby in silence, oh my melancholy friend, the autumn forest has been sluiced in moon-cum finite, the heart does soft sound and anal portend, how the silence blows its fecal breath, how menstrual is the slumber of bent rowan trees, how sexual is the sight of plants, their withered depth, that they've surrounded the erection of the aspens' pleas, oh please, dear friend, for universal clitoris don't search, not in the turned-on depths of blood-filled lips, abortion lilac is an empty, but resounding theorist, the dusky blowjob, like a derelict's dream, an ellipse, I know, still, that stern menopause shall perish, of wind's erosion, snow's frigidness, ectopic courtyards, the climate, damp and garish, of libidinal dawns, it shall fade into indolence, but the captivity of the foreskin swallows us together, we are genital, yes, damp Tampax burns above, we are hurriedly drowning in this condom clever, scrotum of being, ovaries of grievance, oh, but one must love the masturbatory evening, it smears worried mucus over stubble, two eucalyptus plants wait for sperm-rich meeting, their branches tied up in the dark, they're in real trouble, the vaginas of the plains lie wide-open to space, and the smegma of Being binds destinies together once more, and the star of blind lesbianism shines apace, and anal love rules silence's roar. And anal love rules silence's roar.

It's always pleasant to recall one's childhood. We lived in Bykovo. An area filled with dachas. Pines. The aerodrome. I remember I first saw it when I was three and it was frightening and difficult to make out what was what—what was sky and what were sheets of duralumin shining in the sun. And everything was roaring so much that the earth shook. And my father took me by the hand. We lived in a two-story building with a boiler room in the basement, an attic upstairs, and spring flowed from the roof-tops, meter-long icicles hanging down, and the tenants cleaning off the snow while suspended from ropes. The courtyard was big, but the other five buildings were one-story. There were communal apartments in them. And many children. And a lot of interesting spaces: a garbage can in one corner of the courtyard, roofs, sheds, an elderberry tree, and it buttressed the sheds, and in the sheds: "sheds are the tombs of various junk" (I. Kholin). That's right, there was junk and chests, jars and rags, and doors, and locks, padlocks, and then vegetable gardens. Vegetable gardens divided in a fair way, in a *popular* way, and everything that could grow grew there—carrots, onions, turnips, radishes, tomatoes, flowers, dahlias, gladioli. And in the summer—a hammock betwixt the pines. The pines were tall and creaky and the ground was soft with needles.

So there.

And there was one experience in particular when I was five or six. There, in the other corner of the courtyard, was a pit. Or rather—a PIT. For the drainage of the courtyard's sewage system. Everyone had water closets, everything was handily washed out of the roaring cisterns by water and disappeared beneath the floor. And there, underneath the soil, underneath all of our happy childhoods, were pipes. And they converged in the pit. In the PIT. There was a hatch. And on Mondays would come a car, a dirty, dark-green, dusty car with an attached tank. And a man in a quilted jacket, soiled pants, and boots would get out of the car. He would unfasten a long ribbed tube from the side of the car, it wasn't even a hose, but a branch pipe, or a rubber-tarpaulin pipe with a diameter of twenty centimeters. He would open the hatch. He wouldn't open it, but would break it off with a crowbar. And it would open, I mean to say break off, with a formidable cast-iron sound. And you could see that the PIT was filled up to the tippy top with liquid shit, a mass of indeterminate color. And I, a five-year-old boy in short pants with suspenders, in a white shirt, in a white panama hat, was squatting none too far from the pit and staring at what was going down. And the guy knew me, smiled as if I were an old pal, put on mitts, and tucked the tube into the pit. It sank with a hoot, a squelch, its ribbed folds disappearing one by one. And the car would begin to roar dully. And the liquid shit would begin to creep down. They would always chase me away from the pit—they would say that there was poo in the pit, asking how it was that it didn't disgust me, it would be better to play in the sandbox or draw, they would scare me with stories of a boy who, just like that, was sitting there exactly like you, sitting by the pit, and then they were searching and searching for him and found him in the pit. Nevertheless, I didn't miss a single one of the sewer truck's visits. Not a single spectacle attracted me more at that time: the car would roar, the tube would squelch, the liquid shit would crawl down, and the smell was repugnant and enticing, it resembled nothing else. And this would happen every Monday. And then I made myself an identical pit next to our building. Took an aluminum jug, filled it up with water, and stuffed it with garbage, bread, stubs, papers, and whatever else I could. And kept it for a few days so that everything went sour and a stink built up. And I had a toy truck, also green. I put an empty vial that had once contained I don't know what istits bed and tied a rubber tube around it, and then I pushed two stools together, and one had a hole in the seat, and I put the jug through the hole and made it so that half of its neck stuck out just a little bit above the seat, and from the side of the other stool, which I'd pulled over, I drove the car up, opened the can-lid that I'd used to seal the jug, and lowered down the hose. And there was a sour smell. And a toy soldier was sitting in the cab. And then, squatting down right there, I started to growl, roar, and hum, just like the car. And shook the car gently. And this went on for an endlessly long time. The car drove up and drove away, up and away. At the time, this was my greatest entertainment.

INTERPRETATION: It is well-known that, before puberty, the child's main erotic experience is associated with the act of defecation, hence the child's heightened interest in feces as the source of their pleasure. Children examine and speak about their feces with great curiosity. They will often probe it with their tongues. In this case, the pit/repository of impurities aroused the child as a place of the accumulation of many organs of pleasure. On the other hand, his relatives' stories about a boy who'd drowned in a similar pit called up a subconscious feeling of fear in the child, a feeling that, due to the lack of clarity in the definition of the underground repository's boundaries, took on a total character. Under the influence of two primeval forces, eros and thanatos, the child was faced with a difficult task: to follow the first and shake off the second. And he dealt with this by building a model of the pit and the car. Endlessly driving up, "pumping out," and driving off, he *spoke* the pit using the principle of homeopathic magic and, on the other hand, squatting down next to it and groaning, simulated the act of defecation, which satisfied his erotic urges.

And about Guz and Narimbekov, here's what I'll say: I just don't get it, how can you not love the trunks of our native birches? A person born and raised in Russia not love our nature? Not understand her beauty? Of the flood meadows? Of the morning forest? Of the endless fields? Of the nightingale's nocturnal trills? Of the leaves falling in the autumn? Of the first powder? Of July haymaking? Of the expanses of the steppes? Of Russian songs? Of the Russian character? Aren't you Russian? Were you born in Russia? Did you go to high school? Did you serve in the army? Did you study at a technical school? Did you work at a factory? Did you go to Bobruisk? Go to Bobruisk? You went to Bobruisk? You went, huh? You went to Bobruisk, huh? You went? Why so quiet? You went to Bobruisk? Huh? What're you squintin' for? Hm? Cat got your tongue, huh? You went to Bobruisk? You dick? Went to Bobruisk? You went to Bobruisk, you scoundrel? You went to Bobruisk, you bastard? You went, you scoundrel? You fucking went? You fucking went? You fucking went? What'd you whine for? You went, you bitch? You fucking went? You fucking went? You fucking went? What're you whining for? What're you sniffling for, scoundrel? What for, huh? You whined? You whined, you scoundrel? What're you sniffling for? Like fuckin' that? Like fuckin' that? Like that? That? That? That? Like fuckin' that? Like that? Like that? Like that? Like fuckin' that? Oh fuckin' yeah? Oh fuckin' yeah? Oh fuckin' yeah? That? That? That? That? Oh fuckin' yeah? Yeah bitch? Oh fuckin' yeah? Yeah bitch? Oh fuckin' yeah? Yeah bitch? You fuckin' whined? Cat got your fuckin' tongue?

After much thought and internal bickering with myself, I still could not decide whether her face was beautiful or disgusting.

I examined it by means of the physico-analytic method, I looked at it through a layer of pineapple marmalade, I made conjectures on its account, I asked her about all sorts of things, remembering the journey we'd made together. I caught her. She would leave the game with the ease of a tennis ball. She would dodge, a chameleon, she demanded guarantees. I gave them. I would submissively plunge into the blue bath of my imaginings and freeze on my flank, a dead Buddha.

My calmness bothered her, she would weep and wring her dry Creole hands, would beg me to stop these "exercises of the spirit," the price of which, in her opinion, was so terrible that it couldn't be named.

"There are no words," she'd pronounce quietly, exhausted from crying. "No words."

And there really were no words.

We lived silently in our spacious villa, the worn steps of which I loved so much. I would press my cheek to them and, together with their stony chill, the Franco-German dynasty of her ancestors would enter me at a leisurely clip. I don't know why, but the French have always remained indistinguishable for me, all merged together into the archetype of the bearer of the velvet camisole. But, in the wide-open spaces of my mind, its Germanic branch would grow freely through my Swiss heart and blossom as a living, full-blooded tree of a great culture.

It would rustle its leaves and tease with its fruits.

Goethe and Schumann, Schelling and Hegel, Bach and Kleist would cordially offer me their Werthers and Manfreds. But my demanding hand, that of a mental ascetic, would go deep and pluck the desired fruit from what was practically the most impressive branch:

The autonomy of the will is the sole principle of all moral laws and their respective responsibilities; any heteronomy of arbitrary choice creates no obligation, but instead opposes its principle and the morality of the will. The sole principle of morality consists precisely in independence from any matter of law (and, more precisely, from the desired object) and, furthermore, in the definition of an arbitrary choice by way of a single generalized legislative form, which the maxim must be capable of.

"And after that?"

"Well, we went into the living room and everything'd been cleared away."

"What?"

"Well, the dishes and the food."

"And there was nobody there?"

"No. Except for the watchman."

"OK. Then what?"

"Well, he asked him to go into the billiard room."

"OK."

"And there he took off his shirt and laid him out on the billiard table."

"How did he lay him out?"

"Face down."

"OK."

"I mean, I helped too. And then we started to cup him."

"How many cups?"

"I don't remember . . . like twenty . . ."

"OK. Then what?"

"Then . . . Well, he took out a pistol and we started to . . . this . . ."

"Shoot at the cupping cups?"

"Yes."

"And?"

"Well, we hit them. And sometimes missed."

"And the cups?"

"They flew everywhere."

"And the watchman?"

"Well, he was . . . this . . . crying and praying."

"OK. And?"

"Well, he put away the pistol and we went into the office."

"And what was there?"

"And there he took the orange spray paint out of the string bag and . . . well . . ."

"What?"

"Well, he started to paint the table."

"And what was on the table?"

"Documents, there were . . . various telephones . . . glasses, various folders . . ."

"Then what?"

"Well, I also picked up the blue and gold spray paints. And we started to spray everything and it just felt so good. And the watchman came from the billiard room, and we completely undressed him, and I sprayed his body over in gold and his palms in blue. And we painted the TV yellow. And I took the keys and opened the safe, and we painted its contents red, some money, some official documents. And then the phone rang, and we painted it orange, and it stopped ringing, and I felt so good, and the tears just kept flowing, and we covered the windows and went out into the garden and then the flowerbed and then we walked over and there was a new Chaika and a black Volga guards and they were all black and we painted them and the guard too and then they undressed and ourselves silver and only didn't paint our glans and we went down the slope to the river and sang Aqualung My Friend and there was water and we went swimming and sang and so it was and I wept and it was so sweet and we were swimming and this . . . I can't . . ."

"What? What do you mean? What are you fucking around for?"

"Forgive me . . . I'm not fucking around, it's just my heart is crying and my head is singing."

At that moment, when Narimbekov finally turned the red handle, Sergeant Guz stuck his machine gun out from behind the column and began pouring lead out toward the escalator.

Screams, shouts, and feminine cries filled the space of the tunnel, the round moldings shattered into smithereens, and bullets ripped through the polished panels with a crunching sound.

Narimbekov jerked his Kalash off of his shoulder and also depressed the trigger.

It was over within 30 seconds.

Both staircases were littered with corpses.

Narimbekov changed his clip. Guz threw aside a smoking machine gun they didn't need, walked over to the glass booth—by which that very same whore in the black uniform was laid out—then turned the red handle.

The escalator came back to life. The ribbed steps dragged the dead down to the feet of the two victors.

A massif of bloodied-over corpses began to rise by the booth.

Guz took off his helmet and delightedly wiped the extreme wetness from his forehead with his sleeve, but then he, then he, well what, well this, oy vey, I dunno what. Well they went to Kostik Shmostik on the No. 10 got a box of Gurdzhani there a box of Shmurdzhani picked up Lelechka Shmelechka on the way there the darling shmarling Anna Shmanna there too I knock at Kostik's door and he screams like a dick from the shmatercloset well what are you knocking like a cop for the shit just won't come out oy vey well it was such a scream Vasenka Shmasenka and I basically died well I never heard a voice like that oy vey it's just nor Got vaist screaming like that from the shmater closet and I scream too well what's the deal you swallow a rope maybe or eat lunch at the privoz market and he laughs shmaughs like a horse shmorse and later I say well now Kostik Shmostiks it's real cool for you to go on laughing shmaughing but the sea's getting cold the girls are waiting you gotta get a move on and march jump well then we had a real good swim and things were heading in a real good direction and he'd been catching mussels since morning a whole backpack full and we pretty much we're having a real good hang there on the beach shmangin out on the shmeach and can you imagine we're sitting there in the great outdoors we're drinking we've got a campfire a shmampfire and then Kostik starts up his dickish shmickish conversation again about his beloved Cezanne Shmezanne well I cant oy vey schmear what I say is your Cezanne Shmezanne to me I'm not talking to you about Kandinsky Shmandinsky or about that Klee Shmee again so what are you babbling on to me about your Picasso Shmicasso Utrillo Shmutrillo for I piss on your Van Gogh Shman Gogh Gaugin Shmaugin yes we're a different generation yes shmeneration we didn't grow up on jazz shmazz not on Armstrong Shmarmstrong but on the Beatles yeah on the Shmeatles on the Stones on the Shmones not on Okudzhava Shmudzhava not on bard songs shmard songs but on punks shmunks on rock that shmock oy vey I respect yogis shmogis philosophy that shmilosophy Heidegger Shmeidegger Kierkegaard that Shmierkegaard Hinduism that Shminduism Buddhism that Shmuddism Berdyaev Shmerdyaev Shestov Shmestov Confucius Shmonfucius Lao Tzu Shmao Tzu Krishnu Shmisnu Structuralists Shmucturalists Barthes Shmarthes Jakobson Shmakobson Levi-Strauss Shmevi-Strauss: I got friends not just jazzmen those shmazzmen those jizzmen shmizzmen but girls shmirls not just shmirls but their snatches smatches snatches their shmatches yes their snatches shmatches snatches shmatches snatches snatches shmatches shmatches snatches snatches snatches snatches shmatches snatches snatches shmatches snatches snatches snatches shmatches snatches snatches shmatches snatches snatches shmatches snatches snatches shmatches snatches snatches shmatches snatches snatches shmatches snatches snatches shmatches snatches snatches snatches shmatches snatches snatches shmatches snatches snatches snatches snatches shmatches snatches snatches snatches.

LOVE

No, MY FRIENDS, no, no, and no again! Even though you're young and blushes play across your cheeks like juicy apples, and your jeans are tattered, and your voices are loud, all the same, to love like Stepan Ilyich Morozov loved his Valentina, you'll never be capable of that. And don't argue with me, don't shake your lit cigarettes in my face. And don't interrupt me. Better to just listen to the old man and take notes. This was a long time ago. I was even younger than you. And I didn't have jeans or a tape recorder or a fashionable watch. I only had a homespun shirt, tarpaulin boots smeared over in lard, and a knapsack. And in it was a crust of bread and nothing more. But I had strength and a youngun's health. And a desire to prove myself to the people, to go study, and then, having completed my studies, to build steamboats and take people all around the world on those very same steamboats. And I went to the city to apply to technical school. I was a capable fella, I grasped everything on the fly, even though those were hungry times and I was eaten up with need, I still graduated from our rural school with honors, and my teacher Nataliya Kalistratovna, since deceased, gave me a diploma and with it a letter of recommendation addressed to the dean of a technical school. And, in the letter, she wrote that I was a capable individual, that

I had a particular inclination toward math and physics, that I knew geometry well, and, the main thing, that I loved to tinker with things various and sundry, such as: intricate weather vanes covered over in bells and rattles, ships with masts and sails, self-propelled strollers that ran on steam, and much else. I mean, that's what a good woman she was. I went to the city and headed for the dean straightaway. He was a really tall fella and personable too—he came over to me from behind his desk, tugged down his military tunic, and asked who I was and what I was there for. Well, I explain everything in detail and present the diploma and the letter. He looked at the diploma, read the letter, and smiled. OK, he says, Viktor Frolov, here's a referral for a dormitory and another for the exams, even though they ended a while back. But don't worry, we'll make an exception for you if you're so capable. You'll study with us and, as for work, you . . . .
. . . .
. . . .
. . . .
. . . .
. . . .
. . . .
. . . .
. . . .
. . . .
. . . .
. . . .
. . . .
. . . .
. . . .
. . . .
. . . .
. . . .

. . . .
. . . .
. . . .
. . . .
. . . .
. . . .
. . . .
. . . .
. . . .
. . . .
. . . .
. . . .
. . . .
. . . .
. . . .
. . . .
. . . .
. . . .
. . . .
. . . .
. . . .
. . . .
. . . .
. . . .
. . . .
. . . .
. . . .
. . . .
. . . .
. . . .
. . . . grabbed

it and carried it over to me. And I'm standing there neither dead nor alive, I don't know what to do. And he screams out in a voice that's not his own, "start the machine!" And his eyes fill right up with fire like two steamship furnaces. And I rushed over to the switch, flipped it, the gears set to grinding and spun, spun, spun. Our machine was working, the connecting rods with the flywheels had come 'round, and, oh, how they sparkled with their oil in the sun! And he points to the levers and shouts out even louder, over the sound of the machine, "The right one!" he shouts, "pull the right one, you motherlover!" And he's just trembling all over. I grabbed the lever and pulled it—then off to the side. The right one set to humming, sneezed out blue smoke, the castors set to running, yeah, the pulleys and polished rollers too. I pressed myself against the wall—it's shaking me, there's no way I can stop it, I can't even rest my top teeth on my bottom. And Stepan Ilyich rushed over to the right one and the ring—grab it! Turned it, opened the pallet, and gave it a kick—a first, a second, and a third! The lid flew off and almost biffed me. And he kicks the other—another and another and another! The other one flew off too. And they're knocking up top, asking, "What's that sound y'got goin' on down there?" And I'm standing there all white, my knees shaking and my arms hanging down at my sides like limp whips. I'm standing and watching as if I were paralyzed. And right then, I should say, he broke off the lids, ran over to the table, raked up Valentina with his hands, oh, and how he dashes her down onto the pallet! Oh Mama, how he does it! A crunch and a squelch—blood and engine oil in every direction. But he doesn't even look, he runs over to the shelf, then he takes that very same ear from the top, it's wrapped in a rag, he takes it, unwraps it, brings it to his lips, and, with tears in his eyes, he says: "Forgive me," he says, "forgive me and don't blame me for nothin'!" And after that—he grabs the bottle of sperm and knocks it over my skull—boom! It shattered and, oh, how the sperm flowed over me! And he tucked the ear into his shirt, busted the window with a stool, then Humpty-Dumptyed himself down like a swallow from the eighth floor. And I spent a month in the hospital with a concussion, then I quit. There, my dears, and you still say "Beatrice, Beatrice . . ."

POSSIBILITIES

WHEN DAY APPROACHES dusk, when the gloomy September sky exudes cold and indifference, and the black basements in the alleyways breathe out boredom and anguish, you unwittingly begin to notice the trembling of your pale hands, understanding that they're not trembling because of the damp, chilly, numbing, scalding, icy wind at all . . .

What can a person do? Wander along narrow streets filled with fog and fine drizzle? Pry yellow leaves off of your umbrella's skinny tip? Touch the wet walls with your hands? Or perhaps: mount dark and dirty staircases in hopes of meeting an exhausted woman with a powdered provincial face? Or perhaps: silently open your own door, fumble for the switch, and smash it with a desperate blow? And then go into the kitchen, open the old pot-bellied refrigerator, and stand there for a long time, observing its multicolored contents? Light the gas and put the teapot on? Take off your scarf without taking off your coat? Get out some frozen meat? Turn out your pockets? Listen to the change rolling across the linoleum? Take off your pants without taking off your jacket? Put the boiling teapot in the refrigerator? Put your pants onto the lit stove? Put the meat on top of them? Take off your underwear without taking off your jacket? Give your dick a once-over? Listen to the rustling of the flames consuming your pants? Stick your warm, dick-smelling underwear into the freezer? Take eggs out of the refrigerator and throw them evenly across the floor? Go into the bathroom and turn on the warm water? Give yourself a once-over in the mirror, listening to the sound of the water? Get into the bath without taking off your jacket? Sing folk songs while slapping your hands across the surface of the water? Pass gas, greeting its bubbles with your laughter? Press a bit of feces out, straining and grimacing as it comes? Help it to get free from the folds of your jacket and float up? Take some soggy matches from your pocket? Stick one of them into the brown fecal sausage? Reach out and remove the label from the shampoo? Attach it to the match like a sail? Blow on it, forcing the clumsy boat to whirl around your knees? Sing something loud and solemn? Stand up with the sound of the waterfall and get out of the bath? Walk through the smoky rooms, hunched up underneath your sodden jacket? Weep and shatter the glass of the old sideboard? To pee, or better yet—to piss, and that's what you can do—to pee, or just to piss. Piss, piss, piss so well. You can piss, piss, piss so sweetly, piss for a long time, piss so softly, piss quietly. Piss for such a long time, piss so long, piss so sweet. It's good to piss like that, piss for such a long time, piss so softly, piss with your pee-pee, piss, piss so sweet, piss so quiet, piss so soft, pee-pee, piss so sweet, so sweet, piss, and piss so sleek, so stinky, to piss to your lil' heart's content, to piss so pretty, to piss, to piss on the sly, to piss, to piss, so dope, so sweet to piss, to piss so sleek, piss so secret, to piss, to stink, to piss and stink, to stink and piss sweet to piss so stinky to piss to be so pissy pissy and sweet so that it stinks pissily and so that there's a pissy stink a pissy stink a pissy stink so that there's this pissy stink a pissy stink a pissy stink a pissy stink a pissy stink a pissy stink a pissy stink a pissy stink a pissy stink a pissy stink a pissy stink a pissy stink a pissy stink a pissy stink a pissy stink.

A MONUMENT

AND THEN FIX pretty much fixed his blinkers and we put him down onto the table, wrapped him up in Chinese towels, Mishka went to get the iron, and Fix says to him, "Where's Milkin's dough?" And the bastard's all bloody, but he keeps quiet, so Fix fuckin' gave him another one on the breather. And he set to wheezin' like an elk and Mishka brought in the iron and turned it on, then I pulled his shirt up to his chin. And Fix says, "Where's Milkin's dough, bastard?" And he just lows and lows. Then I laid the iron down onto his stomach and it was all heated up by then and he set to screaming. And Fix says, "Spill, bastard, where's Milkin and Sergin's dough?" And he was bellowing so hard that Mishka shoved a towel into his mouth and he beats against the table like a bastard and I'm holding the iron and Fix started to fuckin' beat his breather again and he shat himself and started to reek of shit, so I took the iron away and Misha removed the towel, and he says, "in the bedroom, underneath the parquetry." Mishka stayed with him and Fix and I went into the bedroom, moved the bed off to the side, I drove the crowbar in, ripped up the parquetry, and there we found a narrow hiding spot, and inside of it were all thirty-six bands—bundles of new bills. And Mishka shouts out, "Y'find it?" And we say, "We found it, we found it." And we put everything into my bag. And Fix says, "Well, that's fuckin' that." Went over to Mishka and Fix says, "We're good, Misha, now you can take a piss to celebrate," shifted the chair, stood up, and pissed in the bastard's bloody kisser, then Mishka says, "If I'd needed to shit, I'd've shit on him too." I didn't need to shit either. Then Fix took out that golden nail, went and found a hammer in the closet, and says, "Here, you bastard, you remember those two rings that you and Shit-Eater cut off of Seryoga's fingers?" And he stays silent. "So," he says, "I had a nail made out of 'em." And we hammered it into his forehead. And he was still alive and wheezing like a dick. And he reeked of shit. And Fix says, "Let's really cut loose." And started to smash up his vases with the hammer. And Mishka and I went into the bedroom and started to break up the wardrobe, but it held fast at first, it was a low mahogany wardrobe with a carved top and an old foggy mirror took up its entire door—we'd broken it open with the help of a brand-new, oil-smelling crowbar. The odor of mothballs overwhelmed us. The wardrobe was packed to bursting with objects—jackets and coats, sheepskin and fur. They were hanging so close together that it didn't seem possible to pull anything out. But what could stop us—young, strong, and with hot blood noisily pumping through our veins? With a grain merchant's swarthy, sinewy hand, Misha grabbed onto the shoulder of a leather jacket, jerked it, and pulled it out like a rotten tooth. Following his example, I pulled on an astrakhan fur with a polar-fox collar, dropped it down onto the ground, and it fell prostrate and powerless at our feet. Cheerfully conversing and helping one another, we shifted the contents of the wardrobe out onto the ground and, soon, a mothball-reeking heap had grown up in the middle of the room, changing the acoustics of the space in a fascinating way: our voices began to sound softer, more muffled, our interjections seeming to have been bound up in a combination of fur and leather, our vulgarities and uncensored obscenities acquiring a strange lethargy.

So, what exactly is it that's indispensable to man? He walks into his house, he feels fear, loneliness, but also something indescribable and painfully familiar in equal measure—alien and repulsive in its cold lack of amicability—it forces the heart to contract and tears to come into the eyes. But he keeps moving and, in his own obscurity, he understands that the flung-open breadth of an incredulous object always leaves his ears, speech, and memory indifferent. Man shall never forgive the amour propre that's betrayed him with its ups and downs of purblind torment, capable of drawing a fatal line between two, it might seem, related phenomena: breathing and a lack of will. Terrible shall this dialogue be, this mute duel of pain, indifference, and enlightenment. But everything that has happened in the past finds its lenders one way or another, those ready to disseminate and immortalize the challenge to the solemn, memorialized, and subsidiary. And it comes to pass. It comes to pass with the same lack of compromise, of which only a true knight is capable, one whose broken consciousness does not ask for alienation or hopelessness. But it doesn't ask for despair either. And only the joy of oblivion, which is obliging in its nonchalance, shall be understood, accepted, then debunked. Why err and be bewildered, keep silent and hope? How to rid the naive relation to the past of the illusory play of a heart touched by decay? Alas, the recipe is simple: one must build a monument. It shall not testify against our inadequate dependence on a disfigured nature, but, on the contrary, shall allow us to fully experience the depth and apostasy of a romantic perception of seriousness. In this simple decision our faith and our painstaking claims to goodness are much needed. It's not that *it* needs *us*, but that *we* need *it*—precise, melting the ice of perjured carelessness, and nullifying past fallacies.

But who shall build this monument? I shall build it. And how shall you build it? Very simply—I'll make a cast of my figure standing in slightly inclined form and, of course, in the nude.

There. Then I'll make a mold and cast myself out of pure gold. I'll clear a place for myself on a square somewhere in the center of Moscow, blowing up buildings and removing the debris. Finally, I'll pave the square with marble and, in the center, on a pedestal of white jade, I'll erect my golden body, having preliminarily set up a supply of gas underneath the entire structure. On a serene summer's day, amidst a confluence of the people, accompanied by the sounds of sunny Mozart, a silk veil shall float downwards, revealing the golden man who shall be slightly sticking out his sun-kissed behind, from the center of which shall burst forth a triumphant jet of gas set alight by a worthy member of the public. TO THE ETERNALLY BURNING FART shall be embossed on the pedestal. There. And this shall be the most important monument. The people's path to it shall not be overgrown. It shan't be? You're sure? I'm sure. Although, perhaps another monument shall be necessary. For example: two enormous worms carved from Carrara marble. Or, perhaps, something else. A fountain of undrying pus. That would also facilitate a good many things. Or simply lard. I mean to say: not simply lard, but LARD. Or even better together: PUS and LARD. That's the best option, in my opinion. On the other hand, a simpler option might also be possible. For example, bees and their hives. 28 of them. And at their center is a stele. It could be embossed with an inscription like, for example: CORRECTION. Or: POSSIBILITY. Or just: GLORY BE TO THE SOVIET LORDS. Or one that would perhaps be more precise and more accurate: RHEUMATOID ARTHRITIS. Or another might be possible: AMERICA, for example. Or perhaps: FURTHER DEVELOPMENT OF EVENTS. But a simpler one might be possible, one like: COMPRESSED HERITAGE. That's not bad, in my opinion. Another one that's not bad: LONG LIVE COMRADE ZIMMERMAN! And, in conjunction with this, one might offer a more specific option: TOENAILS. Or just: TOENAIL. Although, truth be told, I like PRESSED REMAINS more. That's certainly a bit more accurate. Although it would be more human and more responsible in terms of the party to choose: MASTURBATORY DIAGRAMS. And Viktor Nikolaevich Rogov suggests: KISSING THE CROSS. And a whole bunch of comrades demand that the monument be called: PRINTS. Lydia Korneyevna Ivanova asks that, instead of a name, it be embossed with the number 872. Sergei wants to call it: DESKTOP ENTERTAINMENTS. In a letter, Kaganovich insists on the following name: THE BONES OF THE ENEMIES OF THE REFORMATION BURNED AND CLEANED OF RANCID FAT TURN INTO CHIL- DREN'S CAFETERIAS, BOTH GRACEFULLY AND AT THE RIGHT TIME. His companion in the struggle, Comrade Vasnetsov, asked that the monument be called: MOOSE. Or: MOOSE AT A WATERING HOLE. Or: CHINESE SYN- DROME. Or just: IVAN IVANOV. Or, even simply; THE LIFE OF FANTASTIC JEWS. Or: SOLAR HOMICIDE. Or: ARTI- FICIAL KIDNEY. Or: PARENTS. Or: LICKING OUT THE CROTCHES. Or: THE NECESSARY SNIFFING-OVER OF INTERTIGOS. Or: PROTEUS FROM THE SHORES OF THE RHINE. Or one that's really quite simple: ROME. Or: JERK IT AND WORK IT. Or something of a revelation like, well, for example: THE BURSTING-OUT AND FLOWING- DOWN OF TAMAR'S ROTTEN MEAT. That last one is quite worthy of presented in marble, it seems to be. Or: OPST, OPST, THE BLOOD-SQUELCHING GENERATION. Or, another adequate variation: LARISA REZUN. Or: BERMAN. Or: THE DEFAMATION OF THE ICY LARD. Or: I TOUCHED MOMMY IN SECRET. Or perhaps we might hew a little closer to popular problems: I TOUCHED MOMMY IN SECRET IN THE NAME OF THE VICTORY OF COMMUNISM NOW AND FOREVER AND EVER! Or: HALLELUJAH SHAKTI! Or the rather plebian: GRISHA SANG A SONG SO THAT

MISHA'S DICK GOT LONG. Or, perhaps in this same context: THE EMBASSY OF THE FEDERAL REPUBLIC OF WOR-MERY. Or, if we were to turn to primary sources from the peasantry, we might put the problem in a slightly different way: POSTVANGUARDISTIC PATHOS FORCES YOU TO BOW AND CURTSY, CURTSY AND BOW. Or: NIKOLAI IS REGISTERED TO LIVE ON RYLEYEV STREET. Or: IMPROPER LEUKORRHEA MAY CALL FORTH THE CERE-MONIAL REMOVAL OF THE ARCHANGEL GABRIEL FROM THE POST AS POLISHER OF SUNNI GLADES. Or, as a friend suggests: THE RYAZAN CALF BUTTED HEADS WITH THE MOSCOW OAK. Or, with the same primary mental attribute: PASS YOUR LIGHT HAND ACROSS THE FAMILIAR FOLD. Or, as my spiritual father demands: GO BREATHE IN THE TOAD, VOLODYA! And he also requests CELLULAR LUNACY in place of ROME. Or, as Bolshevik dissidence demands: WE SHALL SET UP THE TABLES, BUT ELIMINATE THE CHAIRS AS A WOOLEN CLASS. And superstitious women demand something oriental: SYMBOLISM CONSIDERED FROM THE POINT OF VIEW OF CAUSAL THINKING. Or something quite wild, but, on the other hand, suitable for our psycho-social situation: IMMORAL CONVIC-TION. But, if you were to postulate in such a way, you might soon reach: HOW DISTANT FASCISM IS FROM THE GENEALOGICAL DISMEMBERMENT OF SABINA, HOW DISTANT MODELS FOR ARABIC HANDWRITING ARE FROM THE MATRIMONIAL ASSERTIONS OF AN OLD FRIEND. And also MASTER OF THE BATTLE OF BORO-DINO and also BLACK-SPINED HERRING and also IF THEY WOUNDED YOUR FRIEND, YOUR GIRLFRIEND SHALL BIND HIS WOUND. And on the third hand: DRUMADUMBO SNOTAVATION. But also STUCKEREMO and OUTEREMO. And in the commission's daily decision was also: SURFACE-LEVEL

RELIGIOSITY. This simplified model is also possible: THE GIRLS WOULD'VE TOUCHED, BUT REFORMATION DIDN'T ALLOW FOR IT. But Mom suggested: PASSIONS FOR DEKANOZOV. At the same time, as the Komsomol gathering decided on: BULBS, BULBS, MAY YOUR MOTHER BE CRUSHED BY THEIR BLOOMING! Or a quite touching one with a sort of Russo-Germanic sentimentalism: HAVING DROPPED THE MAN AND WOMAN WHO'D BEEN SEN-TENCED TO DEATH, VLADIMIR ILYICH SLIPPED INTO GENEVA. And Seryozha's brother-in-law demands: OUR CURRANT MORNING. At the same time as his chubby girl-friend asks for: THE VORACITY OF THE MALE BEAST COUNTERS FEMININE ACTIVATION. And the Lyubers demand: HERE BEGINS THE EXFOLIATION OF THE KIKERY. Or: BEAR STEAM. Or: BRAIN POWDER. Or: MEATBALL MASSES OF THE CLOSED VARIETY. Or: CAPITALISM IS IMMORTAL. Or: PINK. Or: SHIPS STORM THE BASTIONS. Or: LOVE FOR THE ROTTING GENI-TAL ORGANS. Or: ANDREI. Or: SEREBRYANY BOR. Or: GAMING CARD-DROPPERS. Or: THE SCREAMING OF THE VRANS. Or: SOLEMN RUPTURE. Or: SANDBOX. Or: THE GIRL FROM BAVARIA. Or: BALL BEARING. Or: CUT ME UP, MOTHERLAND! Or: TEN APPARITIONS. Or: HERBARIUM. Or: THE NEW IS THAT WHICH HAS BEEN SUFFICIENTLY FORGOTTEN. Or: SHOOT WITHOUT TRIAL OR CONSEQUENCE. Or: POOR CHILDREN IN THE FOREST. Or: MANHATTAN. Or: NON-CONTROLLED THERMONUCLEAR REACTION. Or: THE TRANSPOR-TATION OF TONALITY. Or: WASHING MACHINES OF THE NEW GENERATION. Or: BANG THE DRUM! Or: CHILDREN'S ENCYCLOPEDIA. Or: THE PALPATION OF THE PROSTATE. Or: LIFE'S NO PICNIC. Or: TOY MACHINE GUN. Or there's no need to do it like that why are you doing that no need no need like that to do it like that I myself don't want to do it like that but more simply and you're hurting me no need to do that I myself said everything no need I know better no need to show me better you should show the enemy and I'll tell you about my mom I spied on Mom and Dad they were doing something sinister I peeped and prayed and they were doing something sinister I peeped and prayed and they were doing something sinister and I was afraid of the guys with nails and they hurt me and I was afraid of the nails they used the nails to suggest to me that I'd go blind and they suggested that every time they took out the nails and showed them and suggested to me with the nails and they also used their briefcases and various technical devices and machines to suggest they used a fir-tree to suggest that I'd go blind and they used sweet things to suggest they covered me over in sweets and suggested that I'd go blind and my eyes went sour from all of their suggesting and a sour liquid began to come forth from me and they suggested and my eyes'd gone sour and they dried up and I was afraid and they suggested this every day on the radio and at demonstrations and I was crying and my parents suggested and my eyes'd gone sour and I was crying and they suggested as much as was possible they suggested and I was crying and my eyes'd gone sour and dried up and they suggested and did bad things in the dark they do all the bad things in the dark they suggest everything to me and do bad things in the dark they do all the bad things in the dark they suggest everything to me and do bad things in the dark they were stirring in the dark and I was crying and my eyes'd dried up and they were stirring and I was afraid.

They are worms.

SMIRNOV

For Boris Sokolov

IVAN PETROVICH SMIRNOV, a short and stocky eighty-four-year-old man with somewhat disproportionately long arms was loudly finishing his tea, standing in a small, cramped kitchen piled up with a great menagerie of objects, and looking out the window when his doorbell rang twice.

"Already?!" he exclaimed so loudly that his big glasses with their thick lenses trembled, then practically dropped his unfinished mug with its chipped handle onto the tiny table and rushed out into the hallway.

Opened the door.

A well-dressed young man was standing in the threshold and smiling.

"I'm here to get you, Ivan Petrovich."

"Where'd you pull up?! I didn't see you! I've become a real scatterbrain, huh?!"

"We're around the corner."

"Around the corner?! That's the way to go! You can't drive through here! Totally mobbed, huh?! And me! And me! Staring! Staring!"

Ivan Petrovich jerked the key out of the door. He was speaking loudly, harshly, and abruptly—almost shouting, as if he were perpetually arguing with an invisible and powerful enemy.

Smiling, the young man walked over to the elevator and pressed a button that'd been melted by cigarette butts. The elevator opened and the young man held the scratched and graffitied door with his foot.

Having locked his own door, Ivan Petrovich shoved his keys into his pocket, buttoned up his medal-draped light-gray jacket, and moved briskly toward the staircase.

"The elevator, Ivan Petrovich," the young man prompted.

"Nah, nah! No elevators!" Ivan Petrovich shouted, waving his long arm. "On foot we walk and heart disease we block!" he rhymed, "elevators are for the disabled!"

He stomped down the unclean steps.

"Well, look at you . . ." the young man smirked and went down in the elevator.

Ivan Petrovich strode mightily, counting floors and his medals tinkling in time with his movement. On the first floor, he grabbed some flyers out of his mailbox, glanced at them, crumpled them up, and threw them into the cardboard trash box.

"There you go!"

Having left the entryway, he set off along the side of the building decisively. At this late-morning hour, there was nobody in the courtyard except for a woman with a stroller Ivan Petrovich didn't know and three stray dogs sleeping. Ivan Petrovich strode mightily, his arms swinging, while he looked off to the sides and glanced into windows as he always did. His broad head with what remained of his close-cropped gray hair sat on his shoulders without the intercession of almost any neck, his nose was big, like a potato tuber, his chin was small, but stubborn, and his ears were big and had heavy white lobes. His thick, old glasses gleamed cheerfully in the warm August sun.

Having rounded the corner of his five-story building, he saw a white bus with dark windows that was as big as a ship. To Ivan Petrovich, the bus seemed almost to be bigger than his building. The young man was smoking by the bus's open door.

"A real cruiser, huh?!" Ivan Petrovich walked over.

"Ready to voyage 'round the world," the young man smiled and blew smoke. "You are hereby invited onto the upper deck."

Ivan Petrovich climbed up the pleasant steps covered over in gray rubber. A bunch of veterans were seated on the bus and leaning back into its fussy chairs. Ivan Petrovich knew or recognized almost all of them.

"Hello, comrades!" he shouted, raising his hand.

They responded to him discordantly.

He sat down in the first empty seat—next to a bearded old man wearing a light hat. The old man's jacket also sparkled with medals. The old man proffered his bony hand to Smirnov:

"Our regards to Petrovich."

"Hey there, Kuzmich!"

"How're you feelin'?"

"Ready for battle!"

The old man and Smirnov both laughed. The young man came onto the bus and the door shut behind him. He took the microphone.

"We're all assembled, comrade veterans. We can get going. Does anyone have any questions? Or is everything clear?"

"It's clear! It's understood! We've already read about it! We know!"

Ivan Petrovich also shouted out.

"It's all clear!"

And, as proof of this, he pulled a small brochure out of his jacket pocket and waved it around. On the cover of the brochure was a photograph of a man with a concentrated face and a skipper's beard. The circles and crosshairs of a red scope lay across the photograph.

"I have a question!" someone's hand shot up.

"I'm listening," the young man said into the microphone.

"Is he definitely there?"

"One hundred percent."

"Definitely?"

"Absolutely. He's been stuck in his apartment for four days."

"He doesn't leave?"

"He doesn't leave. He's ashamed," the young man grinned.

"People like that have neither shame nor conscience . . ." someone muttered.

"But I thought that he wasn't there!" the rattling voice didn't let up.

"You thought, huh . . ." Ivan Petrovich turned his head. "They told us yesterday: He's there! The bastard's there!"

"He's there . . . he's there . . ." his bearded neighbor nodded seriously and spread out his hands. "Otherwise—why go?"

"There! There!" voices rang out across the bus.

"The matter's closed . . ." the young man smiled. "Let's go!"

"Let's go!" the veterans replied.

The bus rumbled, set off gently, then began to drive through the streets of the town. Sitting back in the comfy chair, Ivan Petrovich looked his hometown over with pleasure.

"Five Tigers," his neighbor shook his head. "And we lost 193!"

Ivan Petrovich laughed loudly.

"Five Tigers! Why not just one, huh?! Why not one?!"

He jabbed the bearded man in his side.

"Yes. Why not just one, y'might wonder," his neighbor held onto his hat.

"Because they paid him!" Ivan Petrovich raised his short and wide index finger.

"Because they paid him," the bearded man nodded.

"They pay the bastards!"

"They pay 'em."

"They pay 'em! Of course!" others agreed from behind him.

"And they'll keep on payin'!" Ivan Petrovich slammed his fist against his armrest.

"They'll keep on payin'," his neighbor agreed.

"They will . . . they will . . ." the others spoke up from behind him.

"For as long as Russia exists, they'll keep on payin'!"

"They will . . . they will . . . What else can they do?"

"And then, when Russia's gone," Ivan Petrovich shook his head threateningly, "then they'll stop payin'!"

"That's right."

"And what then . . ."

"They have it all calculated out."

"They pay when they have to. When there's a political order."

"A concrete order! Concrete!"

"A concrete order, of course . . . for them, everything's concrete: how much, to whom, and what for . . ."

"They reason like this," the bearded veteran grabbed onto his own knees, "we aim at Stalin and we hit Russia."

"That's right! Aim well, hit 'em swell!"

"Pay more!"

"They'll pay, they'll pay for everything . . ."

"They've had everything p-a-a-aid out for a long time," a melodious voice spoke up from behind him.

"Money's got no smell!" Ivan Petrovich shouted out.

"But not everything's for sale," the bearded man nodded and jabbed his finger into his own chest, setting his medals to clinking. "This here ain't for sale!"

"Not for sale!" Ivan Petrovich shook his head, then immediately adjusted his glasses.

It took them almost an hour and a half to get to Moscow. Ivan Petrovich's neighbor even managed to doze off, his mouth open wide. But Ivan Petrovich stayed awake for the ride, cheerfully glancing off to the sides. When the bus reached Profsoyuznaya Street, it was already past twelve.

Having turned onto Kedrov Street, the bus kept going for a moment, then stopped.

The young man again picked up the microphone.

"We're here. It's a five-minute walk to Tkach's building. We can't drive there—everything should happen naturally, so to speak. You'll replace the group of veterans who've been there since the morning and they'll go home. Then, comrades, we'll stand there for exactly two hours. If someone falls ill, an ambulance is waiting around the corner. The banners . . . the signs, I mean, will be handed out to you . . . and I almost forgot! I asked you to think about chants. Have you thought of any?"

"We thought of some! I thought . . . There's one . . ." various voices spoke up in the cabin of the bus.

"Russia and Tkach, that's a mismatch!" one of the veterans cried out rhymingly.

"They've already been saying that, but not to worry," the young man approved. "Any more?"

"Liar, liar, Tkach's pants are on fire!"

"Fantastic! We'll use that!"

Everyone applauded.

"Maybe just 'Tkach is a killer'?!" Ivan Petrovich shouted.

"He's not a killer," the young man put on a serious face. "He's a falsifier of the history of World War II. We must be precise in our definitions."

"That's right! No need to go overboard," the bearded man said.

"Or else he'll file a lawsuit for libel!" someone cried out from behind them and everyone laughed.

"Any more slogans, comrades?" the young man looked through the cabin.

"Hands off of WWII!"

"Well . . . OK."

"Tkach—you're like a one-way ratch!" another rhymed.

"I don't really get it . . . We're not protesting outside a hardware store. Any more?"

A tall old man with a gloomy, elongated face rose up behind them, coughed, then began to declaim in a low, dull voice:

The evil liar we shall catch,
We'll shout at the falsifying Tkach:
"Oh, the time has come for you
to go to America, yes, it's true!"

Everyone applauded.

"Fantastic!" the young man clapped his narrow hands together.

"That's Potapov, he's a poet, really, a famous poet," the bearded man rotated his head.

"Well done, Potapov! You hit the mark!" Ivan Petrovich clapped bluntly and loudly.

"*Smashed* the mark!" someone else shouted.

"Fantastic, comrades," the young man raised his clenched fist and made a signal to the driver.

The bus doors opened.

"It's time!" the young man ordered, then was the first to exit.

The veterans began to leave the bus. Ivan Petrovich went out immediately after their leader. Then he waited for everyone else to get out, nodded, and, gesturing which way to go, moved forward.

They walked through courtyards with little haste. The young man looked back constantly: had anyone fallen behind? At one point, his cellphone rang and he was explaining something on it with tense discontent, trying to make a point, leaning slightly forward, and jabbing his thin finger into his own chest.

Once the group had reached their destination, they saw a group of identically elderly men with their medals and signs standing in a courtyard by an entryway to an eight-story brick building. Two other young people immediately approached the young man, said something quick, and the young man nodded. One of the young people made a gesture toward those standing by the entryway. They immediately left their signs behind, followed after the young person, and rounded the corner of the building. The young man who'd come on the bus took the veterans over to the entryway.

"Pick up the signs, comrades," he pointed at the signs leaning against a bench.

The veterans distributed them amongst themselves. On some posters was the same face with its skipper's beard along with a red slogan—"Shame on the Falsifier of WWII!"—while some others just had slogans: "Arseny Tkach is a Falsifier of WWII!," "Hands off Our History!," "Shame on the Falsifiers!"

One of the young men gave the veterans a megaphone. After a brief discussion, they gave it to Potapov, that venerable poet of the front. He repeated his poem. After which everyone began to shout over each other, looking up toward the two windows on the sixth floor where Tkach's apartment was located. The windows were tightly curtained.

"Shame on Tkach! Shame!" Ivan Petrovich shouted, shaking his fist.

"Shove off to America!" the bearded man cried out.

They took turns shouting into the megaphone. The two young men stood side by side and handed out leaflets to the occasional passers-by, leaflets on which the history of the falsification of the Battle of Kursk by the military historian and Doctor of Historical Sciences Arseny Tkach was pithily laid out.

This went on for more than an hour.

Some passersby lingered and started conversations with the veterans. The veterans explained the purpose of their protest to them. An old man wearing glasses and the uniform of a major of the artillery troops explained it in detail to two women—one young and one elderly.

"On the 12th of July, 1943, the greatest tank battle of all time took place near Prokhorovka, as a result of which our tanks stopped the German offensive on the southern face of the Kursk Bulge, which influenced the entire outcome of the Battle of Kursk, of the greatest battle in the history of mankind, this, so to speak, decisive battle, during which the Germans wanted to take revenge for their defeat at Stalingrad. After the battle, the Soviet troops launched a counteroffensive, defeated 30 German divisions, and liberated the cities of Orel, Belgorod, and Kharkov. Stalingrad and the Battle of Kursk broke the fascists' back, as they say, once and for all. And the man living behind yon windows," the old man pointed at the sixth floor, "claims that, during the battle of Prokhorovka, the Germans lost only five tanks, while we lost 193! Which is 38 times more than the Germans!"

"Five tanks . . ." the women exchanged a look. "That really doesn't sound like much . . ."

"It isn't much!" the old man smiled with his gold teeth. "To us veterans too, it doesn't sound like much. But to Tkach, a Doctor of Historical Sciences, to him I'm not sure. He's written more than one article on the subject, he speaks at international conferences, he travels around the world and lies, lies, lies. And what do you think—how many of our people died in World War II?"

The women exchanged another look.

"Twenty million people?" the young woman asked the elderly.

"Around twenty," she nodded.

"No, my dear ladies!" the old man shook his head. "Forty-three million! What do you say to that?"

"Forty-three? That sounds like kind of a lot . . ." the elderly woman smirked.

"But it doesn't sound like a lot to Tkach."

"Why is he doing this?"

"That's what we want to figure out! Why!"

One guy with a bike didn't understand the point of what was happening for a long time and kept repeating:

"But still, what did he, like, actually do?"

Ivan Petrovich recklessly forced his way over to him and sternly raised up his stubby finger.

"He shat all over World War II! Shat, shits, and shall shit if he's not stopped! Got it?"

"Got it," the guy said, then sped off.

Some of the veterans began to get tired and take turns sitting on the two benches. Ivan Petrovich didn't get tired, but, on the contrary, became livelier: he was shouting, energetically conversing with the other veterans, explaining the deal to passers-by, and walking through the courtyard, looking like he'd grown up in it.

Suddenly, the doors out onto the balcony from Tkach's apartment opened up and Tkach himself went out onto the balcony. The veterans grew livelier, shouted, hooted, and shook their signs.

"The bastard couldn't resist!" Ivan Petrovich laughed angrily and victoriously, pulled a bit more air into his lungs, then, clenching his fists, let forth a protracted cry: "Sha-a-a-ame!"

"Shame!" the old major standing next to him cried out.

"Sha-a-a-ame!" Smirnov let forth another protracted cry, now screaming his head off.

"Shame!"

"Sha-a-a-a-ame!"

"Shame!"

"Sha-a-a-a-ame!"

A flat rectangular object appeared in Tkach's hands. He turned it around and the sun flashed across the object: a mirror. Tkach aimed the mirror at the crowd of veterans. A large splotch of sun crawled through them. They began to turn away and to cover their faces with their hands or their signs. The venerated poet of the front grabbed the megaphone from someone and began to speak through it with his muffled voice.

"Get out of our country, Mr. Tkach! You don't belong here! You shat in the glorious well of our Victory! Scoot off to your masters across the sea!"

"Get out! Go! Double-dealer! Scoundrel!" the veterans cried.

Ivan Petrovich stepped forth from the crowd and shouted louder than anyone else.

"Sco-o-o-o-o-oundre-e-e-eel!

Tkach directed the splotch toward him. The blinding light flashed into the thick lenses of his glasses and flooded Smirnov's eyes. But he didn't cover his face and didn't turn away.

"Shine it on me! Shine it on me, you bastard! Shine it!"

The light of the sun filled Smirnov's eyes. He opened them more, as if wishing to suck all of the power of the sun into his body.

"Shine! Shine! Shine, coward! Shine, traitor!"

Tkach shined it onto his face. This duel continued for several long minutes. Then Tkach put down the mirror and retreated from the balcony. He was accompanied by shouts and hoots. Ivan Petrovich continued to stand there and repeat:

"Shine! Shine, bastard! Shine!"

He couldn't see anything, and red flashes swam across his eyes. The young people took him by the arms.

"Are you alright?"

"I feel great! I feel fantastic!"

Ivan Petrovich took a step, couldn't see anything, but kept going. His feet in their old boots scraped across the asphalt.

"Just a sec, guys, just a sec . . ."

They took him over to a bench and sat him down. He tried to turn around, twisting his head and rolling his unseeing eyes, but then suddenly went limp and fell onto the veteran sitting next to him. The ambulance immediately drove over, Ivan Petrovich was taken into it, then it disappeared around the corner.

"A spell of fainting as a result of overexcitement," the doctor explained to the young people after looking Ivan Petrovich over. "He'll lie down for a little while, then he'll be fine."

And it was true: Ivan Petrovich soon came to his senses. They gave him a couple of injections and drove him over to the bus. He walked up the steps himself and sat down in the empty cabin. The driver was dozing in his seat.

Ivan Petrovich sat there looking out the window. Having sat like that for fifteen minutes, he got up and left the bus. And started off along Kedrov Street. Then turned and began to walk through courtyards, past a building site for something or another, past garages and a playground . . . He walked, waving his long arms at his sides as was his habit, and looking from left to right. Stopped, seeing a rusty Volga with a broken windshield and flat tires being dragged onto a motor transport.

A pigeon landed on a low concrete wall near some dumpsters.

"There you go!" Ivan Petrovich winked at the pigeon and nodded toward the Volga.

The pigeon cooed softly.

Ivan Petrovich kept going, now bypassing the courtyards, crossed the street, and found himself on a spacious square. There was a new supermarket on it, next to which Tajiks were laying asphalt.

Ivan Petrovich stared at the supermarket. Its entrance was decorated with a garland of blue and red orbs, under which a yellow inscription read: "WE'RE OPEN!"

"We're open!" Ivan Petrovich nodded in agreement.

Stood there for a moment. Moved toward the supermarket. The glass doors parted before him, and he went into the supermarket. The interior was bright, spacious, and smelled new. Pushing their carts, lonely shoppers wandered through long aisles filled up with groceries.

Ivan Petrovich also took a cart and began to roll it across the supermarket's clean new floor. Passed by the fruit and vegetable department, stood in front of the juices, reading their names.

Kept going, passed by a rack of grains and pastas, stopped by a long rack of canned goods.

"Baltic Gold!" he read the inscription on a can of sprats. "There you go!"

He nodded approvingly, kept going. Saw the glass display case in the meat department and approached it.

"Hello!" the tall saleswoman smiled at him.

"Hello!" Ivan Petrovich's glasses trembled.

"How can I help you?"

Ivan Petrovich looked the meat over, moved along the glass case, and read:

"Zrazy . . . steak . . . ground lamb . . ."

"There's also ground beef, pork, and chicken," the saleswoman moved in parallel to him, looking at his medals.

"There you go!" Smirnov shook his head approvingly.

After the meat department began the sausage department.

"Sausage!" Ivan Petrovich stopped.

"Sausage," the saleswoman stopped with a smile.

"So," Smirnov sighed and adjusted his glasses. "Little sausages too."

"Little ones too. What kind of little ones do you like?"

"Doctor's sausages."

"There they are, right in front of you."

"How much?"

"360 rubles per kilo."

"There you go!" he nodded.

"How much shall I weigh out for you?"

"For me? Weigh me out . . ." he thought for a moment.

"Half a kilo?"

"No," he shook his head. "Weigh me out a hundred and ninety-three sausages."

"A hundred and ninety-three sausages?"

"A hundred and ninety-three!" he nodded.

"Whatever you say," the saleswoman's smile grew wider.

She pulled out a heap of sausages and began to count. Ivan Petrovich stood there, staring at the display case. There weren't enough sausages in the heap and the saleswoman disappeared behind a white door with a round window.

"Braunschweiger," Ivan Petrovich wrinkled his forehead.

"There you go!"

The saleswoman returned with another heap of sausages and continued counting.

"Braunschweiger," Ivan Petrovich shook his head and whistled slightly. "Mhmm . . ."

"Exactly one hundred and ninety-three sausages," the saleswoman finished. "Which comes to eight kilos and four hundred and twenty grams. Do you want it in one package or maybe two?"

"You can . . ." Ivan Petrovich muttered as he stared at the display case of sausages.

"I'll do two so they're easier to carry."

He didn't reply.

The saleswoman wrapped up the sausages and handed him two weighty packages. He took them and put them into his cart.

"Anything else?" the saleswoman asked.

"Else . . . and this . . . Braunschweiger . . ."

"How much?"

"Five sticks."

She silently pulled out five sticks of Braunschweiger, weighed each one separately, stuck price tags onto them, and handed them to Smirnov. He put the sausages down into the cart in a neat little row.

"What else?"

"Ah . . . nothing . . ." he shook his glasses and pushed the cart further on.

Passed through the dairy department, turned, and found himself at a dead end with a large poster in front of him: a dog and a cat eating from the same bowl. The shelves of the dead end were lined with pet food. A girl in a white coat was shifting packages of dry food from cart to shelves. Looking the shelves over, Ivan Petrovich moved closer to the girl. She looked back at him, then immediately turned away, continuing her work, bending over, and stuffing the bottom shelf full of bags.

Ivan Petrovich took a stick of Braunschweiger and hit the girl in the neck with the sausage as hard as he could. The girl collapsed onto the floor.

"There you go . . ." Ivan Petrovich muttered, looking at the girl lying motionless on the floor.

"There you go."

Chewing his lips concentratedly, he stood there for a few seconds. Then fixed his glasses, bent over, and carefully placed the sausage onto the girl's back. Took four sticks of Braunschweiger out of the cart and also placed them onto the girl's back next to the first in a neat row.

Turned and pushed the cart out of the dead end. Pushed the cart to the checkout. The cashier took one package of sausages, then the next, and added everything up.

"Three thousand twenty-four rubles and forty-three kopecks."

"There you go!" Ivan Petrovich brought his middle finger up to the cashier's face.

She stared dumbfoundedly at his middle finger, then turned her gaze to Smirnov and his medals.

Smirnov took the packages of sausages and moved toward the exit. The cashier stood up and opened her mouth. The two guards by the exit were discussing something explosively and with much laughter, one showing the other a shape with his fingers. The cashier shook her head ruefully, sighed, brought her palm to her mouth, then bent over. A small grayish-brown egg fell from mouth and into her palm.

"I can't do the schism that fast!" the cashier pronounced, almost crying, and shook her head.

One of the guards, red haired and with a cruelly masculine face, suddenly began to fuss about and whisper to himself, his head shaking, he pulled a folding knife out of his pocket, and slashed his left hand with it forcefully, still whispering incomprehensibly. The other guard covered his face with his palms and let forth a deep, harsh guttural sound.

Smirnov was walking toward the guards. His movement slowed. He was moving his legs as if they were immersed in liquid glass. It was with the greatest difficulty that his old boots tore forth from the floor and swam forward, like outdated amphibious hovercraft.

Customers jumped protractedly through the supermarket, hovering in the air.

Remaining suspended through the course of a long jump, a plump woman in a bright dress tore up a loaf of wheat bread and threw the shreds at the other customers with solemn joyfulness. They didn't attempt to dodge these shreds; their faces were filled with bliss and joyful tears flew across the store in a slow rain.

Smirnov was walking toward the guards.

Some mustachioed bald man grabbed firmly onto a ten-year-old boy's back, jumped up together with him, and, roaring and weeping, slowly, but with terrible strength, smashed the boy against a refrigerator filled with chilled soft drinks. Having broken through the glass, the boy's head began to crush through the multi-colored bottles, the contents of which slowly erupted forth in energetic jets. The boy's blood and brains were thereafter distributed among these streams.

Smirnov was walking toward the guards.

In the fish department, a short saleswoman solemnly lifted her associate up over her with outstretched arms, then, with a protracted scream that decayed into long sounds, brought her down onto the display case full of fish. Frozen with delight, her associate slowly crossed her thin arms across her bosom, closing her eyes gratefully. Having torn off her associate's apron, pants, and panties, the saleswoman grabbed a live sterlet and began to shove it into her vagina with incredible strength and tenderness.

Smirnov was walking toward the guards.

An old woman using her cane to lever herself powerfully off the floor flew slowly and concentratedly over a shelf of grains and pastas and hovered up above the meat department. Here, a short-haired saleswoman with two long knives in hand and a solemn wordless song was already waiting for her. Taking her cane warningly between her teeth, the old woman descended, exposing her back to the saleswoman. Making joyful exclamations, the saleswoman sunk the knives into the old woman's back and shoved her as hard as she could, directing her toward the wine department. With a patient moan, the old woman floated across the store, accumulating energy like a tensely *potential* threat. The old woman's contact with the shelves of wine bottles was grandiose: explosions of dark red, splashes, a scattering of many drops and shards.

Smirnov was walking toward the guards.

Jumping up all the way to the ceiling, a young man was kissing his own palms furiously. His distant relative threw glass jars filled with eggplant pâté at him, kneeling, singing, and praying as she did. Miraculously missing the young man, the jars slowly exploded against the ceiling, showering the praying woman with their contents. Not noticing this, the young man was kissing his palms passionately, whispering mysterious, indispensable words that came right from the heart into them.

Smirnov was walking toward the guards.

Having torn off all her clothes, the swarthy-skinned, black-haired cleaning lady solemnly put a blue plastic bucket over her head and began to jump around the store with protracted cat-like leaps. A menacingly solemn howl came forth from beneath the bucket. She passed gas in time with her sweepingly daring jumps, as if she were propelling herself with the gas. A gray-haired, but still youngish customer was chasing after her, trying in vain to flag her with a slab of chilled beef. He gnashed his teeth with such delight and bewilderment that they crumbled, these fragments showering down onto the fresh meat and sticking to it.

Smirnov was walking toward the guards.

The two packers left their post with delighted singing, one holding a large piece of lard and the other a steam radiator—this latter object torn off of the wall by them both. Having run ahead of the other, one of them threw herself onto the ground, the lard held beneath her as she did. The other jumped onto her back, lifting the radiator over her head. Using the inertia of their bodies and the slipperiness of the lard, they moved across the floor and toward the checkout. By the entrance, the packer hurled the radiator at the kneeling customer. The radiator took off half of her head, spattering brains onto the cashier with the egg.

Smirnov was walking toward the guards.

Holding the grayish-brown egg in her palms as before and completely oblivious to the customer's brain sliding down her back, the cashier pulled a brass hairpin out of her hair and began to gently palpate the egg with it, sobbing and murmuring:

"Schism . . . schism . . . a quick schism . . . we all need a schism . . ."

But the egg had no intention of schisming.

Smirnov had reached the guards.

Roars and triumphant cries rang out through the supermarket. The red-haired guard waved his cut-up left hand theatrically. His blood dripped onto Smirnov's face.

"There you go!" Smirnov nodded approvingly, not bothering to stop. His glasses bobbed up and down.

"Schism, schism, a quick schism, a good schism . . ." the cashier muttered, weeping.

The red-haired guard shook his bloody hand theatrically and whispered something in a rapturous tone. Still covering his face with his hands and bending down slightly, his associate let forth harsh, abrupt sounds from his throat. There was singing, weeping, and praying in the supermarket.

Smirnov left the supermarket with the two packages of sausages in hand.

DAY OF THE CHEKIST

For Galina Dursthoff

IVAN AND MARK are sitting at a table covered over in Russian zakuski (pickled cucumbers and mushrooms, herring, lard, boiled potatoes, and sauerkraut). An old Soviet overcoat with an MGB captain's shoulder loops lies thrown across Ivan's shoulders. Mark is in a light beige sweater. He opens a bottle of vodka and pours it into their glasses.

MARK. You were a Chekist?
IVAN. I was.
MARK. And you're not ashamed?
IVAN. No.

They clink glasses, drink, and chase vodka with food.

MARK. Did you arrest the innocent?
IVAN. I did.
MARK. Did you beat false confessions out of them?
IVAN. I did.
MARK. Did you torture?
IVAN. I did.
MARK. Did you fabricate collective plots?

IVAN. I did.
MARK. And you're not ashamed?
IVAN. No.

They clink glasses, drink, and chase vodka with food.

MARK. Did you send *provocateurs* out into the people?
IVAN. I did.
MARK. Did you take hostages?
IVAN. I did, oh, I did.
MARK. Then shoot them?
IVAN. Duh.
MARK. And did you yourself participate in mass executions?
IVAN. How could I've avoided it?
MARK. And you're not ashamed?
IVAN. No.

They drink and eat.

MARK. Did you confiscate every last kernel of grain from the peasantry, condemning them to starvation?
IVAN. I did, oh, I did.
MARK. And then arrest the peasants who begged in the cities?
IVAN. I did. Tons of 'em.
MARK. And you served with the barrier troops during the war?
IVAN. There was some of that.
MARK. Did you shoot deserters with a machine gun?
IVAN. I can remember just how I did: tra-ta-ta-ta-ta.
MARK. You're not ashamed?
IVAN. No.

They drink and eat.

MARK. And after the war, did you arrest Soviet citizens who ended up in German-occupied territory?

IVAN. I did. Thousands of 'em!

MARK. Did you expel the Crimean Tatars, Chechens, and the Ingush?

IVAN. I did. Echelons of 'em. Choo choo-o-o-o-o-o . . .

MARK. Did you fabricate the Doctors' Plot?

IVAN. I did.

MARK. And you're not ashamed?

IVAN. No.

They drink and eat.

MARK. Did you kick Solzhenitsyn, Voinovich, Vladimov, Brodsky, and Bukovsky out of the country?

IVAN. I did.

MARK. Did you kill Mikhoels?

IVAN. Yeah, we had to run him over with a truck . . . ugh, this thing's making me sweat. Your turn.

He stands up, takes the overcoat off his shoulders, drops it onto Mark's shoulders, then sits back down.

IVAN. Were you a Chekist?

MARK. I was.

IVAN. And you're not ashamed?

MARK. No.

They clink glasses, drink, and eat.

IVAN. Did you torture Meyerhold (the director), Vavilov (the academician), Vinogradov (the professor), and Babel (the writer)?

MARK. I did.

IVAN. Did you drink the blood of monarchists through a straw?

MARK. I did.

IVAN. And fry the brains of great princes?

MARK. But of course. In vegetable oil. And butter on holidays. First, you boil 'em in salted water with a spoonful of vinegar, pepper, bay leaves, and cloves, let 'em cool, roll 'em in crushed breadcrumbs, fry 'em, pepper 'em, sprinkle 'em with lemon juice . . . m-m-m . . . delightful! A fantastic food to chase Żubrówka with.

IVAN. And you're not ashamed?

MARK. What're you jabbering on for? Ashamed, not ashamed . . . let's drink!

They clink glasses, drink, and eat.

IVAN. Did you juggle with the battle standards of the Reich?

MARK. I did.

IVAN. Did you frighten women in underground passageways?

MARK. Ah! With great pleasure! Wow! Wow! Kill 'em ow!

IVAN. Did you ask your daughter to draw a circle on a white wall?

MARK. Of course I did. And it turned out real pretty.

IVAN. Did you spy on the copulation of Pioneer leaders in a haybarn?

MARK. I didn't spy, I eavesdropped. It was . . . hot damn! I was walking from the boathouse where a guy from the 5th detachment had literally given me a kick in the pants. And said, "get outta here!" The older detachments were taking boat rides with their girlies and, once again, there weren't enough boats for Rudik and me. Rudik went to Veniamin Ivanovich in the forest for an entomology lesson, but I trudged over to the playfield, thinking I'd play some ping-pong. And when I was walking between the barracks and the inventory warehouse, I saw that the door into the warehouse had been left ajar. And people were talking in there. Two voices: a man and a girly. And it seemed to me that the girly was sobbing. I stopped. Marat, a senior Pioneer leader, was talking to Sasha, a leader from the 3rd detachment. Sasha was real tall, with strong legs, a big behind, a broad face, and a harsh voice. And played volleyball super well. And when she scored, she'd say, "not fast enough, you millet-brains!" And now she was sobbing and repeating:

"No, no, that can never happen again."

"But why, can't you explain why?" Marat was asking.

"Because . . . it can never happen again . . . never!" she was repeating.

I was standing by the door and listening.

"But what? What happened?"

"Nothing happened."

"You don't like me?"

"I like you."

"Why'd you switch to *vy*? We've been on *ty* terms for two days. Or did you forget?"

"No."

"You don't like me anymore?"

"I do like you."

"*Ty* . . . that's better. Am I disgusting to you?"

"No."

"You don't want me anymore?"

"I don't . . . no . . . I don't right now."

"It doesn't have to be right here. Or right now. Well?"

"I dunno . . ."

"It'll be wherever we have the chance to give each other pleasure. In peace."

"And where will that be?"

"There's a haybarn over by the dam. It's not far, but there's nobody there. Ever."

"I won't go."

"So, I'm disgusting to you?"

"No."

"Then why?"

"I won't go."

"Sasha, well what . . . I mean . . ."

"No . . . Marat . . ."

"Sasha . . ."

"I . . ."

"   "
. . .

"   "
. . .

"Well? Is that how it is? You're already a woman—not a lil' girly."

"Please don't . . ."

"   "
. . .

"   "
. . . . . .

"   "
. . .

"   "
. . . . . .

"You're just so . . . tender . . . so womanly . . ."

"Please don't . . . I'm begging you . . ."

"I fell in love with you right away, like a little boy . . . I'm going insane . . . I stopped being able to sleep at night . . ."

"C'mon . . . don't . . ."

"So . . . oy . . . such tenderness . . . and here . . ."

"Please don't . . ."

"You're a woman . . . you should enjoy life . . ."

"   "
. . .

"   "
. . . . . .

" . . . oy . . ."

"Well? Better, right? Oh baby . . ."

"Um . . ."

"Say what you mean to without 'um,' Sasha, without 'um.'"

". . ."

"My sweet . . . my beautiful . . ."

"I'm . . . not very beautiful . . ."

"And stupid . . . so stupid . . . and tender . . ."

". . ."

"There . . . you've got nips like a grown woman's . . ."

". . ."

". . . my angel with her nips . . ."

". . ."

". . . and here . . ."

". . ."

"Sashenka . . . my angel . . ."

At that moment, the bugler Misha played the signal to get into formation for lunch.

"I gotta get to my detachment . . ." Sasha muttered.

"Go. Then, as soon as quiet hour starts, walk over to the pillars."

I backed away from the door, walking on tiptoe, then started to run.

On the square, around the flag, we began to form up into rows. Sasha came too. Her face was red. Marat came later, when everyone had already formed up—he stood near the flagpole. The commanders of the detachments began to make their reports to him. The Pioneer leaders stood off on their own. I was watching Sasha. She was wearing shorts and a military shirt with a red tie. She had white-heeled shoes on. The reports having been declaimed, everyone set off for the cafeteria. The Pioneer leaders had a separate table. Marat sat with them. I saw that he was saying something funny, and all of the Pioneer leaders were laughing. And Sasha was laughing too. Then they announced quiet hour. I went to our barracks, took off my pioneer shirt and tie, and slid into bed. Two leaders walked down the aisle between the bunks, then left.

The guys started jabbering and I made as if to "go for a leak."
In fact, I left the barracks and ran to the place where two pillars
were dug into the ground, pillars we often had to climb. And saw
Sasha pass between these two pillars, then, a little ways into the
bushes, saw Marat too. He turned and started walking. And she
followed after him. And I ran after them. They walked past the
basketball court and went into the forest. I followed them. Once
they were in the forest, they started to walk together. Marat took
Sasha by the hand. Then they turned, passed through a clearing,
and approached a haybarn. It stood at the edge of the forest—the
periphery of a meadow. I stood in the forest and watched. The
haybarn was locked. Marat unlocked it, then they went inside
and closed the door. I walked cautiously up to the barn. It'd
been knocked together from rough boards, between which were
cracks. Hay stuck out from between the cracks. Nothing was
visible through the cracks. But things were audible. I watched
the protruding hay and listened.

"Well, there . . . here, y'see how . . . no one'll bother us . . ."
"I . . ."
"Come here . . . like that . . . like . . ."
"But . . . um . . ."
"Say what you mean without 'um,' baby . . ."
" . . . "
"I'll do it myself, myself . . ."
"No . . . it's hooked . . ."
"There . . . there . . ."
" . . . "
"Baby . . ."
" . . . "
"Yes . . ."
" . . . "
"Yeah, baby . . ."
" . . . "

"Yeah, baby . . ."

"Oy, that hurts . . ."

"I'll do it slow . . . slow like that . . . your pussy still can't take the dick . . . take it . . . take it . . ."

"Oy . . ."

"Take it . . ."

"Oa . . ."

"Take it . . ."

"A . . ."

"Take it . . ."

"Ao . . ."

"Take it . . ."

"Ai . . ."

"Slow . . . good . . ."

" . . . "

"Good . . . good? Good, right? Does Sashenka like that?"

"Yeah . . . ao . . ."

"Good . . ."

"Ao . . ."

"Good . . ."

"Ou . . ."

"Good . . . baby . . . I adore you . . ."

" . . . "

"There . . . how good it feels to Sashenka . . . beautiful Sashenka . . . like that . . ."

" . . . "

"There . . . now turn over onto your tummy."

"Ao . . ."

"Like that . . . lie like . . . it's softer here . . ."

"But . . . ah . . ."

"Lie with your booty up . . . your sweet booty . . . I'll kiss your booty . . . so that my girly Sashenka feels real tender . . . feels real good . . ."

"   "

"Like . . . that . . ."

"No . . . what for . . ."

"Now it'll be even better . . ."

"Not there . . . it hurts!"

"I'm not rushin' . . . slow . . ."

"Please no!"

"Don't be afraid. I'm here with you."

"It hurts!"

"Don't be afraid . . . it's all good . . . all sweet . . ."

"It hu-u-u-urts!"

"No, it doesn't hurt . . . it doesn't hurt anymore . . ."

"It hu-u-u-urts!"

"OK, I stopped. Quiet, quiet . . ."

"But, it hurts . . . it hurts . . ."

"I'm already there . . . it's all good . . . I'm not doing anything to Sashenka . . . to sweet Sashenka . . . I'm just lying here . . ."

"Please don't . . . ah, please don't!"

"But I'm already there. That's it."

"Please do-o-o-on't!!!"

"You better quit it! If you shout like that, I'll choke you to death, you dumbass! I swear to God! I'll choke you to death and burn down the barn. Here, look . . . here's my lighter. There! I'll burn the shit out of it and you too. If you're such a dumbass, you'll be kindling for the blaze! Make another peep, then watch!"

"   "

"I'm doing something good to you, I'm teaching you how to be a free, sexual woman. And you're screaming like a fifth grader. I'll never do anything bad to you. Never."

"It . . . hurts . . . me . . ."

"It doesn't hurt. But, soon enough, it'll feel good. There. Sashenka's sweet booty."

"......"

"And what a booty. A sweet booty. Te-e-nder . . ."

"It hu-u-urts . . ."

"Ah, quit it! Quit it! Repeat after me: it feels good! Well!?"

"It feels go-o-od . . ."

"Sashenka likes it."

"Sashenka likes it."

"Sashenka's so sweet."

"Sashenka's so sweet."

"Tender booty."

"Tender booty."

"Marat's all up in Sashenka's booty."

"Marat's . . ."

"Well!"

". . . all up in Sashenka's booty . . ."

"In her booty."

"In her booty."

"In her bo-o-oty . . ."

"In her booty."

"In her bo-o-oty . . ."

"In her booty."

"In her bo-o-oty!"

"In her booty."

"In her bo-o-oty!"

"In her booty . . ."

"In! Her! Bo! Oo! Ty!!! Aaaaaahhh!!!"

"......"

"A-a-a-a-h . . . aaa . . . aaa . . ."

". . ."

"Well, there . . . aaa . . . my sweet . . ."

". . ."

"There . . . I spilled . . . spilled and spilled into Sashenka's sweet booty . . . Sashenka's . . . aaa . . . spilled . . ."

"... me ..."

"Wait, please, don't move ... don't budge ... shut up ... shut up!"

"   ..."

"Sashenka ... oy ... how ... this ... there ..."

"   ..."

"There ..."

"   ......"

"   ..."

"   ..."

"   ......"

"Careful ... now ... Sashenka's got nothing to fear ... now ... there ... there. And that's that."

"   ..."

"And that's that. Doesn't hurt, right?"

"   ..."

"The sweet booty doesn't hurt ... I'll kiss it ..."

"   ..."

"   ......"

"   ..."

"What a ..."

"   ..."

"Sweet ... sweet ... booty ... I won't give it away to anyone ... my booty ..."

"   ..."

"Turn over. We're done now. Well? Like that. Come closer ... like ... like that ... I won't give my sweet girly away to anyone."

"That ... was ..."

"What?"

"Painful ... why ..."

"You're OK. There's no blood—no nothing. I told you: I'll never do anything bad to you. Only good things. You'll grow up and thank me. Today, you became the freest woman in the whole school. All the other girlies are just snotty little virgins compared to you."

"I'm never gonna do that again."

"Hold on . . ."

"Never. I swear!"

"Well . . . hold on . . . my sweaty little thing . . . your upper lip's covered in sweat . . . Sashenka . . ."

" . . . "

"There's still a lot you don't understand."

"I'm never gonna do that again. And you and I are . . ."

"Don't call me *vy*, remember?"

"OK, well, *you* and I are never gonna go out again."

"Here . . . listen. Let's be quiet for just five minutes. Five minutes."

" . . . "

" . . . . . . "

" . . . "

"There. You calmed down."

"Mhmm."

"If 'mhmm' is all you've got, then listen. Listen carefully. I'm in love with you. Very much so. Do you understand that?"

"Yes."

"If a man is in love with a woman, he wants to take pleasure in her. Is that clear?"

"I'm not gonna do that again."

"Next time, it won't hurt you at all."

"I'm not gonna."

"It'll just feel good."

"I'm not gonna."

"You will, Sashenka."

"I'm not. Give me . . . gimme my . . ."

"Hold on."

"I've gotta go."

"Well . . . hold on . . ."

"I've gotta go!"

"Shut it!!!"

" . . ."

"And listen to me. Carefully. Just lie there and listen. I'll put my hand on you like this . . . may I? You're a grownup, you've finished ninth grade, and you know who's in charge of our country right now. Yuri Vladimirovich Andropov. Before, he was in charge of the USSR State Security Committee. The KGB. So there, my darling Sasha. The mightiest people in the country right now are KGB officers. They're the smartest and the most cunning. The most penetrating. And they can do anything. They can give someone a career and they can destroy another like an ant. My uncle Pasha is a KGB general. An old friend of Yuri Vladimirovich Andropov. I'm his only nephew and he doesn't have any children of his own. He loves me very much. And helps me. I got into the Moscow Aviation Institute myself, without using my connection. But climbing up the Komsomol ranks . . . he helped me with that. I'm already a member of the Bureau. I love the Komsomol, love lively work with other people. I'd like to become the second secretary of the Komsomol Institute. I think that I will. In a couple of years. If someone wills something, they can attain it. My uncle helps me. I can always sense his support. So there. You pretty much know what the KGB is. But I know *exactly* what it is. It's a mighty organization. And, in our country, it can do anything. You were saying that you actively participate in the drama club. You act in school plays. I noticed that you were a born actress right when I saw you. Even when you play volleyball. You could really be an actress. It's complicated. Very! Because, at the Russian Institute of Theater Arts and at the Shchukin Institute, there's a lotta competition. Hard to get in. Again with the connections. But if I tell my uncle: Uncle Pasha, my sweetheart is real talented and wants with all her heart to act in movies, please help her out. Then Uncle Pasha will help his nephew. And, in a year, my sweetheart will start out at the Shchukin Institute. And, during that year, you'll get so ready, you won't even recognize yourself. Uncle Pasha has a lot of actor-friends. Tabakov, Efremov, and Ulyanov, for example. They go hunting together, go to the banya. I once saw Efremov at his birthday party. A real man of the world! He drinks like an animal, he could drink a whole cistern, but, still, he'd be joking and laughing. He told such a funny joke, all the ladies slid under the table! He said some interesting things about his new movie . . . So, then, we'll get you tutors from the Shchukin Institute itself, they'll train you, work on your diction. You'll stride into the exam like Doronina: 'do you love theater like I do?' And they're all entranced, A+, you're on the list. And you and I go to a restaurant, we celebrate, we drink champagne . . . Sashenka's an actress! And a shining new life. That's what I can do for you. And this is just because you and I are gonna meet in the same secret place every Monday. And give each other pleasure. And I'm gonna get pleasure from my sweetheart Sashenka."

"And your . . . sorry . . . *your* wife?"

"What do you mean my wife? Why bring *her* up? Yes, I'm married. I got married early, when I was a freshman. It happens. I can't say I'm that happy about it now. I could've waited. But what can you do. Passion! I'm a passionate person, Sashenka. What's done is done. Nina is a great friend. We have a family. But passion sometimes flows aslant from family life. I'll tell you what: don't get married young. Better to wait. Have some fun, enjoy yourself. One must know how to enjoy life. Have a *real cool* life. There, Sasha. And the last thing: my uncle can help, but he can also take a shit on you. In a big way. A shit you won't be able to wash off for your whole life. For example, someone can get fired. And never get set up with that kinda job again. Your dad works at the State Defense Enterprise, right?"

"Yes."

"So, Sasha. The cards are on the table. And the decision is yours. Think. Today. And tomorrow give me just one word: 'yes' or 'no'. That's it. Get dressed and go out first. And I need to lock up the barn."

The rustling of hay became audible, I tiptoed away from the barn, walked into the forest, and ran back to camp. I was holding a small dung beetle in my fist. While I was standing and listening, it'd slid out from a crack in the barn. And I'd grabbed it. It was small, clearly a youngun, completely blue, and shimmering beautifully. Usually dung beetles are black, but this one was blue—very unusual. I took it into my fist and it kept turning and tickling my palm. And when I was running past the cafeteria, one of the dishwashers shook her finger at me. And one of the two Pioneer leaders shouted out from the window of the director's building.

"Hey, get to bed!"

I ran into the boys' barracks, quickly zipped into my bunk, and got under the sheet. Unclenched my fist and saw that the blue beetle was no longer there. It was so strange! I'd never stopped feeling its stirring. Then suddenly—it was gone. Where could I've dropped it? When could it've fallen out of my fist? It'd just disappeared. I lay there and looked into my palm. And cursed myself. Tears welled up in my eyes and I wept silently. Thank God that the guys next to me were already asleep. I suddenly felt an enormous sense of exhaustion. I'd probably gotten overheated when I was standing by the haybarn. We were having a hot July. I fell asleep. And had a dream:

I'm at camp, I'm walking to the river to go boating. I walk onto the shore. It's not a river, but an enormous lake, its opposite shore not visible. That same guy who gave me a kick in the pants is standing by the boathouse. But now he's a *deeply* old man with a wrinkled, motionless face. There's a red Pioneer tie hanging over his chest.

"I need a boat," I babble with no hope of my request being granted.

"If you need one, take it," the old man says and gestures at the boats.

Not believing my luck, I walk over, sit down in a boat, grab onto the oars, and lean in. And I'm not floating but slipping and sliding across the lake. It turns out it's frozen and iced over. The boat flies across at the lightest touch from the oars. A chill, ice-smelling wind blows into my face. I sweep along, squealing with pleasure. I make out a figure before me. Someone's skating quickly across the ice. I catch up with the skater: it's our math teacher, Vera Kharitonovna. She's completely naked! She's wearing long ice skates, has one hand behind her back, and the other is smoothly swinging at her side. I catch up to her and begin to tear along next to her. From the boat, I can clearly see her *all*—a naked body with a generous bosom, a firm behind, and slender legs. Her dark pubis flickers between her evenly moving thighs. I rush along next to her, steering with the oars. She grins at me and begins to mutter with her plump, always ironically twisted lips.

"Well, Shamkovich, are we gonna make fools of ourselves again in the third quarter when you forgot the kefir equations with two suitcase variables you forgot to discover through a tour of duty in Viktor Viktorovich's gym-class office in the direction of the blind bisector and the diary was cut out and composted through by red doctors immediately after a hearing of the council of the squad of the parents of the Pythagorean Theorem?"

But I don't listen to her muttering. I suddenly understand that I can do absolutely whatever I want to with Vera Kharitonovna with absolute impunity. I reach out and touch her dark, hairy groin. Paying no attention, she slides over the ice, muttering and grinning. Her groin flickers between her thighs. I reach for it and grab it. It hides itself from me between her pumping legs.

Vera Kharitonovna slides, mutters, and grins. I grab her by her warm groin. My heart beats wildly. I try to align the boat to get closer, closer, closer, closer to her dark, dark, soft, hairy, groin. The boat rocks, slides across the ice, disobeys. My teacher skates evenly. I catch her, come up alongside, suppress my trembling, grab her groin with my left hand, then drop the oar and grab on with my right hand too, thrusting up from down below—between her chill, evenly moving thighs.

"You're an aluminum-cast C-student, Shamkovich!" Vera Kharitonovna laughs from up above.

I woke up.

There was no one next to me, only empty bunks. The sun was shining through the window. I sat up in my bed. And realized that my underwear was wet. I looked down at them: a dark stain on the groin. I touched it. It was sticky. I stood up, put on shorts, a shirt, and my Pioneer tie. And left the barracks. Guys and girls were coming out of the cafeteria and the afternoon snack was ending. I walked into the cafeteria. At our table, Table No. 4, were only the Three Fatties—Big Fatty Gamble, Middle Fatty Drunko, and Small Fatty Lefty. They were finishing their second portions of a cottage-cheese casserole and washing it down with kissel. Cottage-cheese casserole is better than a semolina meatball. My portion and my glass of kissel were at the other end of the table. I sat down and pulled the plate of casserole over. It had raisins in it. I took a swig of kissel, picked up my spoon, scooped up a loose piece of casserole, brought it to my mouth. And suddenly saw that, in place of raisins, that very same small blue dung beetle had appeared in the casserole. I looked at the beetle. It was dead. I looked at the Three Fatties. They continued chewing, indifferently looking over at me. I don't think it was them who'd planted the bug there. But how had it gotten into the casserole? Somebody had put it there. But who? Vitka? Zhenka Gopnik? Or maybe it'd made it there on its own? It'd flown away from me, flown in through the kitchen window, then fallen into the casserole? And gotten baked into the snack? I looked at the beetle. The Three Fatties finished their casserole, got up, and trudged over to the exit. They stuck together, not just because they all got bullied, but also because Gamble and Drunko were in the same class and Gamble's mom gave Lefty violin lessons. I looked around and there was no one. I pushed the beetle deeper into the casserole, pushed the plate away, and drank more of the kissel. A skinny dishwasher with a swarthy, elongated face pushed her cart over to the table.

"What? No appetite?" she asked, picking up the empty plates and cups and putting them onto her cart.

"I just don't want it," I said.

"The boy who's late comes not in a hungry state," she rhymed, took my plate, then set it apart from the dirty ones.

I finished my kissel quickly and ran out of the cafeteria.

TRANSLATOR'S NOTE

FUCK THE *SKELETON Key to Finnegans Wake*. Such a text explains nothing.

The *Skeleton Key* to this book is Turgenev's *Sketches from a Hunter's Album*.

Or maybe Hemingway's *Complete Short Stories*.

Maybe both.

Those are alright.

Eternal thanks to Yelena Veisman, my extraordinary дичь-consultant. Your comments are, as ever, indispensable.

Thanks also to Andrei from The Untranslated (esp. for "Car Crash"—really whiffed at that last-paragraph pitch to begin with) and Ben Hooyman for their comments.

And what an honor it is to have your words at the beginning of this book, dearest Will! Your contributions to the so-called *Sorokinaissance* deserve a MONUMENT of their own (a bronze cast of you getting boned by the Tom Cruise lookalike).

Thanks to everyone . . .

. . . and stay tuned for the Dalkey Archive editions of *The Sugar Kremlin*, *Roman*, and *Marina*!

VLADIMIR SOROKIN was born in a small town outside of Moscow in 1955. He trained as an engineer at the Moscow Institute of Oil and Gas but turned to art and writing, becoming a major presence in the Moscow underground of the 1980s. His work was banned in the Soviet Union, and his first novel, *The Queue*, was published by the famed émigré dissident Andrei Sinyavsky in France in 1985. In 1992, Sorokin's *Their Four Hearts* was short-listed for the Russian Booker Prize; in 1999, the publication of the controversial novel *Blue Lard*, which included a sex scene between clones of Stalin and Khrushchev, led to public demonstrations against the book and demands that Sorokin be prosecuted as a pornographer; in 2001, he received the Andrei Bely Award for outstanding contributions to Russian literature. His work has been translated into more than thirty languages. Sorokin is also the author of the screenplays for *Moscow*, *The Kopeck*, and *4*, and of the libretto for Leonid Desyatnikov's *The Children of Rosenthal*, the first new opera to be commissioned by the Bolshoi Theater since the 1970s. He has written numerous plays and short stories, including the O. Henry Award winner "Horse Soup," which appeared in *Red Pyramid*, a volume of stories published by NYRB Classics. His most recent novel is *Doctor Garin and his Heirs*. He lives in Vnukovo and Berlin.

Born in Brussels but raised in the American Midwest, MAX LAWTON is a writer, musician, and translator. He is currently working in close collaboration with Vladimir Sorokin to publish all of his untranslated works in English. Max is also working on translations of works by Michael Lentz, Antonio Moresco, Alberto Laiseca, Fyodor Dostoevsky, and Louis-Ferdinand Céline. His novel *Progress* is forthcoming. He lives in Los Angeles.